MW01258078

THE
NIGHT
IS
NOT
FOR
YOU

By Eman Quotah

Bride of the Sea
The Night Is Not for You

THE NIGHT IS NOT FOR YOU

EMAN QUOTAH

RUN FOR IT

This book is a work of fiction. Names, characters, places, and incidents are the product of the author's imagination or are used fictitiously. Any resemblance to actual events, locales, or persons, living or dead, is coincidental.

Copyright © 2025 by Eman Quotah
Excerpt from *Red Rabbit Ghost* copyright © 2025 by Jennifer Nicole Julian

Cover design by Alice Clark
Cover image by iStock
Author photograph by Hillary Deane

Hachette Book Group supports the right to free expression and the value of copyright. The purpose of copyright is to encourage writers and artists to produce the creative works that enrich our culture.

The scanning, uploading, and distribution of this book without permission is a theft of the author's intellectual property. If you would like permission to use material from the book (other than for review purposes), please contact permissions@hbgusa.com. Thank you for your support of the author's rights.

Run For It
Hachette Book Group
1290 Avenue of the Americas
New York, NY 10104
hachettebookgroup.com

First Edition: October 2025
Simultaneously published in Great Britain by Wildfire, an imprint of Headline Publishing Group Limited

Run For It is an imprint of Orbit, a division of Hachette Book Group.
The Run For It name and logo are registered trademarks of Hachette Book Group, Inc.

The publisher is not responsible for websites (or their content) that are not owned by the publisher.

The Hachette Speakers Bureau provides a wide range of authors for speaking events. To find out more, go to hachettespeakersbureau.com or email HachetteSpeakers@hbgusa.com.

Redhook books may be purchased in bulk for business, educational, or promotional use. For information, please contact your local bookseller or the Hachette Book Group Special Markets Department at special.markets@hbgusa.com.

Library of Congress Control Number: 2025934691

ISBNs: 9780316595810 (trade paperback), 9780316595827 (ebook)

Printed in the United States of America

LSC-C

Printing 1, 2025

In memory of Alison, Clark,
and other beauties lost too soon to violence

CONTENTS

فأعيد كل ليلة
مشاهدة شريط موتي

Night after night,
I play my death reel.

—"Nights" by Mona Kareem, in *Poetry* (May 2023),
translated from the Arabic by Sarah Elkamel

CHAPTER 1

Heartless

First victim.

Imagine his eyes when she came at him, wild and unholy with disbelief and terror. Imagine the pure evil rushing through her as she raised her blade and then thrust it into him, ignoring his screams and pleas. Imagine her cackle as she hacked into his neck a gaping wound like a distorted second mouth. Next, sliced into his chest. Left a raw and glistening hole, left him to die, his lower body as naked and exposed as the day his mother bore him.

No one in town disputed the terrifying details of what happened late at night in the alley behind the Murad family's twenty-four-hour corner store. Whoever the murderer was, she stabbed her victim over and over, carved out his heart, and wrote a note on his forehead in lipstick:

"Love kills."

It would take a week to clean up the blood, feces, and guts that had transformed the alley into a grisly butcher-shop scene, and longer to even begin to erase the neighborhood's memory of what she had done to a man right outside the store where most people shopped daily.

She. The murderer had to be a *female*, Mr. Murad said, because the scent of ambergris and jasmine in the alley was stronger than the stench of rotting banana peels or death, and her coral lipstick was smeared on the poor man's body, along with all that blood. She had to be an outsider, too, someone passing through with a vendetta, because no God-fearing person in town, whatever their faith, would murder someone. Not like that.

His certainty was somewhat strange. Even stranger was that he swore to God he'd found a set of bloody, Pepsi-y, hoofprints on the sidewalk tile, and had shooed three emaciated stray cats away from the victim's pulsing heart, which had been wholly removed from his body.

The cutting out of his heart was simply vile. But no one knew what the hoofprints could mean. A marauding donkey? A murderer on horseback?

"Half-woman, half-jinn," whispered Mr. Murad's father, a man of ninety. No one latched on to the idea, because who believed in those old-timey stories anymore?

The corner-store owner claimed he hadn't retched at the sight of the naked and mutilated corpse. He hadn't even gagged. He'd seen everything and served everyone, he said. Rich, poor, and everything in between. Nothing in the neighborhood got by him—except this murder, it seemed—and nothing surprised him. He was up at dawn to serve coffee to the early risers. After school, he stopped secondary school children from stealing snacks. In the evening, he sold milk for tomorrow's breakfast to busy mothers with just a few bills in their purses.

Most people were good, he said, but he watched satellite news all day on a little television behind the counter. He'd seen horror films. He knew the evil in the world.

The truth of what had happened when Mr. Murad found the body was different from the tale he told. He'd opened the back door, a trash bag in one hand, and stopped at the sight in front of him, as though he had been transported to another, more violent place, a place inside a screen. One where men were carved up, their hearts served for dinner.

The murderer, whoever she was, had set the heart on top of the green dumpster. It throbbed, and the corner-store owner's live, hardworking heart nearly skidded to a stop. Then his heart sped up, beating faster than he ever thought it could, pounding against his insides, as though it wanted to escape his chest. He fell to his knees, sobbing, unable to move, unable to escape the alley, a wave of fear nearly drowning him. Nearly killing him right there.

That could have been me, he thought. *That could have been me.*

The municipal workers in their green suits scrubbed away the blood, bit by bit, washed it away with soapy water, imagined how it had all got there. They were told, "Keep quiet. Don't share the gory details."

Their silence went unnoticed. No one else wanted to contemplate, for longer than they had to, the awfulness of how the body in the alley had met its end.

Still, people had many questions. Questions about how to avoid a similar fate, about why it had happened to *him*, about how he'd ended up in that alley.

No one could say. The victim's family hadn't seen him since lunch the day before—he was thirty-five, divorced, living in his parents' block of flats, the pink one on Green Forest Road. His friends who got coffee with him every day said they'd wondered where he was the morning Mr. Murad found him. His boss at the plastics factory said he'd been regularly tardy for work, on his way to losing his job.

No one in the neighborhood wanted to tell his mother he was dead. They especially didn't want her to know how gruesomely he'd died. They'd never heard of a death so terrible! Not here, in this semi-rural town, in this neighborhood. They didn't want to watch as the mother's escalating worry over her son's disappearance transformed into shrieking grief. Everyone, her distraught husband and other grown children included, let her believe her son was merely missing. In a cheek-by-jowl neighborhood in a small town, everyone could rally together, even as devastated as they were with terror and sorrow. Keeping the man's mother in the dark was not hard. For days folks hid the truth from her, and for days she insisted her boy must have gone to the city to look for work. He'd talked about that a lot. Then one day, his oldest sister sat their mother down and said, "People are coming to mourn my brother."

Passersby on the street that day paused to stare upward as the mother nearly threw herself out the third-floor window and the daughter yanked her back by the waist, both screaming in agony like goats.

Of course, people blamed the victim for his own death. "What did he do to deserve such a thing?" And they blamed the victim's family—especially his mother—for raising a man who would give into who-knows-what temptation and be murdered for it.

No one in the neighborhood or the town wanted to believe the killer would return. Some came to agree with Mr. Murad. She had to have been a malevolent, vengeful stranger. She had to be long gone. She couldn't possibly strike again. No one deserved a death like that—and if anyone did, well, he was gone now. They pushed fear away, bit by bit, day by day, and went on with their lives.

Still, those who prepared the desecrated body for burial, and those who heard their first-person accounts, woke up night after night, shaking and sweating from nightmares that looped through their minds and followed them throughout their days. They saw the murdered man first from above, as though they themselves were the killer, saw him shrinking back from them as though he could escape down, down through the concrete. Then, they *were* him, cowering in the alley, with some monstrous creature hulking above. A veil or blindfold over their eyes kept them from seeing her, but the searing pain, the nauseating smell of a perfume that had once been whale excrement, the gallop of fear in their chests—

They knew they were dying.

CHAPTER 2

Donkey of Donkeys

Seven-year-old Layla meets a beast.
Adults begin to fear.

My name is Layla and here is how I come to be: I grow up in a neighborhood on the edge of town, in a town on the edge of the hilly countryside, on the edge of change, on the edge of time.

How do I come to be?

How do I come to be that is different from how *you* came to be?

I start as a little girl with hopes, just like anyone's, but all my own. Earliest memory: When I am seven, I ask my father for a donkey, fully believing that because he loves me, he will say yes.

Since I can remember, I've wanted more than anything to be self-sufficient. To think for myself, walk on my own two feet, get myself wherever I'm going. So, I convince myself that trotting to school on a donkey would suit me much better than taking the bus or riding in Baba's white pickup truck with my brothers and sisters.

Baba loves his truck, and often tells me I should grow up to be a teacher. *Why in God's name,* he must think, *does Layla want a beast of burden?* It isn't a normal thing for a little girl in our town to want. Riding a donkey is a vestige of the past unless you're a farmer. And fewer and fewer people in our region farm anymore.

Most of my parents' generation have moved to town from the country, looking for better jobs, more reliable electricity, modern plumbing, even though our little town has few industries and few resources, unlike the port city a few hours away. When one family member moves to town, others follow, often settling in the same neighborhood or the same building and working in the same professions or selling the same goods and sharing one car or truck among several branches of the family until everyone saves up for their own.

That's how my family got here. The animals that prowl or scurry or strut around our neighborhood are stray cats with patchy fur, geckos with missing tails, and pigeons with French fries in their beaks. Not donkeys.

None of that matters to me, a child who stares out the open window for hours a day. A child who speaks her mind. I have thought long and hard about the benefits of a donkey. My reasoning goes like this:

I am too young to drive a car.

I really, really want a pet.

My brothers are allergic to cats.

Baba is always late to pick us up from school.

No one else in my second-grade class has a donkey.

Also, in my young imagination, a donkey's life represents freedom. A donkey, I imagine (though as an adult I'll realize it's not all true), can go where he or she wants, pull a heavy cart, eat when she wants, be ugly, be smelly, never bathe, live alone. If a donkey is late, it's because the donkey wants to mosey, wants to sniff the world around her as she goes. When a donkey is sad, she eats clover.

As much as I want to *have* a donkey, I want to *be like* a donkey, too. Want my ears to grow long and sensitive to the sounds of crickets and birds, want my nostrils to widen, my teeth to thicken, my hands and feet to harden into hooves. I want a tail to shoo away flies.

That such a transformation can never happen leaves me with the same bone-deep sadness as not getting to eat sweets every day, never being able to be the eldest child, or knowing no human has ever learned to fly.

"Layla, Layloula," my father says when I tell him I want a donkey. He smells like the smoky incense he burns every morning in a shiny incense burner he plugs into the wall in my parents' bedroom. The incense annoys my mother, who prefers cleaner scents—perfume for her, cologne for him, bootlegged French and American brands.

I love his smoky smell.

"Baba," I say.

I rub my forehead on his goatee and kiss his cheek. When I perform these small affections before I ask him for things, he almost always says yes.

On the topic of a donkey, he's skeptical. "Why do you want a donkey?"

"I told you why."

"Who will take care of this animal?"

"I would take care of my donkey. I would never be late for school."

"Where will we keep the donkey?"

"Tie her up in the alley!"

"How about your bedroom?"

"She'll poop in there and my room will stink."

"What if someone steals the donkey from the alley?"

"Baba! Stop teasing!"

My father will not give in, but he never wants to disappoint me. One weekend morning soon after I ask for the donkey, Baba packs thickened cream and jam sandwiches, two bananas, two clementines, and a thermos of Lipton, straps me into the passenger seat of his pickup on top of several volumes of the dictionary he inherited from my grandfather, and sets out for a farm twenty minutes outside town. The cab of his truck is like a tiny home for the two of us. Outside my window, the balconied five-story buildings of town give way to cute little brightly colored houses and date and citrus farms, greenish hills crisscrossed by low stone walls, and a trickling stream that arrives only once or twice a year after the rains. In all other seasons, there is a dry, rocky bed. Today is a warm winter day, not hot like summer and not chilly enough for a sweater like it will be later this evening. The inside of the cab heats up like a greenhouse and smells like vinyl. I press down the window button so the breeze can touch my face; I breathe in the scents of greenery and loamy soil. It's a treat to be out with my father without my two younger brothers, my two older sisters, and my mother, who usually sits in the cab while we children ride dangerously in the truck bed, the boys on my sisters' laps. Without cousins or aunts and uncles in a caravan behind us, probably gossiping about us, finding fault, conjecturing, even though they love us as they love their own parents and children. No, today it's me and Baba, on our way, I believe with all my heart, to buy a donkey.

EMAN QUOTAH

At the farm, Baba's friend, whom I call Uncle, waits in the dirt yard wearing an old-fashioned cotton robe. He has a little knife on a belt, the kind all men used to arm themselves with in the old days. Behind him are a chicken coop and a goat on a long, fraying rope tied to a fencepost without a fence. A hen and a rooster roam around, kicking up their feet like Spanish dancers. A duck and its babies sleep in a cozy circle. An orchard of palms stands to the left, ahead of us a small barn, and in the back, rows and rows of spindly bushes. On later trips to the farm, I will see and smell these plants in full bloom: roses.

I'm disappointed. There are no donkeys in the yard. On the barn's roof, a white, brown, and orange cat dozes with its belly offered to the sun.

My father and Uncle kiss each other on both cheeks. Then the farmer bends his knees, as grown-ups do to come face to face with a child. He shakes my hands with both of his.

"Donkeys are misunderstood," he says. "Most people think they're worthless, smelly animals, but we know they're beautiful and useful in their own way."

"Thank God for donkeys," I say. "I'm going to ride mine to school."

Uncle laughs and puts his arm around my father. "Your father won't let me sell you my donkey, and to be honest, I don't want to lose my strong beast. I grow wheat back there, and watermelons. Tomatoes. Fig trees over there. And my wife grows ginger, for stomach ailments, and flowers and herbs for perfume: roses, lavender, lilac, sage, basil. We need our donkey."

There's a kernel of anger in me ready to unfurl itself and grow. My father has betrayed me.

"I've got a lot of birthday and holiday money," I say. "I can pay for the donkey myself."

The men laugh. They think I'm being cute. My father asks if I want to pet the donkey, Bumbo. Uncle sweeps his arm toward the barn, inviting me forward. I rush ahead. I'll figure out a way to take Bumbo home!

Behind me, Baba and Uncle's conversation sounds like *wiss, wiss, wiss, wiss, wiss*. Their voices are too low for me to make out the words at first, but then Uncle starts to sound agitated. He struggles to keep to a whisper. I pretend to ignore them, taking in the smell of manure, the scritch-scratch of hay under my jelly sandals. A high-pitched braying comes from the far corner of the barn. I follow the sound.

Here is something most children know how to do: Pretend they are invisible to adults when they are right in front of them. It works half the time. On this day at the farm, the more the two men talk, the less they remember—or care—that I'm underfoot.

"Horrifying," Uncle says. "My wife and I can't sleep at night. We've told our older sons to stay away from town. I'll run the errands myself. The other children only go for school. No visiting friends anymore."

"God protect us, I think it's safe in town," Baba says. "Only one incident. We shouldn't exaggerate it into more than it is."

"If I lost one of my children—to that. No one could console me. God protects us, *and* we have to tie up our animals to keep them from being stolen. We have to keep our children under our watchful eyes."

"Sure," Baba says. "Protect your children and your possessions. But don't lock them away from the sun. They'll wither."

"More people think like me than you're aware, Dr. Sami."

While they talk, I find Bumbo, his chin resting on the door of his stall as though he's been waiting for me. I rub his long gray-brown forehead, his white blaze, his velvet nose. His lips grab my fingers and his tongue licks between them. He's hoping for a taste of sugar that I don't know to offer. The wet, sloppy tongue on my skin makes me giggle—and yearn even more for my father to listen to my wishes.

"Look, Baba," I say. "He'll fit in the pickup!"

My father's distracted, already telling me it's time to go when we just got here. I've hardly spent a minute with Bumbo, hardly had enough time to admire his fluffy ears and pet his scraggly mane, or to work on Baba and beg him to take Bumbo home. I want to tell my father he's being mean and unfair. But Uncle is standing right here, and my father won't put up with disrespect in front of another adult.

I growl. I blink long and slow, hoping the men don't see my tears.

"I'm hungry," I say.

"We'll eat in the car," Baba says.

Uncle points to a stump and tells us we can sit and eat there. He has a field to mow. His son brings sodas and sweet biscuits to round out our meal.

We eat our sandwiches and fruit in the sun with our backs to each other, bees buzzing at our knuckles and in our ears, while my father thinks about a dead man and God's plan and mortality, and I fantasize about stealing a donkey, about independence, about leaving and never coming back. How far could I get? How fast could Bumbo go?

Baba turns on the car's air conditioner on the way home, and

I fall asleep with the seatbelt pressing into my cheek. When I wake up, he's carrying me upstairs to our flat. My head is on his shoulder. I lift it, because I'm still angry, but I'm too sleepy to try to get down from Baba's arms.

"You fell asleep," he says, as though I might not remember that the last moment I was awake, we were in the truck.

Mama is at the open door at the top of the shadowy stairwell. "Thank goodness! I was worried you wouldn't get home before dark."

Baba puts me down. I stumble inside.

"It's not even four o'clock," he says, kicking off his slides, in a rush to be home. "This one met a donkey today."

Mama kneels and hugs the air out of me. "You're the donkey of all donkeys," she says. "The goat of all goats."

Stubborn, she means.

"The eye of our eyes," Baba says.

"Our moon," Mama says.

Beloved, they mean.

I keep thinking about Bumbo, about roads, about the world outside.

My parents worry about murder, about safety, about things I cannot yet grasp.

CHAPTER 3

"The Devil Is Male"

Second victim.

On the mirror on the lift's back wall, in the aging block of flats across from where the corner store used to be, a message had been scrawled in blood or nail polish—no one was sure which at first. It said:

"Lust kills."

One year had passed since the murder in the alley, and most people had gone back to spending their days and nights as they had before, feeling safe again. But now, on a cool fall night, a man had been sliced in two.

The ingenious killer had pilloried her new victim with the tarnished brass grate on the building's rickety lift. The horrific killing was difficult to believe unless you saw it with your own eyes. And if you saw it with your own eyes, you could never forget. The body, somehow, miraculously, remained standing, hugging either side of the grate, stiff and motionless as a wax statue. With a knife or sickle, she'd carved deep trenches into the victim's cheeks and back.

Up and down the building, the dying man's screams had violently severed residents from their dreams, but only Zaynah, a seamstress and mother who lived and worked on the third floor in the flat nearest the central stairwell, heard the clop-clop-clop of hooves. For the rest of her life, she would keep the sound a secret, convinced it was a hallucination, the trick of a terrorized mind.

While the screaming went on and on, everyone huddled in their beds, frozen with fear. When the screaming stopped, mothers and older sisters held young children close as fathers and older brothers opened their doors, peered into neon-lit hallways, and carefully investigated the scene, wondering who among their neighbors they would soon be mourning and what had brought the monster back. Soon, some people let their consciences overtake them and propel them downstairs, though in their hearts they wanted to hide in a wardrobe with a flashlight, their spouses and children, and their elderly parents. A scream like that, torn from the soul, could only be caused by murder, could only be caused by a monster of a human being, these dwellers of the upper floors told each other as they tiptoed down the steps toward the ground floor.

"I saw a stranger loitering about, a woman with silky black hair," someone whispered.

"Like any woman here who hasn't gone gray or dyed her hair?" Zaynah said.

"She held a sharp, curved blade."

"You lie. You didn't see a thing!"

"What if the killer is still among us?"

They had not arrived at the body in the lobby yet, but they'd had twelve months to speculate on the reasons behind the monstrosity of the Corner Store Killer. To stare across the street at the alley, full of shadows, and imagine her triumphantly standing with a human heart in her cupped palm. Mr. Murad had moved the corner store around the block, and the old place was empty, its metal gate vandalized: "Leave our neighborhood alone."

Uncountable theories had circulated in the beginning, like incense being fanned into a pitcher of water. A spurned woman, a jealous husband, a maniac, the secret service, a business or romantic rival, religious fanatics, an overseas gang. One of the Murad sons made fun of his grandfather's superstition by weaving a spooky tale to scare his younger siblings and their friends: The murderer was a cunning, vengeful jinn who had once been almost human and so yearned for human flesh!

No one had said "serial killer" over the past year, though a few had wondered, *Could it happen again?*

Now, the neighbors were in the lobby, a new victim before them. The body was starting to slump, its innards to ooze out. The neighbors looked away, looked back, retched loudly, ran upstairs or into the night, believing they could forget by running away from a sight that had, already, etched itself into their brains. Those who stayed covered their faces. A few people muttered prayers, even some who weren't much for religion. Then they peeked, breathing rhythmically to try to keep from gagging.

They knew the halved man, of course. He lived on the second floor. A father with young children who would grow up without him now.

The threat of a serial killer bloomed in the neighbors' minds like mold. Could this happen to them? Someone they loved?

Someone breathed deeply and said, "Smells like Chanel!"

A stifled laugh. More retching. The retching was contagious. Someone was sobbing.

"She's back among us. The murderess from the alley."

"He angered her somehow. Angered the monster."

"The Devil and most murderers and abusers are male," said Zaynah. "But you'll blame a woman for the worst crimes."

No one debated Zaynah, but everyone could smell the counterargument, the feminine scent emanating from inside the lift.

And then another scream that could have cut out your appendix, from the lungs of the victim's wife, who appeared as though from nowhere brandishing an antique sword. She looked fearsome, rageful, ready to kill every bystander before her. They wrestled her to the ground and the sword skittered to the victim's feet. If only, when alive, he'd been armed, warned, vigilant enough to escape.

At last, the dead man's father and sisters, who lived next door to him, arrived, convulsing with grief. To spare them, a group of nightgowned and pajamaed women stood side by side in front of the corpse, forming a human screen.

At their center, Zaynah held the sword high and proclaimed, "Keep vigilant! Whatever monster killed him is on the loose. Don't let it get you, too."

CHAPTER 4

"She Prowls at Night"

Best friends. A parent's death.
Mourning. Changes at school.
A late-night plan.

For the past year, since my first visit to the farm with Baba, I've been telling my best friend, Susu, about my donkey. About his soft face, his funny donkey smile, his love of sugar cubes and alfalfa, his donkey smell.

We're in third grade, and since kindergarten we've walked to school together every morning. Now that we're a little older, my sisters—who are twelve and thirteen—and the other older kids walk ahead, waiting for us to be distracted by our conversation with each other and not notice they have turned a corner and left us far behind. Sometimes, they pop into Murad's Corner Store, which switched corners a year ago and is now on our route to school, away from where our parents can spy on us. Mr. Murad has retired, and his sons will sell children anything—even cigarettes, but not in the morning, only after school. Sometimes Susu and I go in there, too, and buy candy bars for breakfast.

THE NIGHT IS NOT FOR YOU

Whenever I bring up Bumbo, Susu makes a raspberry sound with her tongue.

"We could ride him to school," I say.

"Gross," she says. "Stop talking about the donkey."

I'm beginning to understand that other people don't love all the things I do. That to keep a friend, you have to try not to bore them. I try to limit my donkey talk to once a week, but it's hard because even though I've only gone back to visit Bumbo a couple of times, I constantly go on imaginary adventures with him. Bumbo takes me to school, the grocery store, the mountains, the beach. Bumbo nuzzles my hand when I'm sad. Bumbo is my other best friend. To prevent myself from annoying Susu too much, I let her lead the conversation. If I love what she wants to talk about, I jump in and talk about it too. We talk about jelly shoes, bananas, which cartoons and video games we like and are allowed to play, which ones our older siblings have sneakily let us watch, our favorite dragon books and jinn stories, hedgehogs, guinea pigs, elephants (you can ride them, like a donkey, but much higher so you can see the world!), cats, dogs, ice cream. Susu and I talk to each other about everything. I will never again have a friend like Susu, but I don't know that. Like any eight-year-old, I haven't yet learned how precious a single friendship can be, like a flowering plant that blooms once a decade, bright purple or white or red, for a day or hours, and then dies.

And then, one morning a month or two into the school year, Susu's not at the corner when I arrive. I'm late because my sister Rana hid my lunch box. I couldn't find it, and ended up leaving home without my lunch. I will never understand why she chose this day, of all days, to be mean to me. I will wonder if it was a blessing that she did or a curse.

I lean against the sandstone façade of the building on the corner. I'm mad at myself and at Rana, and Susu's not here to make me laugh and forget how annoying Rana is. I rub my back against the wall, trying to get the right angle to relieve an itch on my shoulder blade. I turn my face to the sun and a sky as blue as the swimming pools I've seen in movies but never in person.

Maybe Susu gave up waiting on me. If I don't leave now, I'll miss the late bell.

I start walking. I'm hesitant and vigilant. I've never walked alone to school, or anywhere else. I watch out for bulges in the sidewalk that might trip me, older children who might be hiding round a corner to leap out and shock me, tree branches low enough to flick my face, pigeons on power lines readying themselves to poop on my head. I look up, down, and all around, which of course slows me. I look both ways five times when I cross the narrow street toward Murad's market. A calico cat named Biss crosses the street with me, trotting with purpose. Biss usually expects bits of turkey and cheese from our lunch sandwiches, but I have nothing to give her today. When we reach the curb, Biss looks up at me, then back behind us, her eyes round and questioning, her ears twitchy, her whiskers taut. *Where's Susu?* she seems to ask.

"Sorry, Biss. I don't know where she is, and I don't have anything to feed you."

Biss meows at me, her green eyes shining like marbles. She's too cute not to stop for. My mother told me never to touch Biss because strays bite and they might have rabies. Biss would never hurt me, though. I hunch down and touch the top of Biss's head. She leans into my fingers to get me to scratch her. I give her a few scratches, and it feels as good to me as it does to her. She purrs and I hum.

I tell Biss I really do have to go. Susu is probably at school waiting for me.

I get going at an unhurried pace, backpack bopping. Past blocks of flats packed one after the other in jumbly rows. Our classmates live in these buildings, but I don't see anyone coming out or going in. This route avoids the main road. I don't detect any strangeness, but in my memories, many years later, I will see things more clearly, and notice that something seems off. The sun too bright. The air too clean-smelling and fresh. The traffic quieter than it should be at this hour. A bicycle bell tinkles in the distance. Since I started walking, I haven't heard a horn honking or a motorcycle vrooming. Maybe long-ago me does sense some quiet, vague threat, because I decide I should get more of a move on. I jog, holding on to the straps of my backpack. What if I'm late? Mama will kill me!

Biss jogs along beside me, sweet as a donkey.

No one is going into Murad's, ringing the little bell on the door, or coming out with their cups of coffee and cinnamon buns and bottles of orange juice and breakfast sandwiches and chocolate bars. I notice, in my memory, as I hurry past, that this is another thing different about today. I'm worried about being late for school, but I'm easily distracted. There's a little yellow flower in the crease between the sidewalk and the brick of the store. I stop to contemplate this lone bloom, and my worries evaporate like beads of sweat off my arm. Biss sniffs the petals, nibbles their edges, sits on her haunches, and stares at me. We start to walk; we hustle along. The sun warming my scalp feels good. The freedom of walking on my own starts to lift me, as though I'm floating a few centimeters off the ground, gliding along.

Much later in my life, I will I hold on to that memory of floating. I will see myself doing it, my sneakers walking on air. I will think, *In my childhood, there was this moment of freedom.* If I could, I'd return to that day and snap a Polaroid of my freedom. I'd shake the photo until it developed, greenish and smudgy, and slide it into an envelope, to keep with me.

I go past a park that smells like the sewer water the town government uses to irrigate the patchy grass and leggy bougainvillea and spindly palms. Biss doesn't normally come this far, and here is where she turns around. There's a whole family of gray cats living here. Unlike Biss, they're feral and hostile. I see them and count them: Mama, three babies, a tom that may or may not be the dad. There's a skinny yellow dog with no collar that gets loose and chases the cat family. Without Susu to hold my hand, I'm afraid the dog will come for me. I rush past the park and up the hill.

For a child, even a walk to school is filled with fears, with dangers.

Past my school, I see the bright white school building my older sisters go to, bigger and boxier than my school, and across from it the boys' upper school. There's no one outside. As usual, Rana and Lajwa have left me far behind, failed to do their duty of dropping off me and Susu. If something has happened to Susu, it will be their fault. The idea of tattling on them to Mama and Baba cheers me up.

Never mind that my parents hate tattling. Telling them what happened this morning won't be snitching. It will be the truth. They won't punish me for telling the truth.

In front of my school, The Lower Garden of Knowledge for Girls and Boys, are two spindly evergreens with peeling bark. Behind its outer wall, the school is made up of two former residential buildings with little outbuildings around them. Our classrooms have balconies and flocked wallpaper. From the third-grade balcony, you can see into the other neighborhoods beyond ours, their white villas with walls hiding gardens and, probably, swimming pools. My classmates and I can only imagine the lush green and sparkling blue.

If I were on time, the doorman would be standing at the open gates to the schoolyard, arguing with one of the parents about nothing important or telling a child to stop crying and get inside. He'd be surrounded by gaggles of families, walking caravans of children who live in the same buildings, the littlest ones holding on to ropes with loops on either side. And there'd be the little white shuttles that transport students from the borders of the neighborhood. The mothers and fathers would be hurrying to say goodbye and head to work or back home to care for the younger children strapped to their stomachs and backs.

This is the last time, for many years, that I will be able, be allowed, to walk through the neighborhood alone. Or even in a pair. This will be the day, if I trace events backward, that everything starts to change.

I'm late. The front of the school is empty and quiet, and I am alone. The doorman is nowhere to be found. If someone snatched me or attacked me or threatened me or stared at me with evil intent or touched me, no one would know. I try the gate. It's locked. My stomach tumbles. Where is the doorman? He never leaves his post. He's been snatched, probably. My liver and kidneys throb with fear. I wonder where Susu is, where the other students and the teachers and the head of school are. I tell myself, *You are brave, Layla. You will knock on the door and they will let you in. The doorman is probably using the toilet.* I need to use the toilet, too. I hope someone will let me in soon.

I knock a few times more, wait a minute, knock again. The steel door sounds hollow when I bang on it. I plop my backpack on the sidewalk. No one comes. I knock. "I need to pee," I shout. Mulish grass pushes up through cracks in the dirty gray concrete blocks. Black blotches on the sidewalk mark the spots where bad children spat out their wads of gum, and some other unsuspecting child stepped on them, flattening them, and then dirt and grime colored the flattened gum wads and unstickied them. I walk on the black splotches. I sit on the curb and lean back to look at the sky for the first time since I left the street corner where Susu was supposed to meet me. A dark-brown bird, a hawk or a kite, floats lazily. Can it see Susu from up there?

Just when I think no one is ever going to come and I will have to walk back home alone, my sisters come running, panting, from the direction of their school. My parents walk briskly behind them. Why are they here? School is closed, my sisters say while my parents catch up, and all the children have been sent home, and they were worried silly about me. I should never have gone off like that.

"I was walking to school," I say. How can they be angry at me for doing what I was supposed to do? "I need to pee. Can we go inside?"

"Everyone went home," Lajwa says. "School is closed." Her face is red and wet; her eyes shine with tears.

"Susu, too?" I ask.

My parents have arrived, and we repeat the conversation: *School is closed, why did you wander off, where is Susu.*

"Susu..." Mama starts to say.

I want to be closer to my mother; I want her comforting smell. I sidle up to her, and she puts an arm around me.

"Susu is home today," my father says.

Rana throws herself at me and hugs me. My ribs squeal. My bladder shudders and threatens to empty. I shove her away. I'm still mad she stole my lunchbox.

"Is Susu OK?"

"Yes," says Baba.

"No," says Mama.

"What happened to her?"

"Don't scream."

How can Mama say that? I walked all the way to school, unaware anything was wrong. How could they let that happen to me?

Baba stoops to hug me and hushes me. He's the only person who could possibly calm me right now. They're not going to explain any more than what has been said so far. I'll have to ask my sisters when we get home.

The sky has gone dark in an instant, like a storm is coming. We squeeze into Mama's little car, and Baba drives, and the things no one is saying are in the car too, crowding us. We go past the park, the cat family. Rana hums; no one talks. At the flat, I rush to the bathroom and let everything out of my bladder. When I join my family in the living room, my parents are gathering up their work things, getting ready to go back out and leave us here. Our little brothers, Fadi and Bassam, are at my grandmother's flat, a few blocks away.

My parents whisper to my sisters: "Don't say anything yet. It's rumors and gossip. Don't turn on the TV or the radio. The news will scare your little sister. Don't go outside. Don't even play in the stairwell or on the roof."

I ask if I can call Susu. Mama says no. Baba looks like he wants to say yes, like he's about to dial for me, but Mama pulls him toward the door. She tells Rana she'll call at noon. Don't answer the phone any other time. Our parents leave us, in the prison of our home.

I aim the remote control at the TV. Rana smacks it out of my hand. Whatever happened to Susu and her family must be very bad, if it's something I could find out about on the news. I yell, "You know what happened, but you won't tell me, and Susu is my friend."

I kneel on the couch, which sits against the wall, under a window. I slide the window open.

Rana and Lajwa debate whether they should let me look outside. Or would Mama say that was off limits, too?

"We should tell Layloula what happened," Lajwa says. "She deserves to know."

Rana makes a face and practically shakes her whole body. *No.* She looks like a monkey. *Eee, ee, ee,* I think.

"Come on. Tell me."

Rana locks her mouth with an invisible key. She glares at Lajwa. "You, too," she says, twisting the invisible key. "Lock your trap."

I stand on the sofa cushions and bounce. "You talked! You talked!"

Lajwa stands in the doorway, like she's about to leave the room. "I can't deal with you two. Tell her, Rana." She thinks they should tell me, but she's not the one who's going to crack. Lajwa can keep a secret. And she lets Rana be the leader, does what Rana says, like walking ahead to school and leaving me behind. Rana isn't concerned about protecting me. She likes to be in control. Lajwa is older, but Rana is bossier. We rarely beat her at her game. Rana is also a huge tattletale. She tells my parents when I don't make my bed or sweep up after dinner, which is my job while Lajwa and Rana do the dishes; our brothers are too little to help. Rana tattles on children at school, and teachers love her because she points out the cheaters while they're copying an answer off someone's sheet or the insides of their forearms. Skirting the rules is only OK when Rana's the one who decides which rules to bend.

I badly want to outwit her. Maybe today will be my day. Maybe I can guess what happened, and she'll give it away. I start with a wildly incorrect guess: "Did their building burn down?"

Lajwa laughs and points at me, like she's declaring a winner in a game of soccer.

Rana groans. "Of course not, you can see it through the window, right there."

I look. Since earlier this morning, someone has put up yellow tape in an X across the building's front door, which is outlined in a brass-colored metal and mirrored, like many of the doors in our neighborhood. People who live in the buildings can see out, but passersby can't see in. I look closer. The shades on all the windows are drawn—that's normal. People like their privacy.

Then I notice that the balconies are empty. Days I've stayed home from school with a cold or the flu, my neighborhood's balconies were full of activity. The grandmas and stay-at-home mothers and aunties and retired grandpas and out-of-work fathers and uncles smoking on the balconies, drinking coffee or tea, hanging their laundry, chatting with neighbors who loiter on the street below.

Today is different. There are no boxer briefs and T-shirts and dresses and scarves drying on racks or lines strung from the walls or between potted ficus plants. Everyone's taken down their laundry, or not hung it up. No one's sitting on a plastic chair reading a paper with a cup in their other hand. No one's loitering on the street today, either.

The emptiness of the tableau makes me panic.

I turn around and step onto the coffee table, knocking over the Kleenex box. I'm not supposed to stand on the coffee table, but Mama and Baba are not here to see me, and I ignore Rana when she says, "Get down!" She retrieves the box of Kleenex and shakes it in my face. It's in a fancy crocheted tissue holder my aunt made. She makes them in her flat and sells them to her neighbors. I don't care that I knocked it over. I close my eyes so I can't see Rana shaking it in my face. The yarn smells like my auntie; the tissues inside smell papery and clean. In the future, when I think of my sister, I will think of those smells. Middle-aged lady smells, even before she was a middle-aged lady. I open my eyes and push Rana away, then stand with my knees bent, my hands at my waist, like I mean business. I'm driven by a sense of urgency to *know what happened*. What if they're all gone? What if everyone in that building disappeared into thin air?

"Did her grandma die? Her sister? Her mother?"

I grab the tissue box and beat my sister with it. Asking so many questions at once is a terrible strategy, but the words rush out of me. I'm powerless. Rana's calm has returned. I think she might push me back, but she doesn't. She tugs the box away from me and sets it on the table, next to my foot, like she's daring me to kick it. She looks as satisfied as Biss did this morning when I rubbed her head.

Lajwa is suspended halfway up the doorway, like an acrobat, hands and feet pressed against the doorframe's sides, watching me and Rana face off. She does both things often: climbs the doorjambs and observes me and Rana. Even later, when she's a grown-up, an architect, a mother, too old to climb the walls, she'll seem to me like she's suspended in air.

Rana purrs. She is going to best me. "Susu's grandma is already dead. She died last year."

"Did her Mama die?"

Rana locks her mouth, smiles a thin, immoveable smile, and walks toward the doorway. She stares at Lajwa, who jumps to the floor. Rana leaves the room, knocking Lajwa's shoulder as she passes through the doorway.

"Sorry, little sister," Lajwa says.

The battle is not over. I can be patient—that is my power. I get a piece of paper, a tin of colored pencils, and a hardback book and start to draw a picture of Bumbo for Susu. I lie on my stomach on the couch, one leg in the air, and dream about him as I draw. He is plain brown and gray, which is boring, so I draw a green field and orange flowers and blue sky and a tree with red apples. I give Bumbo a purple bow around his neck. I hope Susu is OK. I draw a sun. I draw dark clouds, black and gray with a bit of mustard yellow, like pee.

Lajwa sits on the sofa and reads a comic book till Rana comes back, her hair brushed and curled, eyes kohled, lips glossed, as though she's going out, not stuck here with her sisters all day. My sisters play Concan, their favorite card game, on the coffee table, and when they're done and Lajwa has won the most points, I ask if we can go to the playground.

"Stop it," says Rana. "Mama said don't go outside."

"Not till Mama and Baba come back," says Lajwa, kindly. "Be patient, Layloulie."

"I hate you," I say. "I'm hungry."

My sisters heat up leftover rice and lamb for lunch. The meaty lamb aroma fills the house. We eat at the coffee table, and I get bits of lamb between my teeth. While I'm worrying the stuff out with my tongue, I spill my juice by-accident-on-purpose.

Rana yells at me and tells me to get a paper towel to clean it up.

I'm ready for her. "Not unless you tell me what happened to Susu."

"Come on, you pest. Clean up your mess."

"No."

Apple juice cascades onto the carpet. Lajwa looks like she might climb the wall like a gecko or a spider and cower in a corner of the ceiling. Rana groans and goes to the kitchen, and comes back with a roll of paper and a sponge. She wipes the table and scrubs the carpet and says I'm a brat.

"I'm sorry," I say. "This is the worst day ever."

"We should tell her," Lajwa says. She's cracking, after all. I'm proud of myself for getting her to give in. "We should tell her what happened."

"No." Rana is holding the wet sponge and a wad of yellowy-damp paper towels. I smell the mildew of the sponge, the sweet-tart apple juice.

"It's about her best friend. She should know."

"No. Let Mama and Baba tell her."

"Right. She's going to find out when Mama comes home. Why can't we tell her? We're her sisters. We should tell each other things."

"Fine," says Rana, leaving for the kitchen, hands dripping. "Whatever. I don't care. You do it."

The whole room smells like apples now.

Lajwa says, "You're sort of right. Someone died."

"It's too awful to talk about." Rana is back. She can't help herself. "Someone murdered Susu's father."

Until now, I have never heard the word *murdered* used about a person I know. Murder only happens inside a newspaper or a television or a computer or a phone or the mystery novels Mama reads. Murder is not something older people talk to little children about, unless they absolutely have to.

"Murdered him dead?" I say.

How does an eight-year-old hear the word *murdered*, hear the word *dead*? If the person who'd died were someone I didn't know or who didn't matter much to me, I would picture a death in a movie. An actor writhing on the ground, and when the cameras turned off, getting up and heading home. Movies are not real. But my best friend's father is dead, and that means a person I know is truly dead, never coming back. A best friend's father is a shadow of a person to a little girl, but he's real to her friend, as real as the little girl's own parents. *The friend*—me— grasps his realness, and his death extends the circle of death to the friend's friends. In other words, for me, Susu's father's death suggests other deaths—not mine; that still seems unlikely. My life has barely begun. But someone I love dying, my mother or father, my sisters or brothers.

31

What if it were my father, not Susu's, who'd been murdered?

Rana says, "Yes, you donkey, he's dead." Now that she's decided I can hear what happened, she's all in. And she wants to scare me. She spooky-whispers: "Whoever killed him left him in pieces. Hacked him up!"

Hacked. The word sounds violent, especially the way Rana spits it out, but its full meaning is out of reach. I imagine Susu's father's arms and legs detached from his body, his head lolling to the side, chin pointing to the floor. No blood. Clean cuts, like a carrot or potato sliced into chunks.

"Shut up," says Lajwa. "We don't know if that's true. Don't scare her."

"She should be scared. We should all be scared. I heard the headmistress say he was *cut into pieces*, so it has to be true."

"Did the person kill him in the alley?"

"He, or she, killed him in a *lift*," Rana says. "You're lucky we don't have one in our building, or the murderer might get you, too."

"Don't make things up," says Lajwa. "I heard he was killed right in his bed."

"The point is, Layla better watch out, better watch where she goes. There's a murderer out there. A murderer who could get *you*." She presses her finger right on my chest, so hard I feel my breastbone give.

My face flames with tears. Lajwa shoves Rana away from me. She lets me sob into her shoulder.

"It's horrible, so horrible, like that other guy who died," Rana says.

"What other guy?" No one has told me about a guy dying *before*.

Lajwa gently lets me go and sets me on the couch. "Shut up, Rana, or I'll stuff a sponge in your mouth."

We hear a clap of thunder, and the sky dumps rain onto our building and our neighborhood. The rain on the roof is like a stampede of elephants. The smell of wet dust obscures all other smells. In five minutes, the rain peters out, turning into a drizzle. The drizzle subsides, and the sun comes out and dries everything, in less than an hour, and I start wishing I could go out.

The rest of the day passes slowly, second by second, minute by minute, in a gray-beige blur of boredom punctuated by excruciating worry. What if the killer is still lurking in the neighborhood? Will my parents come back from work? Will they die today? Will they die one day? What will I do then?

When my parents come home, they deduce right away that my sisters have told me. They're exasperated, but not angry.

Baba says, "Don't believe everything you hear. The police are still figuring out what happened."

Mama says, "We have to be strong for Susu and her family. We can't spread gossip because that will hurt them." At dinner, I beg my parents to let me see Susu that evening. I think for sure Mama will say no, but she says yes. She tells me to put on a nice dress and brush my hair and teeth. She explains that the family is sitting in grief. Neighbors stop by to give their condolences.

I wear a yellow dress with tulip sleeves. I braid my hair. I look at myself in the mirror on the wardrobe and think I look like a princess.

As we're getting our shoes on, my mother lectures me.

"You have to be polite. Don't say a word."

"Why?" I've been to Susu's dozens of times.

"This kind of grief is worse than regular grief," Baba says. "It was a terrible death."

"All death is terrible," Mama says. "All death is the end. All death rips love away from us."

"You know what I mean. The way he died."

They seem to have forgotten I'm sitting on the foyer floor beneath them, putting on my socks and shoes.

Baba will go to the men's open house, at Susu's uncle's flat, and we will go to Susu's auntie's place, upstairs. Lajwa and Rana stay home to take care of the boys.

Shadows lurk everywhere. The fluorescent light in our stairwell flickers and crackles and illuminates my parents' features in stark contrasts, as though tiny shadowy creatures hide in the crevices of their faces. Our shoes squeak on the marble floor. How does our building feel so haunted when nothing bad has happened here?

The street is quiet and cool. A nighttime breeze kisses my face with the cinnamon scent of flowers blooming out of sight, somewhere around a corner. Susu's building is two doors down on the other side of the street; her relatives' building, where we are going, is one door over from hers. Yellow tape still marks the door to Susu's building, and all the windows are unlit. The place looks haunted. No one lingers in front of it, as though ghosts or ghouls have drawn an invisible border around the building, or installed an electric fence. Even the trees in front of Susu's, in their square holes in the concrete, droop sadly, haunted and shadowy.

Baba notices me staring.

"The police are investigating the...crime," he says. He can't say the word *murder*. I think he doesn't want to let it be true. One father's slaying, and the building is full of death.

"Everyone's staying with family," Mama says. "I wouldn't stay in a building where that happened, either."

"Did someone really—" I want to ask about the hacking. I want to ask where it happened. I want to be less afraid.

"Keep walking," Mama says.

Baba whispers. She harumphs. Do they want me to know the truth, or not? Are they afraid, too? How could they not be?

Starting at the edge of the next building, life returns. We cross over, and shimmy between the parked cars that line the street. A taxi idles in the middle of the road until a car honks politely and the taxi driver double parks so the other driver can squeeze by. Now someone wants to get out of their space, so they honk politely and the taxi moves again. My father says the drivers are unusually patient tonight. No one lowers a window to cuss and make rude gestures, as might happen on any other night.

"We have to be kind to each other at times like these," he says.

The doors to the building's foyer have been propped open, and the entry and every window up and down and across are lit to a warm, medium brightness. Shades up, curtains open, as though the building is saying, *Yes, we are sad, but...Nothing terrible happened here. Not haunted. Not haunted at all!* The crowd outside seems to include every adult in our neighborhood. Neighbors congregate, greeting each other solemnly as some go in and others come out. Some are dressed in traditional clothes, others in trousers and dresses and skirts. Many of the women are not wearing make-up. Everyone looks tired. The

35

entire neighborhood is grieving. For Susu's father, on behalf of her family.

A teacher I recognize from school, Miss Khayriyah, exits the building as we enter. She and my mother greet each other in the doorway and seem to tearily read each other's minds. Then Miss Khayriyah says something that makes my mother laugh. A guilty look takes over Mama's face. Is she thinking laughter is forbidden on this night? It feels that way to me, as though we should try to be as serious as possible. What if we laugh and the murderer comes after us, too?

"Susu will be so glad you came," Miss Khayriyah says to me. "She needs friends more than ever now."

In the lobby, someone has taped to the lift door a handwritten sign on printer paper: "Off limits. Use the stairs."

Mama mutters, "This is not even the lift that killed him." She pushes me toward the crowded stairs. "Well, it's healthier anyway to take the steps." She shudders, as though a cold, dead spirit has passed through her body.

No lift will ever look the same to me, or to my neighbors. No lift will ever appear innocent and unthreatening. We are about to become a neighborhood with no working lifts, a neighborhood of people who climb the stairs, no matter how many floors, whose calves and thighs become strong as steel, whose lungs expand.

As we climb upstairs, we pass more people coming down and are sandwiched between several families going up. What should I say to Susu? What can I ask? *Are you OK? Are you sad? Where's your dad's body now? What's your mother going to do?*

What I really want to talk about is roller-skating, candy, all those other things we talk about on the way to school.

Baba and the other men disembark the train of people on the third floor. Mama and I, and the other women and girls, climb to the fourth. Mama pants a little. A wave of bodies pushes us inside the flat where Susu is staying; the entryway smells like incense, rosewater, and coffee. Women sit on cushions along the walls. Women, standing, cover the floorspace and block my sightlines. Women are everywhere, talking, crying quietly to themselves, drinking coffee, fumbling in their purses for tissues. Eyes wide like a skeleton's empty sockets.

Mama kisses women on the cheeks. Some of the sitting women stand to greet her. We pass through fragrant gray smoke; I can't tell where the burners are. Stone-faced, Susu's aunties and older cousins pass out coffee. My mother speaks words of condolence to them, words that sound like gibberish—grown-ups' jargon.

We swim through the sea of women, through a room where Susu and I and her cousins have played video games, watched cartoons, but today the TV is gray and silent. We weave our way to the center of the labyrinth, to a family room in the back, its walls full of crooked, black-and-white family photos of stiff, unsmiling ancestors in their younger days. There are glass shelves filled with knickknacks and wedding favors, little heart-shaped boxes and plaques and ceramic figurines in fancy old-timey clothes and golden swans and little engraved plates on tiny wooden plateholders.

My mother asks for Susu's mother.

"She's in the third bedroom, back that way," an auntie in a white dress tells us. Her hair is slicked flat against her skull, almost as smooth as a black scarf. In a deep, sandpapery voice, she says, "Susu and the others are with her."

"We don't want to disturb them," my mother says. She lays her hand flat on my head. "But this is Susu's best friend, and she'd very much like to see Susu. Do you think we can go in?"

The auntie bends to my level. Her thick glasses magnify her eyes. The brown irises around black pupils fill her lenses to the edges. She parts her lips, but she's not smiling. I think I could fit my pinky finger into the gap between her teeth, and I'm tempted to try. She appears bewitched and otherworldly. She's too much to take in, so I look at her feet, encased in flesh-colored stockings. One toe pokes through a hole in the nylon.

She catches my chin and pulls it up. "Thank you for coming, dear. Susu will be happy to see you."

I stay close to my mother as she shuffles into the dimly lit bedroom. It smells of Vicks cough drops, cucumbers, and tuna. A repulsive combination. I want to leave, but then I see the family, and their grief sucks from me all intention or thought.

As though she's sick, Susu's mother lies in a queen bed against the far wall. Susu's younger siblings, three of them, are in their pajamas, covers pulled up to their shoulders. To their right, along one side wall, Susu's saluki dog, Shams, lies dejectedly, head on its paws, tail hidden beneath its rump. To our left as we enter, behind the door, is a white dresser with a mirror that covers almost the whole wall above and reflects back to us the entire scene in the room. Little fake votive candles flicker on the dresser top and in the mirror.

Unlike her mother and siblings, Susu does not lie in bed. She sits on a red velvet chair in the corner to our right, wearing her school uniform. She holds a reading lamp in her hand, switching it on and off with her thumb. When the light flashes on, I swear her face is the same angry color as the chair, but it's hard to tell, because in another second she's shadowed, and it seems as though she's wrapped in black cloth.

Mama closes the door gently behind us. I wish she would say something. I lean against her legs, and she nudges me straight. She sighs loudly; her breath drops out of her mouth like a stone. Does she sense what I sense? The room is a cocoon of grief. No, a temple of grief. Step inside like we have, and you are mummified, stuck for eternity in an in-between state. We may never escape.

A sob and a series of hiccups pop out of Susu's little brother. Susu's mother pushes the hiccupping child gently forward and slaps him on the back. He stops hiccupping for a moment, then starts again, in time with Susu's light.

"We are so sorry," Mama says.

"Why did they let you in?" Susu's mother says. "I didn't want anyone to come."

"We'll go," Mama says. "We don't want to disturb you. We want you to know how sorry we are for your loss."

Susu turns off her light and sets it down. She balls her hands into fists and thrusts them downward, like she's stabbing her own thighs. "I'm going to kill who killed him," she says, so softly I think I'm the only person who hears her. She's staring straight ahead, fingers of both hands curved like claws now. She inches her bottom to the very edge of the chair and angles herself so her feet reach the ground. One foot stomps.

"I'm going to slice them and hurt them," she says. "I'm going to stab them and stab them."

"I'm sorry, Susu." I echo Mama, because what else is there to say? "I'm so sorry."

"This wasn't supposed to happen," Susu's mother says. "What will we do? Why did this happen to us?"

Mama grabs my hand and squeezes hard, like she needs me as her lifeline, to keep her strong in front of her grieving friend and neighbor, to keep her from crying herself. I squeeze back. I imagine Baba being gone, never coming back. I imagine me and Mama in this room, this bed and chair, instead of Susu and her family. My brain doesn't want to hold on to the image for very long. I ask myself *what if.* I think I owe it to my friend Susu to imagine myself in her situation. What if it were me and my siblings who had lost our father? What if Baba was not downstairs, saying *sorry for your loss* and *God multiply your blessings* to the dead man's brothers and uncles and nephews? What if he were the one being mourned? The thought turns on and off in my mind, like a hiccup or a light bulb.

"God protect you," Mama says. "The neighborhood will take care of you."

Why didn't God protect Susu's dad? Who deserves protection? Don't we all, or do only some of us?

And: Where do bad people—murderers—come from? How do they become what they are? Why do they become what they are?

Mama tells me it's time to go, and I lean in to hug Susu goodbye. The forcefield around her pushes me away. I'm sad not to be able to touch her, not to have the power to comfort her as I've done in the past when she was sad about someone teasing her or losing a coin on the way to school or an older child stealing her hair band right off her head.

We leave the room, descend into the night, and wait for Baba on the sidewalk. Mama keeps peeking at her watch. Minutes tick loudly by. Fewer people come and go. Most have come already and gone. I'm getting bored. I yawn. Mama yawns. I sit on the curb. My skirt pools around me and I feel the rough concrete on my legs. The cool night air blesses my face, the stars shine brighter than ever, and the near-full moon has tears in its eyes.

Her back to the wall of the building, Mama cries quietly, her hands at her sides. I lean against her arm and think about bananas and Susu in the red chair and how I walked alone to school today and then was sent home. When Baba arrives, he ignores Mama's "Why'd you take so long?," scoops me up as though I weigh nothing, and carries me home. His shoulder my pillow. My sisters are already in bed with the lights out. They probably have a million questions, but they turn over and cover their heads. I am so tired and glad to go to bed, fall asleep, and escape the heartbroken world.

In the wake of this second murder in our town in about a year, school closes for the rest of the week, and the parents of my town, who have to keep working, have nowhere to send us children, except to our older relatives, who are lax caretakers. We run wild in the parks. Hang upside down from the monkey bars and climb too high on the covered slides. Ride our bikes, unrestricted, in the streets, blowing through stop signs, popping wheelies, two or three or even four children to a bike. Grandparents and older siblings pay no attention to our shenanigans. They watch the littlest ones, who run around in their underwear and T-shirts. Everyone plays except Susu and her siblings, who watch morosely from the window of their cousins' flat, where they are stuck grieving their father.

I wave, but I don't think Susu sees me. My sisters and I draw a hopscotch grid with chalk. Their friends bring jump ropes, and they sing and jump until it's time for lunch. We run inside and make sandwiches, and come back out for a few more hours with orange soda on our upper lips, then we watch TV or play video games until our parents come home.

Then, some parent or grandparent decides the children should not be outside, because doesn't everyone remember there's a murderer on the loose? So, we stay indoors the last weekday and through the weekend, and it's like the afternoon of the day after Susu's dad died: tense and boring and filled with annoying sisterliness. When the weekend ends, we are so ready to go back to school and our parents are so ready to send us, even if they worry about safety, about a murderer on the loose.

I expect Susu to be at the corner this week, but she's not. My sisters aren't surprised. My parents must have told them Susu wouldn't be coming back to school yet. Why didn't anyone tell *me*? Lajwa and Rana each pull me by a hand and walk me all the way to school. Today, for once, they take their responsibility for me seriously. The other children walk in clumps, instead of fanning out and climbing trees. In every household, there have been lectures over the weekend about sticking together, staying safe, taking care of the younger children.

At school, all the Misses and Madams walk hunched and heavy, like they've got weights on their wrists and ankles and around their necks. Charcoal smudges adorn their under-eyes as though they've had a disaster with kohl or cried for days. Their lids and cheeks and chins have puffed out, their noses grown wider than usual.

Adults have not been sleeping.

Me, I've slept as peacefully as the dead, without a single nightmare. Every night since the murder, I've fallen asleep thinking about Susu and how I will take care of her when we're back at school. Now that I'm here and she's not, I'm disappointed. I hope she's going to be OK. The teachers sleepwalk through their days, but we students get back to work, and third grade is the same as ever, except for the lack of Susu. Unlike the teachers, we're focused, and learning. We're rested from a surprise vacation. For one week, school becomes our favorite place. With Susu and her family out of sight, we can mostly forget the tragedy. For the time being, we're free of it, almost as though it never happened. As though we could go back in time and be the people and place we were before.

Susu and her younger sister return the following week—two weeks after their father's death. The rest of us are already lined up in the schoolyard, hands on hearts to sing the school song and the national anthem, when the gateman swings the gates open and the two sisters climb out of their uncle's blood-red sedan with the spoiler in the back. The car's muffler pops, as loud as a gunshot, and teachers jump and clutch their chests, like their hearts might otherwise jump out through their skin.

"Turn to the front!" the teachers bark.

I sneak a look as Susu and Seema slide to the end of the third-grade line, holding hands. Seema's line, the first-grade line, is to our left. The teachers don't pull her away; they let her stand with her big sister. I look discreetly over my shoulder at Susu, and our classmate Fuad, who's standing next to me, punches me in the arm. I punch him back. I try to mouth hello to Susu, but she's staring at her black oxfords, which shine in the sun, then up at the cloud-streaked sky. I look where she

43

looks. I wave. Susu snares my eyes with hers. She stares straight into my soul. I disappear, sink through the courtyard tile. For several moments, I feel as though I'm in a dark, claustrophobic grave, and then I'm above ground, squinting in sunlight, goose-pimples up and down my arms.

Other children experience the same journey to the nether-world when either of the two sisters looks at them. We talk about it under our desks, in the bathroom, over the lunch table, on the swings at recess. How they're spooky now, changed. How we're all afraid of Susu and Seema. Their presence distresses and distracts us. It reminds us of murder and murderers and mayhem, and the nothingness that must be what follows death. Their sweat smells of death, Fuad says. What does death smell like? He says it's a little like licorice and eggplant and skunk. Things no child wants to be near.

We're too young to understand grief, even if we've felt it. The quietness in the sisters' eyes creeps us out.

Susu and I don't walk to school together anymore. Her family drives her and Seema, and I walk with my sisters. We're not best friends anymore, either. She has a new best friend, a girl named Amirah, whose sister survived cancer last year. I sit on a bench by myself at recess, watching the two friends pretend-cook rocks and feed them to pretend babies. A gaggle of girls asks if I want to jump rope. No, I don't. Later, I wish I'd said yes, but changing my mind, asking *them* if I can play, seems too hard. I should have said yes when I had the chance.

I sit alone and hum a little song to myself about Bumbo. A donkey is stubbornly loyal and honest and hates to make new friends.

On the way home, I tell my sisters I never liked Amirah.

They snap their chewing gum with skepticism.

"You're jealous," Rana says, and for once Lajwa agrees.

The fourth week after the murder, all the third-graders complain of aches in our stomachs and limbs and temples. Susu seems normal, but grief ripples the air around her. Her grief seeps into us, or we take it on for her. Do we wade into those waves of grief on purpose? Whatever the case, we feel it permeating our skin and invading our bloodstreams. It leaches into our bones and lungs and amygdalas. It rearranges the chemical composition of our brains and taints our imaginations. We don't talk to anyone but each other about the phenomenon, because the adults wouldn't believe us and our older siblings would tease us. But the grief can't be contained by our skin. It won't stay inside of us. In art class, I draw bodies rising from semicircular graves. I look over at Hisham's paper, and he's drawing skeletons and dead people, too. All the third-graders, except Susu and Amirah, draw angry swirls of color that end up looking like brown tornadoes. We draw livid faces with black holes for eyes, exploding heads, people with hair like twisting, hissing snakes. I draw Bumbo with claws instead of hooves and pointy teeth drenched in blood. In my head, he growls and snaps and sinks his teeth into his enemies.

Hisham and Fuad are the first to draw knives and severed limbs and blood. Hisham copies my Bumbo's legs and draws a witch on top. Fuad gives her daggers for hands. They fill in the background with thick black strokes. Darkness. There should be a moon, I think. Stars.

"This is the killer, on the loose," the boys say. "She prowls at night." They hunch their shoulders and raise their arms and march in place, pretending to be monsters. They make their voices low and spooky. "Watch out! She prowls at night!" They write the words beneath their drawings. They follow the girls around at recess and wave the drawings in their faces. They whip up more pictures of the witch, as though one of those festival artists who draw portraits on the spot for a few rials has been enchanted by something evil. They wad the drawings up and stuff them in our pockets. We run away screaming, take the drawings out with two fingers so as not to get evil boy cooties, and throw the pictures away. Undeterred and devious, the boys stuff drawings in our backpacks so we'll find them when we do our homework at night. They give me one with a donkey's head and a snake's body and a bear's legs and red, pointy high heels. It holds a severed head in one human-like hand attached to a tentacle. I breathe in the smell of colored markers and tear up the paper, dropping the pieces into the rubbish bin in my bedroom.

Lajwa catches me red-handed. "What's that?" she says.

"None of your business."

"Show me."

"Don't want to."

"Pretty please." Her voice is soft, floaty. If Rana were asking, in her bossy older-sister way, I'd say no. But Lajwa is the good older sister, the one who protects me from bullies. I step away from the bin and let her rummage through it. She lays the pieces of paper on the floor and slides them around, putting the whole thing back together like a jigsaw puzzle.

"What kind of rubbish is this?" she says.

"It's the monster."

"What monster?"

"The one that killed Susu's father."

Lajwa uses her palms to push the pieces of paper into one thick pile. She pats the edges, like she's fixing a deck of cards, but I didn't tear the paper evenly, and she gives up on truly neatening the papers.

"There's no such thing as a monster. The murderer was some evil person, and they're gone now."

"The police caught them?"

"Yes, probably. I don't know." Lajwa pockets the pieces of paper.

"Don't tell Mama and Baba about the drawing," I say.

"Tell those boys to leave you alone."

I nod, and she's convinced I will do it, but it's ridiculous advice. The boys won't listen to me. They live to bother girls. They live to torture us and give us bad dreams. Except Susu. They leave her alone, without the teachers even telling them to leave her alone. Are they, like me, afraid that what happened to Susu will happen to them? They have to be nice to her, or the monster, the evil person, the whatever it is—human or supernatural, real or fantastic—will smite someone they love.

We fear the contagion of Susu's tragedy.

Over the next few months, into the cool winter months and the early warmth of spring, Susu works hard to hide her sadness. She and Amirah appear to be living in an alternate world. Instead of monsters and severed limbs, they draw clouds and trees, yellow suns and birds flying. Susu draws candy, with wrappers that look like bows. She uses up all the yellow-colored pencils to color in tubs of popcorn. She draws girls smiling and holding the hands of their fathers. She draws only happy scenes, as though she has found a time machine and gone back

47

to before. Without ever mentioning the murder, the teachers praise Susu for her strength and resilience.

They send each of the rest of us, two by two and three by three, to the counselor's office. The counselor seems ill-equipped to deal with a mass trauma. Or so I overhear my mother saying one night midway through the school year, when I've gotten out of bed to go to the bathroom.

"Why wouldn't they expect this? Our whole neighborhood is grieving," she tells my father. I creep to the dark hallway outside the living room, where my parents are watching TV with the sound off. They're distracted by their conversation and don't detect me.

"It wasn't like this with the first...death," my father says. "It didn't affect the children. So, I guess no one knew to prepare."

"We should have protected them from the stories and the gossip," Mama says.

"Who? You and me, while we were at work?"

"All of us, everyone. We shouldn't have left them to run around that first week. We should have sent them to school, kept their routine. Now they're all a mess."

"That was the schools' decision. They made it with good intentions."

"They were wrong. Our children needed to be at school."

"It was just one week. And they would still be the children of the adults who lost a neighbor in a horrifying way."

My father unmutes the television to catch the weather report. The temperature is going to be unseasonably hot the rest of the week.

"Why would this evil come to us?" my mother says. "To him? What did he do to deserve it?"

She must be talking about Susu's father. What *did* he do to deserve it? And what did Susu do to deserve losing her father? "Nothing," my father says. Sandstorm on Tuesday. Torrential rain Wednesday. "No one deserves what that monster did to him."

Who should I believe about the existence of monsters? Lajwa or my father? For weeks after eavesdropping on my parents, I have fresh nightmares, populated with more and more monsters. The monsters aren't after fathers anymore. They come after me. A different monster every night: An octopus that walks on land and strangles me in my sleep. An elephant with purple skin and tusks that gouges out my sisters' eyes. A hummingbird as big as my torso with a rapier beak and wings as loud as helicopters' rotors. Before the bird can stab me to death, its wings lift the dust around me and I suffocate.

I wake up wet every night, and my mother becomes more and more terse with me the more loads of laundry she has to wash. After weeks of bedwetting, she takes me and my sisters to school one morning, toward the end of the school year, so she can talk to my headmistress.

My sisters fight over what radio station to listen to. My mother turns the dial to the news, and lowers the volume until no one can make out the words. I lower my window as we pass Susu's old building. It's empty now. Susu is still at her aunt's. It seems no one will ever live in the old building.

"Are they going to tear it down?" I ask.

"Tear what down?" Mama says.

"Susu's old building."

"They should," Rana says.

49

"But then what will they put there?" says Lajwa. "Another building no one will want to move into?"

"They could build a little park there," Mama says. "It could have a fountain, a little vegetable garden, and roses."

"A donkey could live there!" I say.

"Not a donkey," Rana says.

Mama turns off the radio. "It's a good idea. A park. Maybe I'll take it to the town council. But I think first we need a community event. Something to bring the neighborhood and town back together. Help us rise above our fears. Everyone's been on edge, angry that the police haven't caught a killer. It's tearing us apart."

This is the most Mama has said about how she feels about what happened, the way it's affected the adults.

Later that day, after Mama has spoken privately to the headmistress and headed to work, my teacher sends me to the counselor's office. The counselor tells me we will start meeting once a week. But what really matters is that the next day, Amirah stays home with a cold, and Susu hands me a folded piece of paper. I'm giddy; she hasn't talked to me in such a long time. I say thank you and start to stuff the paper into the skirt pocket of my uniform.

"Read it now," Susu says.

Folded into eighths, the paper fits in my palm. I open it and see a moon in a dark sky, a building with a gaping golden mouth, the number eleven, like a pair of flinty monster's eyes, and a field of red and purple flowers with petals shaped like hearts.

"OK," I say.

"Don't be late."

I go through the evening at home thinking about Susu's plan, because that's what the drawing was—a plan to meet at the place her father died. I eat dinner with my family: lentils with rice and tamarind sauce. I smash my rice into a flat oval and drown it with brown, tangy sauce. I ignore the sliced cucumbers and tomatoes on my plate. I drink three glasses of water. I think about monsters monsters monsters and scary ghosts. Susu's father sewn back together, walking stiffly, an embarrassed look on his face. I'm trying to scare myself on purpose, so I'll have bad dreams and wake up in a few hours.

When I go to bed early, my mother looks worried, touches my forehead, and says, "It feels fine. Are you fine?"

I yawn. "Tired, Mama."

I curl up with my pillow. My dreams are vivid and frightening, and I wake up when the glowing green numbers on our radio clock say ten forty-five. My sisters are sleeping in their beds, Rana stiff as a board and Lajwa curled into a comma. Their breathing sounds like the sea. The murmur of the TV as I let myself out of our room tells me my parents are awake, or dozing with the news on. I smell eggs and leeks, my father's favorite late-night snack. Pretending there's a curtain of invisibility pulled around me, I walk toward the front door. The tactic works. Snuggled together on the couch, my mother's head on my father's shoulder, his hand on her head, like he's patting her to sleep, my parents don't notice me.

I carry my flip-flops, padding down the stairs barefoot so as not to make much noise. I draw my cloak of invisibility around me. In the brightly lit foyer, I drop my flip-flops, slip them on, and keep going. Out the door, into the night. Streetlamps spill yellow-green light. When one of them flickers out for a few seconds, I'm in a well of darkness, fear in my belly. I take a deep breath, like the counselor at school taught us, and visualize something nice. Bumbo and Biss, nuzzling each other's faces. I feel their fur between my fingers, smell their animal scents. Then I smell something musky, and a rectangle of air in front of me shimmers and swings toward me, like there's a door opening to Somewhere Else. Like a doorway to darkness is pulling me toward it.

The streetlamp comes on, and I see Susu, waiting at our old corner with Shams leashless at her side.

"Did you make yourself invisible?" I ask. I let Shams sniff my fingers and lick them. I keep the shimmery door to myself.

Susu nods. No one at home sees her anymore, anyway, she says. Her mama sees only the ghost of her father and her auntie sees only the littler children.

I thought Susu and I would never be friends again, and the relief of standing next to her and Shams is like stepping off an amusement park ride that's sent me round and round, adjusting to being still. I need a minute. My body reels; I'm dizzy. Moments later, standing on solid ground has returned to being the most normal, natural thing in the world.

I practically hear Susu's thoughts. She's afraid to go in, but she wants to see where it happened. She worries she's strange to want that.

I kneel and rub my face against Shams's back. I sneeze. I feel calmer, though, so I nuzzle her more.

Susu wants what she wants. She doesn't have to miss her dad the way other people tell her to. She wants to see where his death happened and destroy whoever murdered him. Her desire for revenge hasn't gone away.

The building is locked like a vault. We don't bother with the front door. We sneak in through a first-floor window that someone must have forgotten to close and lock as they fled the building on the night of the murder. Susu has a flashlight. We fall onto a bed, make our way through the dark rooms. Shams sniffs everything, and we push her rump so she'll move along. She whines. She doesn't like it here. Don't worry, girl, we tell her. It'll be OK.

We open the front door and step into the lobby.

CHAPTER 5

Crushed

Third victim.

Nadir Fayez had no fears when he closed up his auto repair shop on the hot summer evening he was crushed to death.

It had been—what? Nearly three years since the lift attack, and people in the neighborhood had started to relax. Nadir loved the sounds of summer, even the racket of the crickets screeching, as loud as a host of car engines at the start of a race. Occasionally, one lone cricket got inside the shop and peeped, like a lost soul. On this night, Nadir had pulled down the garage doors and locked them. He was bending over a decades-old jalopy's engine for a final look of the day when he heard the vroom vroom of a motorcycle. He was alone, so he thought he must be imagining the sound. This imaginary sound seemed, oddly, closer than the crickets. The imaginary engine sounded well-tuned, as lovingly cared for as his own beloved motorcycle, Malikah.

He turned to see what was going on, and fear hit him like a truck with bloated tires. Headlights blinded him from the far corner of the cavernous space he'd worked his entire life to finally buy last year.

He froze like an animal. She came for him, zooming ever closer—an instant that felt like an hour, like the ticking time-bomb of his mortality. He had nowhere to run. He howled with ungodly terror as she hit him straight in the abdomen, as his beautiful machine, polished to a mirror-like silver and fresh-blood red, knocked him to the ground, wracked his body with pain, and kept going. He could hardly cower; he was already knocked flat. She ran him over and over, and the pain, the pain, every part of his body on fire, every part of him dying individually. The killer seemed, to his rapidly dying mind, like she was fused to Malikah, a machine-age centaur who crushed him to pieces, until he was in blackness. Outside his consciousness, she kept driving, cackling, and driving, until he was roadkill, until his body stopped twitching and his heart stopped pumping.

Blood pooled on the floor like motor oil.

The police found Malikah in the shop, blood on her tires, her headlight, her black leather seat. Other things clung to her, too, things that made a few of them sick to their order-loving stomachs: bits of skin, bits of organ.

One officer noticed the nose-tickling yet elegant scent of roses in the air, but of course there wasn't a vase of anything in the shop. Not a hint of fingerprint, either. In a shadowy corner, one guy swore he saw a hoofprint.

"Ridiculous," his colleagues said. "It's a streak of motor oil."

Really, wasn't the whole thing ridiculous? This murder by motorcycle. Who would plan that? A scorned lover? An ex-wife? Nadir had many.

*   *   *

When word got out that Nadir was the latest victim, that he'd died within two blocks of the killings of a few years ago, the most beloved local TV reporter at the time, Khaled Khaled, who'd reported in-depth on the mystery of the first two murders, vowed to get the story. The authorities allowed him to step into the auto repair shop only once, without his cameraman, after they'd removed body and motorcycle and scrubbed the place clean. After his solo inspection of the place, he stood outside with his Channel 1 microphone, in his Channel 1 hat and polo shirt, loudly biting the hand that fed him by asking what the authorities were hiding. The place, he explained to his citywide viewers, had been incredibly clean, antiseptic smelling, and filled with cars in various states of repair. The authorities insisted the death had happened inside, not on the neighborhood's streets. This was a crime of passion, they seemed to imply but would not say outright, not an act perpetrated by a killer lurking in alleys, an indiscriminate victimizer. But how, Khaled Khaled asked, could the killer have gotten enough distance to kill him in the shop? Were the authorities lying about the method of death? Why? And where was the message everyone expected to have been left by the serial killer who had devastated this poor neighborhood (he meant *poor* with all its connotations) for years? Had the police erased it? Why?

The police commissioner, under intense pressure from the mayor to tamp down the public's fears and wild anxieties, squirmed on the inside but kept a stern and authoritative exterior. Yet, no matter how many times he repeated his talking points—only the third murder in four years, three whole years since the last one, doing everything we can to keep the public safe, no reason at all to panic, have you no respect for the man's family—Khaled Khaled wouldn't listen to facts.

"There's a cunning, creative, crazy serial killer on the loose, putting our children, friends, and neighbors at risk. What are you doing about it, Mr. Commissioner, sir?"

It might not have been a serial killer at all, the commissioner wished he could say. But he kept quiet; the PR consultant from out of town had told him not to mention the possible number of killers. Because which, to his mind, was better, eh? One killer or three? The police commissioner couldn't argue with PR logic, and he couldn't decide on an answer. One killer or three?

To be honest, it didn't matter. He had already told his teen-aged children they were never to leave the house at night.

Little did Khaled Khaled know, he'd been scooped. The neighborhood was already ablaze with gossip. The coroner, relatively new to the job, had relayed the gory details of the aftermath to her sister: a man of sixty-four viciously mauled by his own motorcycle, run over half a dozen times on the concrete floor of his shop. The coroner's sister told their aunt, who told a neighbor, who told the butcher at the grocery store meat counter, who told someone or other in the Murad clan, who told anyone over sixteen who walked into the store. (Unlike the police who had tried to piece together a motive for the crime, the neighbors knew Nadir's three ex-wives and his children and grandchildren had moved away to the city at different times over the past decade, and were not available for comment. No ex-lovers came forward.)

The gossips said Nadir Fayez's internal organs were rolled flat as apricot leather, his face crushed beyond any repair the mortician was capable of, unrecognizable even to his closest

57

friends. As though the killer wanted to erase like chalk the smile everyone who came into Nadir's shop knew and some loved, with the one broken tooth and another gold one, the dimple on one side. Wanted to erase the mostly trim physique, the slight belly he sucked in when he wasn't tinkering with a machine. He'd been still handsome, still charming—despite the dental disasters, a mustache he rarely trimmed, his multiple marriages, and his status as an elder. His clientele had called him "well-preserved." Now, he wasn't. He was a bag of bones. A flattened, disgusting, un-human-looking bag of bones. The description sounded funny, and people laughed uncomfortably, because Nadir's death sounded painful, more painful than anything anyone could imagine.

These details of the death were what was left at the end of a game of telephone. What the coroner really saw, and how she felt about what she saw, only she and her sister knew. Nadir's eldest daughter had been the coroner's best friend until they both went off to college and only the coroner returned home to settle down. She had not wanted her friend to know the things she knew. None of the family had come to town for a memorial or burial. The man's remains were sent to them in a box you could have packed books in. If they shed tears or tugged at their hair in grief, if they prayed for his soul, they did so in their flats in the city. But such outward mourning seemed unlikely.

Most in town suspected Nadir's family hadn't shed a tear over him.

Only the coroner's sister, Amal, knew about the years of insomnia the coroner suffered after the murder, years of trying to get a desk job and being told she was the best coroner they had, until she got up the gumption to move to a place where death happened quietly, normally. Only Amal would ever know how crushed the coroner was inside, how changed, how filled with dread, how unable to ever go back to the way she was, to a time when she believed cruelty was uncommon and had limits, even as someone who'd seen and examined and scalpeled and taken apart and analyzed death. Only the coroner's sister, outside of the investigating officers and the coroner herself, knew of the words that had been scrawled on the floor in a mix of oil and blood:

"Kill them with kindness."

CHAPTER 6

Baba's Place

Susu and Layla's place of their own.
Contacting the dead. Need for revenge.
Civic engagement. Departure.

In the last weeks of third grade, Susu and I make a haven of the building where her father died and in which she and her parents once lived. We burrow into the abandoned lobby where his blood was spilled; it becomes our private, secret place. No one else dares come inside, day or night. We are safe here. She tells me she's not friends with Amirah anymore. I'm her only friend.

We call the building—and more precisely, the lobby—Baba's Place. I like how the name suggests Susu and I are sisters. I claim her father as mine when I'm here. I claim her as family, more than a friend. Later, I will see that at Baba's Place, I claimed her more than I claimed my family.

Two or three times a week, we sneak to Baba's Place after school and, occasionally, at night. Why do no adults or older children ever catch us and stop us, little girls who have recently turned nine years old when this all begins? Is it because we

usually have Shams with us? Or because Susu and I believe
with all our hearts that when we go to Baba's Place, we become
invisible? See-through as air. Clear as water. Like supernatural
beings. Like jinn who've stumbled into the seam between their
world and ours. I believe there's a jinn walking beside us,
cloaking us, protecting us. Why else does no one see us walk
right in front of them? How else would I have the courage to
do it, carrying—at various times over the weeks, months, and
years—backpacks full of snacks and art supplies, sleeping bags
and cushions to make the space comfortable, bottled water,
flashlights, a battery-powered essential oils vaporizer I "borrow"
from my sister, slippers, baggies full of lollipops and chewy
candies, packets of crisps and biscuits, library books, stuffed
animals that we leave in the lobby to keep Susu's baba's ghost
company, a hammock, a mini trampoline, a skateboard, a rabbit
in a cage, rabbit food, colored pencils, notepads, modeling clay?
The adults are vigilant about keeping children safe, especially in
the first year or two after the murder—and yet, they don't see us.

The first half dozen or so times we visit the building, we
avoid looking at the boarded-up lift and climb the stairs to
Susu's old flat, where the door had been left unlocked in her
family's haste to leave. We snuggle into her old bunk bed with
Shams and fall asleep. I like being in a flat that's empty of
people except me and my best friend and her dog. I like turning
on the television, and my parents and sisters and little brothers
aren't there to insist we watch something else.

But eventually the electricity goes out, and the place starts
to stink of rotting food and something unnamed in a bedroom
trash bin.

Also, Susu wants to be closer to her father. If his ghost

comes back, it will be in the lobby, she says. He won't come up to the flat.

"Why not?" I ask.

"That's where he and Mama fought."

"Do you miss him?"

"He's the only one who knows who killed him," she says. "And if his killer comes back, she'd come back to the lobby too."

"Why would she come back?"

Susu mouths something that might be "So dumb."

"Criminals revisit the scene of their crime," she says, as though this is common knowledge.

I ask if we can bring Bumbo to live in the lobby. He'll look out for ghosts and murderers.

"Stop being stupid. My father died, and you care about a dumb donkey. How would we get it here, anyway?"

This is the only time she lords over me with her father's death. I never again speak to her of my beloved Bumbo.

From then on, we stay in the lobby. It's dark, no matter what time of day; we use our flashlights to light the space and battery-powered fans and ice water to keep ourselves cool. Shams pants and looks miserable; Susu leaves her at home, except on cooler days.

Susu and I only sort of understand what happened here, in this room: the lift, her father. My parents never say a word, but I fill in the blanks, and so does Susu. The lift is boarded up, so it almost looks like part of the wall. Someone has spray-painted "Stay away, hussy" on the boards. I don't understand its meaning. I wonder who wrote it.

I shiver at the thought of a man dying meters away from where Susu and I spend our out-of-school, away-from-family, all-on-our-own time. I gag at the thought of someone killing him, not from far away with a gun, but physically, touching him, soiling their hands with his blood, smelling his smells, hearing his last gasps, feeling his body lose life.

Over the summer, my mother hatches a plan. Someone has told her a special TV report about the two murders is in the works. Hoping to get on camera, my mother spends hours and hours trying to get other people to agree to organize a neighborhood vigil on the anniversary of Susu's father's death, in late October. Or rather, to agree to let her organize one. Mama thinks a vigil will show viewers a different side to our neighborhood. A vigil will erase the bad rap we've been given. The fear we're hanging on to.

She first tests her idea for a vigil at our family dinner table soon after school ends.

"It would be good for our neighborhood, good for the town, good for the bereft family. It would show the killer he—or she—can't scare us. We'll go on with our lives. We'll meet in public, out in the open. Light and hope challenge darkness."

My siblings and I chew our lamb and green beans. My grandmother feeds the littlest ones. We suspect very strongly that Mama doesn't want our response or care what we think. She is speaking to my father.

He rolls up his sleeves and reaches for more bread to scoop his food with.

"People will say we had nothing like this for the first murder. Why do something special for Imran?"

"It can be for both victims. I'm going to tell Susu's mother I'll organize it. A neighborhood vigil, in front of the building, on the first anniversary. I'll ask the police to block off the street. I'll get a tent, for shade."

Baba wipes tomato sauce from his fingers with a paper tissue. "Who'll come? Imran was a bit of a son-of-a-bitch."

"He was your friend."

"I wouldn't say that."

"Your classmate. How can you say that about a dead man?"

"He's not a saint now because he's dead."

"Murdered."

"Why is this so important to you? People die all the time. Why are these deaths worthy of more recognition, these two men deserving of more remembrance?"

Mama closes her eyes. When she opens them, it's like a stroke of inspiration has come to her, an understanding of something she couldn't put her finger on until now. Her face flashes like a mirror in sunlight.

"Does Imran's death seem to you like a garden-variety death? Do you think we're all going to die violently and awfully as he did? Do you believe these deaths will become normal, old hat? I hope not. I want to die in my sleep. I want to die with my children around me. I want to die at peace, at the end of a good life. That is how I want to die. And when someone is snatched, and everyone's peace is shattered, we should acknowledge the shattering. We should not continue as though nothing out of the ordinary has happened so we can pretend it could never happen to us."

My father pushes his chair back from the table, takes his plate, and leaves for the kitchen. If there is something about Susu's dead father my own father disapproves of, some reason Baba thinks the deceased undeserving of remembrance, he will never tell us. He will take this secret to his grave. He doesn't defile the memory of the dead. He doesn't think they are beyond reproach because they are beyond this world. These two beliefs contradict each other. We can believe two opposite things at once. The fact of a murder makes it harder for my father to resist my mother's urge to bring people together around the dead men's memory. But he doesn't want to remember Susu's father well, so he walks away from the table.

I won't understand any of this till many years later, till I'm an adult who can't reconcile my love of my neighborhood and the people in it with the violence it harbors, the secrets they keep.

My grandma shakes her head and says, "A man is no woman. He doesn't understand suffering and mortality like we do."

As though nothing has happened, as though Baba still sits in his place, Mama goes on: The gathering will be about hope and joy and life. There will be candles in paper cups, speeches about the father, son, and citizen our neighborhood lost. There will be music. There will be black bunting and strings of light in the trees and on the sides of buildings. The mayor will come. The police chief will come. They will pledge to keep the neighborhood safe and find the killer. My mother wants to invite Khaled Khaled from the local TV station. She'll get the permits we need to be outside on the street, where public protests are not allowed but large groups of mourners are commonplace. She will ask her friends to cook and set up tables in the park. There will be big plates of food eaten communally. There will be black and white balloons, and we'll hand out jasmine garlands so the air fills with perfume.

Mama keeps hatching her scheme. All summer, in every tea with the neighborhood ladies, every encounter with her clients at her vet clinic down the street, every transaction at the corner store, she tells people about her idea, and when they express skepticism, she asks how we should remember Susu's father. She's open to other ideas, other ways of mourning together, but no one offers alternatives, so my mother comes up with them herself. Well, she says, he was a son of the neighborhood. There should be a plaque unveiled, affixed to the empty building's façade. Susu's father was an artist. There could be displays of his art, a children's art contest. He was a man of the people, by which she means he was poorer than some and richer than others. My mother envisions money raised for his family, and the establishment of an art academy in our neighborhood, which the rest of our town sees as poor, lacking in culture.

To everyone's surprise, most especially Baba's, my mother's plans begin to gain traction because she refuses to give up. Because she has an iron resolve not to let fear win. Because she doesn't believe in monsters, only in people. She reports at dinner one night in early September that the mayor is on board for a memorial vigil on the occasion of the first anniversary of Susu's father's death. My father continues to have reservations that he voices via questions that make my mother's left eyebrow twitch.

"And Susu's family?" he says. "You still haven't talked to *them*."

"Sure. I should ask them. They'll say yes."

"Because what if they want to move on?"

"Yes, I should ask them. They'll appreciate the suggestion."

"What if they don't appreciate your meddling?"

"It's not meddling." She looks ready to pull out his beard, hair by hair.

"What if they can't face the darkness?"

"That's why there will be candles."

And then, her plans are quashed by the one person she had thought would be on board.

My mother will never say out loud to my father, "You were right." But he is right: Susu's mama says no.

She wants no public displays of mourning. If she'd wanted more than three days of mourning, her family would have arranged it. She wants to move on. She tells my mother all of this over the phone. I eavesdrop on one end of the conversation and Susu eavesdrops on the other, and we piece it all together at Baba's Place the next day.

Listening from the hall, as my mother's voice gets louder the more she tries to pretend she understands, I hear her disappointment. All sense of purpose drains away. She sounds as though she's having a conversation with herself, trying to convince herself that Susu's mother is right to see the world the way she does, so differently from my mother, who has not lost her husband and believes the world can be fixed, every wound can heal.

"Yes, of course," Mama says. "It's important for you and the children to move on...No, you're right, no one else really knows what you're going through...I see. Yes, well, I thought the neighborhood would benefit from grieving with you, showing you and your family how much we care about you, how concerned we are, angry about what happened. But I see what you're saying. It must be so painful to remember...Yes, it's important not to let such a thing happen again...Well, there are other ways we can remember him...Or—ah, I see. Yes. I see."

Susu and I, in our separate hiding places—me at home, her

in her auntie's home—learn something no one has told us yet: Susu's mama and her extended family have decided that it is best for the children to have a new father to protect them. Instead of a vigil, they are planning a wedding.

The two brutal killings have given our neighborhood a nickname in our town: Horrorville. We hear it from kids whose relatives live in other neighborhoods. We hear it on the news, when Khaled Khaled does his special report on the unsolved murders. It airs the week of the anniversary of Susu's father's death, but it's not the positive, heartwarming, healing coverage my mother envisioned. The mayor calls our neighborhood "dangerous," "tough," and "gritty." The reporter calls it "the wrong side of town." The folks from our neighborhood that he interviews are angry that the police haven't solved the murders. And they're scared. One man cries when he talks about the fear he has of the night, how relieved he feels when his deadbolt locks into place when he returns home from work. He'll never go out at night alone. Ever.

That winter, Susu tells me about the potential suitors who visit her mother. Friends of the bride-to-be's husband, brothers, cousins, nephews, and uncles. Men of varying ages and professions and degrees of handsomeness and wealth. Several ask for her hand, not minding—or not minding too much—the fact that she has children. She chooses a man who graduated from school with her deceased husband, and a year and a half after her late husband's death, Susu's mother is remarried. Susu and her sisters are fitted for poofy dresses. Only family are invited to the small at-home ceremony. There's no big reception or display of lights on their building.

In Baba's Place the next day, Susu tersely answers my barrage of questions about the ceremony. The other family was nice. One boy was annoying. Her new stepsisters are cute. The food was so-so. The cake was chocolate. She carried a tall, beribboned candle in the tiny procession. Wax dripped on her fingers and wrist. Her stepfather wore a musky cologne that smelled gross to Susu. He gave her mother a tiny pair of diamond earrings as a wedding present.

While we hide out, Susu's mother and her new husband are moving all of Susu and her siblings' stuff three blocks away. I'm so glad she isn't moving across town. We can go on meeting at the place where her father died.

After her mother's wedding, Susu's fixation on revenge slowly returns. She never lost it, really, but she had kept it stuffed in a pocket in her heart. We're young, but that doesn't mean we don't love and hate and fear. At first, Susu's vengeance looks like remembrance. It's her idea to steal some electric candles from Murad's store. We set them in a semicircle in front of the lift, and every time we come to Baba's Place, we switch on the candles before we do anything else. In a way, these are two-person vigils. In a way, these are our attempts to summon Susu's father.

The summer before fifth grade, we start stashing art supplies so Susu can make intricate and layered abstract collages that represent nothing in particular visually but mean everything. We smuggle in large pads of art paper and a roll of butcher paper, tall tubs of glue, tissue paper, leaves, flowers pressed in the pages of thick novels and dictionaries, cottony seed pods, scraps of fabric, old newspapers, sequins, buttons, bits of bark pulled from the trees in the park on the way to school, watermelon seeds, dryer lint, felt, rickrack, glitter, clay, water colors, oil paints, acrylic paints, paint brushes, sponges, palettes, an easel.

I watch Susu work. I hand her things she asks for.

That summer and into the school year, she makes hundreds of collages of all sizes, from one as small as a postage stamp to another we hang across the entire lobby. We stack the finished pieces all over the floor, so there's hardly any place to sit or step. Everywhere we look, we see artwork that sprang out of Susu's mind and heart and soul. These are not like the sunny paintings she made in school right after her father died. The collages have layers of feeling, texture, even scent. They smell like pine and glue and cinnamon, or like bubblegum, or like bananas and orange peel. Like chocolate, like sweat. I don't know much about art, but I think Susu is talented beyond her years.

"These are so cool," I tell her.

Her collages are full of color and texture, puffy droplets of paint, swirls of ink that resemble words but don't say anything, like fake calligraphy. I tell her the collages look like the work of a grown-up.

My father says Susu and her siblings have had to grow up too fast.

Susu asks if I want to make art too. I say no. I've decided I'm bad at drawing, and as much as I love Susu's collages, as much as they draw me into her mind and her imagination, make me feel like I'm walking inside her consciousness, collage-making doesn't seem like real art—or rather, it wouldn't feel like real art if I did it. Susu's a real artist, so anything she makes is real art.

I'm afraid of what my brain might create.

Susu's need for revenge is contagious. Young as I am, I sense the hurts I've experienced are shallow compared to hers. Name-calling at school, being annoyed by my family, small jabs from teachers, the disappointments of living in town and not at the farm, where my heart is. Even so, my fingers tingle at the idea of hurting someone back. Once, my brother poked me with a play arrow and I broke it in half. When he cried, I felt powerful. I think of the scary monstress-woman the children at school tell stories about to spook each other. She developed out of our drawings, our heads, the tales our parents told us to keep us scared of strangers and the night. She has long blades for hands, a face so beautiful you want to cry, and hair like a veil of darkness. If I were to try to make a collage, or press a piece of soft clay between my fingers, I fear she is what I would make. A monster, an almost-human, with sharp hooves. She sculpts herself in my mind, and I can feel the flat metal blades of her sharp sickle hands under my thumbs, hear the way the blades clink when she rubs her hands together evilly, like a chef sharpening his knives to cut into meat. I smell her odor, as strong as the perfumes Mama wears, as strong as Baba's incense. Although the Monstress is part animal, she doesn't smell like manure or animal breath and sweat or Bumbo's funky furry odor.

She smells like the distilled fragrance of ten different flowers.

During this time, my sense of smell is developing, deepening, far beyond what most people can smell, though I'm not yet aware that my nose is more sensitive than most people's noses. I can't stand sitting next to my father when he eats eggs or my mother when she eats yogurt. Whenever my sisters and I walk past a dumpster on the way to school, or the sewage-irrigated park, I gag and complain, until Rana suggests we cross the street or walk another way. Instead of making art, like Susu, I want to blend fragrances, to create beautiful scents for myself to breathe. I see a TV documentary about the roses grown in the mountains, and how artisans press out their aromatic essence. How they harvest barks and resins that are burnt for their scent. I love the idea of separating a scent from the object that originated it. The magic of making colognes and perfumes. Instead of pulling a rabbit from a hat or a rial from behind someone's ear, you pull fragrance out of a blossom or a branch or an animal's sweat glands or intestines. From petals or bark or evergreen needles, fruit peels or pulp or sap or resin. There's a magic to the process. You can take the smell of a rose with you, take it in through your nostrils and keep it tucked away inside you, long after the rose has wilted and died.

When Susu isn't making art in the lobby, she's plotting the murderer's death. These are conversations we can't have safely at school, or walking to school, or when we're hanging out in each other's bedrooms after school, or buying sodas and candy at Murad's. Someone might overhear, and they might decide there's something wrong with Susu. I've heard my parents say it's normal and right for her to be angry at her father's killer and at the authorities who have failed to catch him or her. But if they knew about her revenge lust, I think they would consider it an aberration, abhorrent, obscene. If she were older, her dreams of slicing the murderer top to bottom with her knife might seem acceptable to the adults of the neighborhood, but she's too young for her anger to be acceptable. At first, after her father's death, she tells the school therapist everything. When she sees the concern in the woman's eyes week after week, Susu backtracks. She understands what adults want from her. Even in the wake of a horrible crime, a child is expected to be calm as an angel. Susu tells the school therapist that she has forgiven the murderer. She pretends she is healing and moving on, doing normal little-girl things like roller-skating on the roof of her building and watching cartoons and playing with dolls and baking cookies with her grieving mother. She never mentions sneaking with her best friend into the belly of the place where her father was brutally murdered.

Susu has learned to wear normalcy like a uniform.

I'm the only person who knows how she spends her time, who is familiar with the horror of her daydreams, not only because she tells me, but also because of what I see in her collages. Red paint and tissue paper, black ink and white paper, tufts of cotton: the murderer's blood spraying like warm rain on her face. Dark slashes of ink in a confetti of gold glitter-glue: the lift that killed her father.

Around the second anniversary of her father's death, still dreaming of revenge, Susu decides to prepare to follow through, even though there's no sign of the murderer's return. It is the fall of our fifth-grade year, and at school we're learning about animal habitats and long division. Susu steals a curved knife from her grandfather's travel chest and proudly shows it to me. She touches the sharp point with her thumb, like heroes do in movies. I admire the bravery with which she handles the knife. It glints in the electric candlelight. I touch it gingerly. Susu shows me how to hold it by the hilt. She tells me to pretend I'm stabbing the monster, avenging her father. She steals a cushion from her aunt's formal salon, lays it in front of me, and says, "Go on. Kill."

The knife is heavy in my hand.

Susu says I'm not holding it right. She adjusts my grip. "What are you waiting for?" she says.

"You do it." I try to give her the knife, and she steps back, her hands up like shields.

"I'd kill the killer in an instant," she says. "If I see her, I'll stab her without even thinking. It will come naturally. I'll know how. But how about you? Could *you* do it?"

I don't want to kill anyone or anything. But Susu sees me as her soldier. I stand straighter, grip the knife hilt. I want to be loyal to Susu and her father. I stab the cushion. On the second thrust, the knife goes through the cushion's batting and pings against the tile floor. I'm flushed, full of pumping blood.

The more I stab, the more I feel like I'm Susu's plaything, her marionet.

"I don't like it," I say.

"What do you mean? It's a beautiful knife."

"I don't like stabbing."

"That's why you have to practice." She makes me stab, stab, stab until the thrust of my arm through the air is as familiar as brushing my hair or eating with knife and fork.

I put the dead cushion in a trash bag. Susu places the knife, unsheathed, among the votive candles.

I say, "Tell me something about your father." She likes to talk about Baba. Her recollections seem to become sharper, clearer, more adamant every time she tells me about him.

She says he let her play with his paints and watch him draw.

He told her when she was older, she could help him paint the walls and ceilings of other people's houses, which was what he did for money. But she'd never gotten old enough. He took her to see the sunrise, outside town in the valley, set up his easel and taught her how to mix colors for him: oranges and corals and yellows and blues and purples and reds. He'd promised one day they'd visit the sea. They'd paint a mural in town. They'd make their own paints out of things they grew in their own garden in a house he'd buy in the countryside.

I tell her she can still walk in his footsteps, start a painting business when she's a little older. And become an artist. Buy the little house. Make the paints.

Susu's father loved to cook, too. Especially vegetables: eggplant, zucchini, ramps, spinach, stuffed blossoms, okra, artichoke, chickpeas, snap peas, beans, broccoli, broccolini, cabbage. Susu loved vegetables because her father did, because a well-cooked veggie, he told her, was like a poem or a painting. It had layers of meaning; it hit all the senses.

"I wish I liked vegetables," I say. I wish I had a father who could make normal things extraordinary.

That year, we find a bunch of translated Agatha Christie books in the school library, and we become obsessed with Hercule Poirot and his mustache. Susu draws a comic about Hercule. He discovers a well of poisoned water. The poison is highly diluted, so people die slowly and painfully over many years.

Then Susu tells me she wishes the real-life murderer would strike, so Susu's father will not be the victim people think of when they think of the faceless monster who may or may not have killed him in Horrorville. She wishes the murderer would return so she can track her down. Because of course, the killer has never come to the lobby, and neither has the ghost of Susu's father. We've been alone in the place where he died, the two of us. Little girls in a place of death.

"You want another person to die?" I say.

"Everyone dies. How will I find her unless she comes back?"

"What if you never find her?"

"I'll find her. She's going to come back, and I'll find her and kill her."

I want to help Susu find the killer because Susu is my best friend and I want her to be happy, though killing someone is not right, not something little girls should want to do. At the same time, I'm scared of the monster. If we find her, I'm sure I'll run for my life, screaming bloody murder, despite Susu's lessons in stabbing things. Still, for Susu I'll do anything.

Then I have an idea: Only Susu's dad can tell us who killed him. I put aside my fear and, for my eleventh birthday, I ask for a Ouija board. My sisters' friend Alya has one that I saw at her house once. She used it to speak to her dead grandmother and find the stash of gold that had gone missing when she died. She swears dead people talk to you through the board. She showed me a gold bangle she wears as proof.

My parents don't believe in spirits and ghosts communicating from beyond. When I hand them my wish list—*Ouija board, dragon books, hoverboard, soccer ball*—they say, "What's an *ooeeja*?" their faces as questioning as though I asked for a pet dragonfly or donkey. On my birthday, they hand me a fountain pen and ink well and a notebook bound in purple leather, the kind with straps to tie it closed and perfectly smooth paper that doesn't blotch ink. I say thank you, and in my room I scream into my pillow. After three muffled screams, I sit up and tell myself I don't need my parents to give me what I want.

That weekend, in Susu's old building, I make my own Ouija board out of posterboard. I draw the English letters and words from memory with my new pen. Yes, No. Hello, Goodbye. I fish a drinking glass, stolen from my kitchen, out of my backpack to use as the planchette. Through the round glass, we'll see what Susu's father has to say about his murderer.

It's hot in here. The only sound, the battery-powered fan whirring. I expect Susu to be as excited as I am to talk to a ghost, her father. But Susu says no. Communication with him should come without the intermediary of my contraption. Like, he'll start appearing to her and tell her the secret she burns to discover: who the murderer is.

We've waited and he hasn't come, I tell her. We need to encourage him. I don't say I'm bothered that I built a Ouija board for her and she doesn't want to use it. Instead, I snort and stomp and get in her way when she starts a new collage.

Susu relents. "OK, use your stupid board," she says.

I lay the board on the ground, and Susu and I sit across from each other, cross-legged. The little electric candles flicker. Susu aims the fan at the back of my neck. I light a stick of spicy incense; its tip glows and slowly burns into ash. I mean it to smell homey, like something's baking. Something delicious Susu's father will want to return for. Impatient, Susu bounces up and down. Her fingers tap her knees as though she's playing piano. A cold breeze rushes past me, extinguishes the incense, and ruffles Susu's hair.

"He might already be here," I say.

Susu scoffs. "Hurry up," she says. "My mama will be mad if I'm late for dinner."

"Don't you feel it?" I say, as the edges of Susu's collages lift and rustle.

She smooths her hair and sticks out her tongue at me.

I set the upside-down glass on the board with a quiet clink, my right hand flat on its circular bottom. I tell Susu to put her hand on top of mine. I count to ten. The glass starts to move, suspended millimeters above the board. Electricity surges through my arm. I shake it and the sensation subsides. Susu has lifted her hand. I tell her to put it back. The tingling zips from my shoulder to my fingertips. The glass doesn't move.

"We have to ask a question," I say.

"Well, ask one."

"But you're the one who wants to know."

"Who killed him? That's my question."

I rub my arm. It's still tingling. "You have to ask *him*. In English. Ask your father the question, not me."

"Who killed you? That's what I should ask?"

The cup swerves to "No," dragging our arms with it. I'm elated. Someone is talking to us, hopefully the spirit of Susu's father.

"Yes," I say. "That's exactly what you should ask."

"Why does it say no? What question is it answering?"

"Are you Susu's father?" I ask.

The cup stops in the middle of the word *hello*:

H-E-L—

"Did you see who murdered you?" Susu says.

The cup jiggles to the side, then swerves to the P.

"Help," Susu says. Her English is not as good as mine, but she understands.

"What do we do?" I say.

The cup jerks across the board: *M-E*.

"That's exactly what we want to do. I'm going to kill your murderer, Baba."

YES.

"But who is she? Where is she?"

GOODBYE, the cup says.

"Ask again," says Susu.

"Susu's father, who killed you?"

The cup holds still, and a shaft of light prisms through it, projecting a wan rainbow on the board.

"Who killed you, Baba?" Susu says. "It's me, Susu. Tell me, and I'll kill her."

"Maybe he doesn't know," I say. "Maybe it happened too fast. Maybe he doesn't want you to seek vengeance."

Susu picks up the glass and hurls it against the boarded-up lift. It bounces and crashes against the floor. Glass flies across the room.

The next day, I sweep the shards into a dustpan. I fold the Ouija board and wedge it under a stack of Susu's artwork.

Susu doesn't give up. She believes the murderer will strike again, and when she does, Susu will be ready. The summer between fifth and sixth grade, she figures out how to get a rifle. Her older cousin, Shadi, shoots gazelle, and he keeps his gun in the back of his truck. One night, we defy the curfew for children and teens that starts at sunset. We sneak out of our rooms and instead of going to Baba's Place, we meet at Susu's cousin's truck to steal the gun. Susu has found internet forums where you can learn how to jimmy a lock and break into a car. But she doesn't need that information, because Shadi doesn't lock his doors. We jiggle the handles, and the doors open right up. Shams and I stand watch while Susu crawls into the back of the truck. On this overcast, starless night, a bit of yellow moon peeks out from behind the silver clouds. Crickets are out in force, shouting loudly, and a train sighs deeply from far away. The evening breeze smells like licorice.

Shams licks my knee as though nothing out of the ordinary is happening. She's happy to be outside with her two favorite girls.

It sounds crazy, two eleven-year-old girls and a saluki stealing a gun, but Susu is determined and angry. The anger doesn't go away with time, though she seems adjusted and normal at school and at home. No one but me knows about her vendetta. She's confided to no one else about her plans to kill a murderer.

I don't feel invisible tonight. I feel like a flashlight in a dark well. I feel like a lumpy bag full of potatoes. Anyone can guess what's inside.

"What if she's out, in the dark?" I whisper.

"What?" Susu says distractedly. Her bum wiggles as she fiddles with the rifle.

"What if the monster is watching us? What if she's prowling around?"

"She's not a monster. She's a human murderer," Susu says. "And Shams will growl if anyone comes near us."

She's turned toward me now, and the rifle is in her hands, pointing out the truck's door, not at me and Shams exactly, but in our vicinity. Susu shifts it downward.

"Do you think she's nearby?" I say.

"I don't know. She'll come back."

An owl calls, *Hoo, hoo-hoo, hoo.* I've never heard an owl around here before. Shams tenses. I hold her by the collar.

"Hold this," Susu says, handing me the gun. She tells Shams to sit, and Shams does.

I step back. I don't want to touch the gun.

"You're a baby," Susu says. She slides the gun under the truck, and turns to the glove box to look for ammunition.

Shams and I are terrible lookouts, because now a neighbor passes by, and it's not till he's a few steps away that Shams jumps up and barks. The man sees me standing there (although the gun is thankfully hidden) and Susu rummaging in the front of the truck.

He stops. I tell Shams to be quiet and sit. She growls a little. I smile a fake smile I hope will keep the man from thinking Susu and I are thieves. He's the old guy who owns the repair shop. I don't like his sneer or the funny way I've seen him look at Mama and some of the other mothers. He talks to them differently than he talks to men. His eyes slither from me to the open door of the truck.

"You shouldn't be out so late," he says. "You're breaking curfew." He winks. He's the kind of grown-up who tries to be friendly with children and fails miserably. Doesn't know that he doesn't know how to be friendly and not scary to children.

I'm ice-cold and shaking from fear of getting caught. The man doesn't notice. He reaches to pet Shams, who barks and scares him a bit.

"Are you and your friend stealing this truck?" the man says.

Susu stops what she's doing and swings her legs out the side of the truck. She kicks my shin, lightly, and I understand what she's saying: *This idiot thinks we're stealing a whole truck. He's nothing to be afraid of.*

"Of course not, Uncle," I say.

"It's my cousin's truck," Susu says. "He asked me to get something out of it."

"Right," the man says. "Well, it's easy enough to hot-wire a car, if you want me to show you."

I can't stop thinking about the gun at my feet. I look down and immediately regret looking down, because now the man might see the gun.

Susu jumps out of the car, slams the door, and pushes me toward her building. She's got Shams by the leash. "We gotta go, mister," she says.

"I'm joking, of course," the man says. "Can't you take a joke?"

We leave the gun under the truck and pretend to go home. We crouch behind a corner, spying on the man, waiting for him to leave. I'm afraid Shams will make a noise, but she seems to understand what we're doing: spying. She lies on her stomach and closes her eyes.

The man walks around Susu's cousin's truck three times. As though he's thinking about stealing it. It's a beautiful white pickup with a painted flower border. But what would he do with it? How would he hide it in such a small neighborhood? Everyone would recognize it as Susu's cousin's truck.

It doesn't occur to me until much later that this is a man who owns a repair shop—this is a guy who loves cars, mechanical things, metal, tires that kick back when you lay into them, shiny tailpipes. Loves them more than he loves people. He's admiring the truck. Taking in its beauty, its beat-up details, the love Susu's cousin gives it. He touches the top of the cab like he's patting the head of a child he adores. Then he looks up at the sky, like he's lost in thought. He turns away from the truck and spits a lump of saliva and phlegm in an amazing long arc that lands far from the object of his affection, right in the middle of the sidewalk, where someone will surely step in the globby grossness.

We're waiting patiently—or Susu and Shams are. I'm sweaty with worry that at some point he'll find the gun and realize we left it there. He heads toward his shop, and I giggle with relief. Susu puts her hand on my mouth. He stops, turns. We sink further behind the corner, out of eyeshot. Wait a beat. Susu lets go of my mouth slowly, and we peek. Thankfully, he's walking away once more. I make an effort to *keep quiet*.

When he's out of sight, Susu rushes to the truck, grabs the rifle from underneath. We hold it between us, like a third, shared arm, like we're Siamese twins, like we can somehow hide it this way. Shams walks next to us, dragging her leash behind her. If anyone saw two eleven-year-old girls walking down the street with a rifle and a dog, they'd holler at us. They'd say, "Do you know how dangerous that is?"

Of course we do. The attraction of a gun is the damage it can do, the fact that you're not supposed to have it, or use it.

If anyone discovered us, they'd lock us up, send us to juvenile detention, take Shams away from us, never let us see each other. The whole way to Baba's Place, I'm imagining myself in a jail cell, alone, with no one allowed to visit me—not my parents, my siblings, my grandma, Susu. I'm eating bread and drinking water and I'm not allowed to read or watch TV, all because of a gun I told Susu to stay away from.

But no one catches us, and we safely ferry the rifle to Baba's

Place. Susu leans the gun against the staircase. Meanwhile, Susu's cousin finds an empty gunrack in his truck, and he tells the police, and everyone's on edge for weeks, except me and Susu, because they think the only person who could have stolen the gun is a killer.

For the next few weeks, whenever we're at Baba's Place after that, the rifle is with us. We never touch it. We don't know how to use it. We keep waiting for the Monstress to return.

Then, Mr. Nadir becomes the latest victim. Run over in his own shop.

I picture him being smashed, squished by Susu's cousin's truck, because it seems like an excellent weapon: large and heavy and easy to steal. The truck's headlamps are like eyes. Its engine growls angrily. The man screams and tears at his clothes in anguish as the truck approaches. The shiny black wheels crunch his bones. His death scene becomes my nightmare. I wake up shouting night after night, and my sisters sing me back to sleep, until they get tired of it and tell Mama she has to sleep with me. Curled up with Mama, I sleep through the night, but my waking hours become haunted. Every car I pass on the street seems to me an engine of death. A weapon. I am not safe.

Susu is not sleeping at all. The whites of her eyes are tinged with red. She talks faster than usual, and her movements are frenetic. A new victim was supposed to be her chance to find the killer, but she's still in the dark. There are too many suspects: Every person she sees. Everyone in the neighborhood. Everyone in town. No one seems to have liked Mr. Nadir, so anyone could have killed him. When we're in Baba's Place, she's constantly looking at the gun, going over to touch it. I'm afraid she's going to use it.

School is starting in a few weeks, and then she won't be able to visit Baba's Place—and the gun—as often. In the meantime, I try to stall her.

"You can't shoot someone," I tell her. "You can't take that thing outside."

"That's the whole point, to take it where the killer is and *kill her.*" She growls, and her sharp canines glint vampirically. She could sink her teeth into my neck and suck the life out of me. I bring my hands up to my chin, a feeble attempt to protect myself.

"I'll only shoot the murderer," she says. "Why would I shoot anyone else?"

"You could shoot me by accident. Or someone else. Children shoot friends by accident all the time. Anyway, how will you figure out who the murderer is?"

"Murderers look guilty. I'll have no doubt."

What does guilt look like? I wonder. Is it the face of a girl who has stolen her cousin's gun? The face of her best friend who helped her do it? Should we have told the truth, Susu and me? Should we have told her cousin we took the gun? Should we have given it back?

Now that the killer has returned, on a motorcycle, no bullet to be found, no gun used, everyone seems to have forgotten about the missing rifle.

Sixth grade begins. One afternoon, Susu and I are walking home from Baba's Place. We do a long loop around the block, to cover our tracks, and our path accidentally takes us past the repair shop. It's boarded up, like the lift in Baba's Place, and the reporter Khaled Khaled stands out front, speaking into a microphone in front of a cameraman and sound guy. There's a white van with all their equipment parked on the street. This block smells like grilled meat; there's a little kabob shop two doors down.

We stop to watch Khaled Khaled. He says, "In this neighborhood known as 'Horrorville,' people are trying to go about their daily lives under the dark shadow of a serial killer's crimes."

He tells his crew to stop filming, takes out a handkerchief and wipes his forehead.

He sees us sitting on the curb.

"Where are your parents? Are they nearby?"

I elbow Susu. I wonder if she'll tell Khaled Khaled her father was one of the victims. Maybe he'd want to interview her or her mother.

"We're going to find the killer," Susu says.

Khaled Khaled laughs. The cameraman and sound guy are busy with their equipment. The reporter says, "A tiny vigilante. You're a bit…disturbing."

Susu doesn't blink. Khaled Khaled attempts to stare her down, but she wins, and he looks away, then back.

"The police are stumped by this case," he says. "How do you think you'll solve it?"

"When I see the killer, I'll know," Susu says.

Khaled Khaled puts his hand out, and Susu takes the bait and shakes it. "Good luck, kid," he says.

He tells his cameraman to film. "Here in Horrorville," he says, "we tried to get residents to tell us how their daily lives have been affected by the horrible crimes, but no one was willing to talk."

*   *   *

Khaled Khaled's report airs, and the parents double down on safety. They start to keep their younger children inside. Mama tells Rana and Lajwa, fifteen and sixteen now, not to let me and my brothers out of their sight during the day while Mama's at work.

When I complain, Mama says bad people are roaming the streets. I tell her letting Rana and Lajwa go out but not me isn't fair. She doesn't listen. She seems not even to hear my words, like my voice has been extinguished, like I'm mute, or she's lost her hearing. But of course, most people who don't hear aren't deaf. They don't want to accept reality or face the truth.

Baba says, "Maybe we should keep them all inside."

"We'll see," Mama says. But the stupid rule stays.

I don't care. I try to evade my sisters, as usual. The next afternoon, while Rana's watching TV and doing her homework and Lajwa's puttering in the kitchen, I put on my invisibility cloak and walk toward the door.

"Where the heck do you think you're going?" Rana says.

Lajwa comes out of the kitchen with a plate of sliced apples. I'm standing with one hand on the doorknob, the other on the deadbolt lock. My shoes are on.

"Go to your room," Rana says. "It's dangerous out there."

"I'm supposed to meet Susu," I say. "Ever since the new murder, she's thinking about her dad. She cries every day."

"That's so sweet of you," says Rana, but she doesn't mean it.

Lajwa says it's dangerous to go out. What if the serial killer is roaming the streets? Then she says something that contradicts her advice: "I think the killer only kills men, not women. Or children. I wonder why."

"There's no pattern," Rana says. "A bunch of random men died. It might not be a serial killer at all."

"See!" I say. "It's safe."

"There could be three different killers. What kind of crappy, awful place breeds three murderers?" Lajwa says.

"If you go, we'll tell Mama, and she will kill us," Rana says. "You don't want that, do you?"

Anyone could be a killer. Even Mama.

My sisters win. Mama wins. I stay home, and the next day at school, I tell Susu I can't come to Baba's Place anymore.

"I think I've got it—who the killer is," she says. "But I can't tell you here."

The lunchroom is loud and chaotic. No one's paying attention to us, sitting with our trays and our apple slices, our cheese pastries and cartons of milk.

"Whisper it," I say. "How do you know?"

"I just know."

"Why should I believe you?"

"Because it's true." She takes a bite of her pastry and makes a *shhhh* finger sign at her lips because Rula has decided to sit next to me. Rula wants to be my friend, but she lives on the far side of the neighborhood, and my mother won't take me there. Besides, until now I've spent all my time with Susu. I've had no time for anyone else. Rula has short curly hair, bites her fingernails, and says she's going to be a poet.

I shouldn't ask Susu, with Rula at our table, but I do anyway: "Did you see her face?"

"Whose face?" Rula says.

"I'm not going to tell you." Susu smiles sweetly; her voice is angry. "You can't keep a secret."

"Is it the headmistress?" Rula says. "Is that who you're talking about?"

"Yes," says Susu. She's hiding her teeth behind her lips, her truth behind her eyes. She's sending me down the wrong path on purpose, to punish me for speaking in front of Rula.

"I hate her," Rula says. "She's such a monster."

"She's terrible," says Susu. Across the cafeteria, the headmistress is talking to one of the fifth-grade teachers, hands folded under her boobs, displeasure on her face, as though she's smelling sewage or rotting meat.

Could she be a killer? Does she transform into a creature of the night, walk on sharp hooves, and stab with bladed fists? At first, I can't imagine it, but then I see her chunky shoes, ankle boots even though the weather has not been cool, her long acrylic nails, painted a slick silver. She wears her dyed black hair in a thick, messy bun; it probably falls down to her waist when she unfastens it.

I convince myself that Susu told the truth to make me think she was lying. I convince myself our headmistress killed Susu's father and two other men. I begin to dread going to school. My mother and father can't understand why I won't get out of bed.

"What is wrong with you?" Rana says one morning.

"I'm scared," I say.

"What are you scared of, sweetie?" Lajwa says. She's kneeling at the side of the bed, stroking my hair.

"What if the headmistress wants to kill me?"

"She's mean, for sure," Rana says.

"She's evil," I say.

"Well, everyone has good in them," says Lajwa. "Does she hit naughty children with a ruler?"

"No," I say. I've never seen her do that. My parents have told us that in their day, teachers hit them all the time, turning their palms red, leaving welts on the insides of their forearms. Teachers aren't allowed to do that anymore.

"Does she yell?"

"Sometimes," I say.

"Sounds like a normal grown-up. They can't control themselves."

"I wish they would," says Lajwa. "Kids shouldn't be afraid of their teachers."

At school, I see the headmistress's silhouette out of the corner of my eye, even when she's not there. I hyperventilate; my heart races. I need to escape. My teacher says I'm having a panic attack. She walks me to the nurse's office, which smells like rubbing alcohol.

"It's going to be OK," the nurse says, and she teaches me how to breathe so the wave of panic washes away.

I begin to be grateful that my parents won't let me go out. The flat feels safe. My family feels safe. My room feels safe. Everything outside the building where I live is dangerous, menacing. But I try to be OK at school. The headmistress is not a murderer or a monster. There's no such thing as monsters.

Now that I don't go to Baba's Place anymore, I see it as others see it. The building where Susu's father died has become a blight. Three years after his death, a shroud of blood and violence lingers. The balconies sag, weeds push up through the concrete outside, and some sort of dark substance is running down the outside walls, like blood. The two trees in front, planted in squares of sad soil that the sidewalk was built around, are drooping and dying, their leaves dropping, forming piles that build up, then scatter when it's windy. The first-floor windows are broken or cracked, though no one ever catches the children with rocks who surely did the damage. Pigeon poop covers the front stoop and the scattered leaves and every visible bit of sidewalk.

It's an eyesore, a sad reminder, a testament to the neighborhood's willingness to live with sorrow.

Mama still wants a memorial. She imagines a park or a community center, a place where children can safely play instead of wandering the streets, as many kids used to do. The winter after Mr. Nadir's death, she asks Lajwa to draw what the place might look like—my sister wants to be a landscape architect. Lajwa draws a gated garden with grape vines and ivy and tulips and hydrangea and sunflowers, with a terrace where people can grow vegetables and a stream children can wade in. My mother loves it. She presents the idea to the town council, and they say they'll have to bring it before the public and then vote on it. Mama goes back the next month and they say there isn't enough money to do it. They tell her to take her ideas to the neighborhood council, which Mama says has even less money and no power to do anything.

Baba tells her to give up. "Nothing will change around here."

I, too, wish she would stop. Baba's Place is the space of my friendship with Susu. I don't want it to disappear, even though I don't meet Susu there anymore.

In the spring of sixth grade, Mama appears before the neighborhood council. She takes me and my sisters with her, for moral support, and so we can see what "civic engagement" looks like. The council includes a Murad, the headmistress's sister, and a woman my mother went to secondary school with. Something happens that my mother doesn't expect. The room is full, and Susu's mother is at the podium. She says she has decided to speak publicly because of Mr. Nadir's death. She says the curfew needs to stay. She wants more police in the neighborhood. She wants the building knocked to the ground and paved over. The space should not be turned into a park. No children should play outside. They have to be kept safe.

"Children weren't the victims," Mama says. "I want my daughters and sons to be able to go outside." As though the park could erase the memory of the three murders.

The widow's burnt eyes bore into my mother's earnest face. Nothing will override Susu's mother's grief.

"No one wants their children to play in that place of evil. No one cares about our neighborhood except us," Susu's mother says.

Mama says, "Who is 'us'? Everyone here cares. We're all in this together, for our neighbors."

The meeting devolves into chaos. Grown-ups shout. The head of the council hits a gavel on the podium and tells everyone to GO HOME.

Susu and I haven't talked about Baba's Place since I stopped going. I think she still sneaks there after school sometimes. I've been hanging out with Rula at lunchtime. Susu often sits alone. After the crazy meeting, I avoid her even more. I feel guilty about our estrangement, and sad, but mostly I ignore the feelings, tamp them down when they flare up.

Weeks later, the neighborhood council makes a unilateral decision. They knock the building down during the school day, on the last day of school. When I walk home from school with my sisters, there's a pile of rubble where the building used to be.

There's no time to find Susu, beg her forgiveness. No chance to go to Baba's Place one last time, to save any of Susu's artwork, to grab the gun. All the art Susu made in the place where her father died is gone. The Ouija board that rescued his voice from oblivion is buried.

A developer says he will build new flats on the site of the demolished building, but while his workers dig a deep hole in the ground, people protest in the hot summer sun with cardboard signs:

"Let evil lie."
"No one wants to live here."
"Nothing can grow where evil visited."
"Tainted forever."

Construction work stops. The town government builds a padlocked fence around the hole. At the end of the summer, Susu and her family move to the city.

CHAPTER 7

The Well

Three more victims.

Into the well the three men fell. At the bottom of the well, they died.

Did they, or didn't they?

Long ago, in a dry valley surrounded by green hills flanked by greener mountains, a spring bubbled up in the shade of a fig tree.

The spring gurgled and sang and spurted out just enough water to irrigate the tree. Just enough for songbirds to frolic in, for travelers to water their animals, clean their clothes, fill a flask. The air around the spring was cool and clean. In this place, a person could breathe deeply, smell green leaves and the fresh essence of water irrigating the earth. In this place, a person could live.

Two of the men survived the fall, but no one heard their cries. Some said they ate each other alive.

Did they, or didn't they?

*   *   *

Long ago, twice a year, a nomad family from the coastal plain visited a spring in the blue-ish shade of a fig tree in a dry valley that may have once been a river. They visited the spring twice a year, every year, between their travels to and from the mountains. Eventually, the family decided to stay in the valley, close to the mountains but not in them, because the mountains were full of jinn with prickly pears in their mouths and flames bursting from their skin, and the desert plain they came from was a hard place to live, with no shade and little water and harsh winds.

Near the spring in the valley, the family dug a well. Around the spring, they built a small fountain, where travelers and pilgrims would come to wash the grime of travel from their feet and faces and necks. At first, the people who came to the spring and its well were passing through, like the nomad family used to do. Or they came to visit the fig tree, which was said to have sprung from the body of a saint. The family fed the travelers and pilgrims, let them pitch their tents, and brought them water from the well to drink, wash up, and water their livestock. The well's water was sweet and crisp and cold, with a mineral scent. Some of the travelers chose to stay.

Into the well the three men fell in the dark, humid night.

Who pushed them? No one knows.

Long ago, in a dry valley, near a spring, a deep, echoey well appeared. A family of water jinn with liquid skin settled in the well, beckoning unsuspecting travelers.

*   *   *

Who pushed the three men into the well? Who laughed as they fell? Their faces, when their neighbors pulled them out of the well, were slashed bloody. Their backs and shoulders, too.

Long ago, in a dry valley, around a well, a town sprang up. The first paths through town were donkey paths, cutting a straight swath for half a mile, then veering left or right or slithering in and out like a snake, because donkeys hated snakes and if they saw one, they jolted, dashing and wending frenziedly out of danger. If the donkey saw a mountain cat, it bolted. The path dead-ended where the wild creature had been, and a new, perpendicular path began.

You might not believe donkeys created the pattern of streets we see today. A donkey's hoofprints don't magically become packed dirt or cobblestones or asphalt. But roads begin under the feet of beasts. Donkeys brought wood and clay and stone for houses. They carried the wares of merchants. The first houses in the town, set right on the streets, were one-room red clay structures that later were painted bright white, and even later repainted pink and green and blue and decorated with murals of flowers and gazelles and a gurgling spring. Later still, the paint peeled and the murals were hard to make out if you hadn't seen them every day since you were young, no taller than a donkey's knee.

When the town first sprang up, the well was small and round with a bronze crown and a small bucket attached to a rope. As people came to this place and the town grew, they knocked down the old well structure and replaced it with something better and more efficient. They deepened and widened the well and built a larger square brick structure around it, and a system of pulleys tugged by camels or donkeys to draw up a deep trough of water all at once. They said, "There's no such thing as jinn, or if they exist, they don't live among people." Townspeople pooh-poohed anyone who retold their grandparents' stories about a jinn family living in the well.

The streets near the well were the best area of the town to live in. People in neighborhoods farther from the well had to cart their water over the bumpy, lumpy streets to their homes, hoping and praying the water wouldn't slosh over and seep into the ground. Then plumbing came to the town, and beasts of burden were put out of work, and stories of jinn came back, not because people believed in them, but because they wanted to scare little children into obedience. Mothers told their children that a tribe of jinn had moved from the mountains to the well to quench the flame of their skins. The mamas let their little ones look over the edge of the abandoned well. The bottom of the well was dark as a monster's pupils, and the little ones believed the mamas were not lying about the jinn, that they knew something true a child simply couldn't imagine or fathom.

Over the years the neighborhood grew and the town grew, and urban planners from the city swung into town to plan streets. The town's richest families built blocks of flats and auto shops and convenience stores and restaurants and places of worship, and the municipality tucked a few small green parks between buildings. The town became an oasis for people who wanted a better life than toiling in the mountains growing dates and oranges and tending goats and chickens. The neighborhood became packed with people who couldn't afford to live in the parts of town with more parks and smoother streets.

The well that was once the center of town hid on the outskirts of a blighted neighborhood, and even mothers stopped talking about it. People forgot exactly where it was, but they'd heard rumors of it from their grandparents.

Who pushed the three men into the well?

She smelled like oud and fennel. She asked the men for a kiss. Her eyes flashed as she pushed them with her raised forearms. Her sickle hands clinked like castanets.

Khaled Khaled had believed the well was an urban legend, but here it was, tucked behind the structure that had once held Nadir's repair shop. Having received a tip about Nadir's murderer, the TV reporter arrived at the well on a summer evening, in the TV station's white van, with his cameraman and sound guy. The three colleagues hadn't given up on the story in the year since it first broke, talking to people throughout the neighborhood, grilling the police chief and mayor at the town hall, documenting the destruction of the places where the three victims had been killed in what *had* to be connected incidents.

Khaled's teen daughter, Zubaydah, wondered why he was so obsessed.

"It's only three deaths," she said. "Out of thousands of people who live here."

Khaled believed sincerely that every life mattered; everyone, including the dead, deserved justice. When he received the anonymous text telling him to come to the well to learn a secret that the town government and Nadir's family wanted to hide at all costs, he showed up in under ten minutes.

Nadir had a secret, the text said. *Only I know what it was.*

Khaled didn't fear the well. He didn't believe in jinn or

monsters or supernatural beings or things that go bump in the night. He believed in what he could see and verify. He'd grown up in town and his grandmother had been a virologist who moved from the city and gave up her profession to marry a small-town baker because her sweet tooth was stronger than her thirst for knowledge—or so Khaled's grandfather claimed. His grandmother never talked about the past. She made Khaled Khaled believe in bacteria—and by extension, other tiny creatures—by swabbing his cheek with a toothpick, smearing his saliva on a glass slide, and jamming his eye into a microscope. He saw the creatures swimming and reached his hand to try to grab one, but of course he could not.

His grandmother had no inkling he would die not from a communicable disease, but from a broken neck in a deep, dark well.

The well was in a dense neighborhood, surrounded on all sides by blocks of flats. The security checkpoint that had replaced Nadir's demolished shop was around the corner. Khaled assured the camera and sound guys the police would come running if anything weird happened.

"Should we tell them we're here? Get an escort?"

"Our subject won't spill the beans if we have a police escort. Get out! What kind of journalist would suggest such a thing?"

"Why do they want to meet here?" the sound guy asked. He was the best listener of the three of them, and Khaled envied his ability to come up with just the right question. He could have been a reporter, but he deferred to Khaled.

"To be close to the site of the murder?" Khaled hoped the informant would not be spooked by the camera. What could anyone expect from the town's best and only investigative reporter? He would show up with his crew. He would get the scoop.

Khaled didn't fear the well, but there was something a bit spooky about the air around it. It was as though the well were a black hole, sucking away the light that emanated from the streetlamps that lined the streets surrounding them. Take four steps from the buildings where lives went on, and you were steeped in darkness.

"It feels hotter and more humid here," the cameraman said. "They say the spring dried up, and the well did too, and a jinn that takes the form of a snake took residence."

Khaled Khaled punched the guy in the arm. They'd been through a lot together in their fifteen years at the town and surrounding area's only television station; they'd covered fires that killed entire families, a locust infestation to end all locust infestations, the migration of families from the countryside into town, and away from town into the city, and, of course, the murders. In his early years as a reporter, Khaled had dreamt of moving to the city, to a bigger TV station, to a place where there was more than one station and other reporters to compete against for scoops. He'd given up these dreams to give his daughter a small-town childhood: quiet, safe, filled with nosy relatives and neighbors. He hoped she'd never chafe under this place's small-town habits. He had realized lately that he loved it here, where his grandparents were buried, where people trusted his nose for news, his truth-telling, his commitment to fairness. Where they watched out for him and his daughter.

The three men stepped closer to the well, Khaled with nonchalance and his crew as though they were approaching the mouth of a lion.

"Let's film," he said, walking backward as he talked. He trusted his guys would tell him when to stop. They would not let him fall.

"This is a bad idea," the sound guy said.

A thunder-like rumble emanated from the shaft, getting louder and closer till Khaled clapped his hands over his ears.

"Are you getting this?" he shouted at the sound guy.

Khaled couldn't make out what the sound guy was mouthing. "HELP ME"? "SHE'S REAL"? "IT'S HERE"? "OH HELL"?

Blood streamed from the crewmembers' ears. Their eyes bugged, their shoulders slumped, and their equipment fell from their hands. The earth shook violently and the bricks of the structure around the well loudly crumbled.

Khaled turned to face the well.

Her black hair pooled like silk, over her shoulders and down to her knees. Her teeth flashed white and canine. She smelled like oud and fennel and apples. She asked him for a kiss. His muscles tensed and he froze, paralyzed by her smile. He couldn't see her hands.

Her eyes sparked as she grabbed his shoulders. Pain shot through him; something sharp tore into his shoulders, the skin of his face. She was pawing at him. He couldn't push her away.

She shoved him into the well with the pads of her palms. Her sickle fingers clinked against each other. Hands grasped at him as he fell. He fell for a long time. The sky above him was full of stars.

His colleagues cried out, fell past him, thudded to the bottom of the well.

No, that couldn't be possible, unless he were suspended in air.

He was. He was suspended mid-well, defying gravity. He reached out, but the sides were too far to touch. Then he fell, so quickly. His heart flew into his throat, and he slammed into the damp ground, and in an instant his neck had snapped in two. Just before his consciousness snuffed out forever, her voice came from above:

No one gets out alive.

CHAPTER 8

Masquerade

Monster Parade. "Monstress." Trouble at the well.

In seventh grade, at age thirteen, I beg my sisters to take me to the Monster Parade during the annual Festival of the Sacrifice. It will fall in April this year, while the weather is still warmish, not hot.

Once, I wanted to see a donkey. Now, I want to see monsters—well, people dressed up as them, cavorting in the streets, spooking passersby. I've seen it on TV but never in person.

I *want* to be afraid. To choose fear, rather than letting it find me.

The world is already scary, and everyone likes to scare teen girls about what might happen to them...if they...do this... or that...or wear this...or that.

Choosing fear will give me control over what I fear and when.

I look at my sisters, and in their feelings about the parade, I see two different responses to the world around us. I see myself waffling between them.

Lajwa doesn't want to go. Last year, the parade gave her nightmares, visions of half-human, half-animal creatures with gleaming teeth and fiery breath and metallic claws and hearts that beat on the outsides of their bodies. She wants to hide from fear.

Rana, on the other hand, wants to meet fear head-on. She loves the Monster Parade, and every year she tells me about it: how scary it is, how creative the costumes are, how the monsters toss candy to the bravest children, how she avoids nightmares by imagining herself as a monster. When I ask her what kind of monster, she won't say.

"Are you tall, or hunched over?" I ask as she makes us cheese sandwiches. I grab the knife and stab the air with it. "Do you have knives for hands?"

"Give that back," she says.

"Do you glow in the dark?"

"A light in the dark is the opposite of scary."

"No, it's super scary. Why won't you tell me?"

"I don't have to tell you anything," she says, which is the kind of thing Lajwa, who is obsessed with privacy, would say. Rana is usually generous with her thoughts, whether you want to hear them or not. Even though she's annoying and bossy a lot of the time, she also loves to make up stories with me and play games like spying on people in the park and imagining their conversations with each other.

Could it be the monster Rana becomes in her imagination is one of the monsters in Lajwa's nightmares? They share everything; why not the creatures who live in their minds?

My parents rule is that we can go to the parade at age thirteen, but unlike with my older sisters, they've *arbitrarily* decided I must make my case to them. And one of my sisters has to take me. I find their rules ridiculous, unfair, inconsistent with what they allowed my sisters to do. Most children go to the parade from the time they're six or seven, I say. My mother points out that every year our teachers spend hours consoling crying children, telling us monsters aren't real, telling us the difference between what's real and what's imaginary. They send letters to our parents and hold poorly attended community meetings at which they lecture the few parents who come, including Mama and Baba.

We keep fighting. Then my parents take me with them to the meeting at school, because they want me to "understand my choice." If they're trying to keep me from going, they're mistaken in their logic: hearing from school officials and teachers won't convince me not to stay home. At the meeting, a few weeks before the festival, I fidget with a little ring on my pinky while the teachers list other, safer ways for families to celebrate the Festival of the Sacrifice without damaging their children: stopping by the homes of family and friends and neighbors; giving children envelopes of cash, but not too much, so as not to spoil them; wearing new clothes, but not spending too much on them; going to the countryside to choose a sacrificial lamb for our families; sharing meat with our neighbors and the poor; stuffing ourselves with meat and rice and bread and date pies and imported chocolate, but not too much, so as not to make ourselves sick; thinking as a family about the meaningful sacrifices each of us has made for ourselves, our families, and our town; helping children to make a list of new sacrifices we can make. I lay my head on the desk so my parents won't see me roll my eyes at this very boring, very unscary list. The teachers tell parents to shield their children, especially young ones, from the sights and sounds of the parade. They say the appropriate age to attend is definitely not four or five, or six or seven, or ten, or thirteen, but fifteen or sixteen—or even eighteen! The headmistress says the scary costumes affect our growing brains, and parents have a duty to protect children emotionally and psychologically.

My mother takes notes on the handouts she picked up from a folding table near the door. My father grunts and says thank you every few minutes.

I lift my head. The all-purpose room full of folding chairs is poorly lit because our neighborhood has electricity shortages these days, and the school is conserving energy. One of the teachers has a flashlight, and whether on purpose or not, she shines it up at her own face, lighting her nose and eyes and cheekbones in a menacing way. She blinks, turns the light toward the paltry audience. One of the fathers is caught in the beam. He waves his hand in front of his face, as though he could shoo the light away. The teacher lowers her flashlight and apologizes.

Someone laughs and says the room is so spooky, they're sure monsters wait in the shadows.

Yes, the upper school headmistress says, don't you see, that's why you should keep your children home. That's why you should speak out against the parade. It may have served a purpose at one time, but now we know more about children's brains. They need psychological safety more than anything. They need your love and care. Keep your children home. Protect them from the trauma of a scary encounter with a fake monster.

When we leave, my father shakes hands with every speaker, tells them how important they are to "our" children's wellbeing.

He used to want me to be free. Now he wants me to be safe.

I want to be both.

None of the headmistress's warnings makes me not want to see the parade. She never wants children to have any fun. She'd like to see us shut up in our rooms, without TV or internet or video games, or any idea what's going on in the world. She'd like us to read books written fifty years ago, about candy lands and happy puppies.

Soon, she'll win her fight, and no one will have the chance to witness the parade. This will, it later turns out, be the last year parents allow their children to go. In a few years, the parade will die out altogether, because people believe we can't banish monsters if some of us keep dressing up as them. They believe we can't be safe in the streets, only within the walls of our homes. They stop trusting each other. Any one of us—any one of the grown-ups—could be the monster.

After the community meeting, I want to go to the parade more than ever.

But because of what the teachers have told them, my parents fabricate a new family rule: we have to be fifteen to go.

When I ask why they're changing the rule, my parents tick off all the headmistress's warnings. I stew for days.

"Why won't they let me go?" I ask my sisters a few days before the parade, while my parents are at work. My brothers would have been too young anyways. This rule change seems like a vendetta against *me* and only me.

"Because the monsters are effing scary," Lajwa says. "It's not a parade for children."

"You're right, it's not fair. I wish you could come with me," Rana says. "The parade is scary and spooky—in a good way.

You'll love it. Teachers and parents are overprotective. Children can handle scary stuff."

I love Rana when she goes on about parents and children, how our mothers and fathers should let us do what we want, should trust us and let us take responsibility and let us learn from mistakes, just like they did. Rana knows how much I want to go, how jealous I will be when she comes home loaded down with bags of candy and describes the monsters in their costumes. In years past, she's shared a little of her candy with me, but she has a sweet tooth, and she keeps most of it for herself. If I go with her, I'll get my own candy. She tells me the first time at the parade is the best, because it's scarier when you've got no expectations. She says even though I've seen the parade on TV, it'll be scarier in person, more surprising.

"Please take me," I say. "Tell Mama and Baba exactly what you said just now. It's not fair I have to wait till I'm fifteen. You and Lajwa didn't have to."

I like the thrill of a roller coaster when a carnival comes to town. I like scary movies and ghost stories. What I hide is this: Even though Susu and I have not been friends for several years, haven't even seen each other since she moved to the city, I continue to be obsessed with the murders of her father and the other men in our neighborhood. I've spent hours online on the local news site searching for information about the deaths, but there's very little to be found, even after three more men died in an abandoned well in our neighborhood. People say the same murderer killed them who killed the others, but the police deny it. They go on forums and record videos to claim they've followed every lead and they have concluded the three previous murders have no connection to the Well Murders.

I like to imagine what it was like to be those three men, walking in the dark into the ruin of what had once been a vibrant town hub, where long ago everyone got water for their donkeys.

Am I imagining someone murdering me—or am I imagining being the murderer? I like the scary thrill of both.

Why the victims went to the well at night and not during the day is a question everyone and their mother asks—as though the three men deserved to be attacked out of the darkness because they'd made a bad choice. People whisper about terrible things the men did, share gossip with their mouths hidden behind their hands, write threads online about the immorality and corruption that led to the men's deaths. Maybe the whispers and online theories are more than uncharitable rumors. Maybe the men weren't good people. Maybe Khaled Khaled, the news reporter who died with his colleagues, had colluded with the police and hidden the truth. Maybe a beautiful woman with black hair lured them to the well and they followed because they thought they could screw her, force her to do things she didn't want to do. Maybe they deserved coming to a bad end. Or maybe it was not that they deserved it, but that it was inevitable, unavoidable once they'd misbehaved.

Here is my thirteen-year-old's theory about why the men visited the well at night: Going during the day would be too easy. The opposite of a thrill. A snore. There would be no shadows to startle at, no fear that a murderer could appear out of nowhere. No sounds coming from hidden places to make them jump. Going in daylight would be like meeting someone for coffee or lunch or to smoke on the corner, and what could be more boring?

Going at night would be like roller-skating down the steps of the town square and along the edge of the mosaic fountain in front of the town hall in the middle of the day, when the mayor himself could walk out and catch you. It would be like vaping in the bathroom at school, or shoplifting from the Murads' store. The buzz of nearly getting caught, the adrenaline of "What if?"

I bet they didn't expect to die, didn't think the danger was so high. They were investigating a string of murders, but they didn't think it could happen to them. If you thought you could be murdered, too, you wouldn't go anywhere in the neighborhood.

Parents are the first to think it could happen to their children. They're the first to lock us in our homes.

I watch old archival videos of Khaled Khaled investigating crimes and bringing people justice in our small town, helping people fight mean landlords, corrupt city council members and utility managers, cheating shop owners and restaurateurs. He seems brave to me, though a little stupid, a bit foolhardy. He doesn't believe anything an official says to him, yet he'll follow a crazy popular theory about an unsolved mystery to its bitter end. He believes the people. He lives to serve and inform them.

Seemed. Believed. Lived. He's dead now, and the murderer scrawled a message around the well: "No one gets out alive." People from outside our neighborhood have taken the words as a warning. Stay out. That neighborhood is cursed. The local paper runs an opinion article saying our whole neighborhood should be razed, not just the buildings where men have died. And parents from all our town's neighborhoods should keep their children inside, safe from killers.

One person writes a letter to the editor in response: "Don't leave us to deal with our problems alone."

Rana talks to my parents at dinner, the night before the parade. She says she'll take good care of me if they let her take me to the parade. She says the streets are safer than ever. Since the triple murder, police are out in force all across town, not just in our neighborhood. And more police, borrowed from the city, are coming for the Festival of Sacrifice and the parade. We've started to see them everywhere, in their khaki uniforms and black boots, guns at their sides, all along the streets we walk to school, in front of stores, surrounding the area that leads into the well. We'll make sure we can see the police at all times. We'll be sure to text if something concerning happens.

"All right," Baba says. "Take her, but be home before dark."

Mama reminds him of the meeting at school. How convinced he was.

"They were persuasive," he says. "But I think they went overboard. One parade isn't going to stunt her."

"Lajwa and I have gone, and I'm OK," Rana says.

"She'll get nightmares," Lajwa says.

"I'm not like you."

"She really wants to go. Let her go," Baba says.

"I should go with them." Mama seems tired of this conversation.

It will be no fun with Mama there worrying and second-guessing her decision to let me go. Rana pleads with Baba to let us go alone.

"They'll be fine," he says, pressing his palm on Mama's forearm as though that will convince her. "Nothing has ever happened at the parade. It's the safest place they could be, with the mayor in the middle of the crowd. The police can't let anything happen, or there would be a mutiny in town. The teachers meant well, but the girls will be OK."

Looking unpersuaded, Mama gives up. She's tired of arguing. She lets us go.

Rana thanks my parents and tells them she will take good care of me at the parade. If I have nightmares after, she'll wake up with me and comfort me.

As soon as my parents have given permission, I do a one-eighty. Anxiety gnaws at my belly and I worry constantly. All the conspiracy theory videos I've watched online have taught me the murderer is wily. Creative. What if the killer blends into the crowd? I don't want to be snatched by a monster or a human. I don't want to be stabbed to death.

Rana is so excited to take me. Soon, I set aside my anxiety and I'm infected with her enthusiasm. In the days before the parade, I ask Rana if we should dress up like monsters. She says no. Lots of people go in their street clothes, and the monsters spend months perfecting their costumes. We don't have time to make ourselves scary enough for the parade.

Before Rana and I leave on the afternoon of the parade, Mama sets the rules: Don't lose sight of each other. Drink lots of water. Back before sunset. Don't talk to anyone.

"How is that possible, Mama?" Rana says. "Are we supposed to pretend we're mute?"

"Go," Baba says. "Before your mother comes up with more rules."

We walk out of our neighborhood and into the part of town that makes sense: streets in a regular grid, boulevards with green medians, bright flowers packed together. The road through the center of town is lined with roses of all colors: lemony yellow, buttery yellow, orange, coral, orangey yellow, orangey red, red, purple, light pink, dark pink, deep crimson, almost-blue. The smell intoxicates me. As we pass the thorny bushes, I pluck a soft petal from one flower on each bush and I squeeze them between my nails. I bring the petals to my nose and breathe.

Rana notices my theft and tells me to stop. "You're not supposed to pick the flowers," she says.

I show her the petals, piled in my open palms. "These are just petals."

She takes the petals, and it looks like she's going to scatter them under a bush.

My need for the petals is a hunger. Their smell will nourish me. "Please, please," I say. "Let me keep them. I promise not to pick anymore."

Rana stuffs the petals in my pocket. "Keep your hands to yourself," she says. "Be good or Mama and Baba won't let me take you out again."

I bring my empty hands to my face as I follow her into the crowd. I'm happy. I smell like roses.

We hear the parade before we see it. The *bum-ba-da-bum-pum-pum* of drums and stomping feet, an occasional triumphant hoot of a trumpet or car horns excitedly honking, whoops and hollers of joyful people. Louder and louder, until we're immersed in sound, ahead of us a wall of people moving through the street, somehow organized and chaotic, like a gardener's carefully planted rows of flowers that bust their colorful petals out in all directions.

The first monster I see has thick, black batlike wings rising from its shoulders, a curved beak, ears that move up and down, claws held out like weapons. The monster is twice as tall as my father, looming over everyone in the crowd, with orange bird-legs, and large, sharp bird claws where a person's shoes would be.

"That's a great costume," Rana says. She thinks the bat-bird-person is wearing stilts; I think she's wrong. It's not a person. It's real. I can't imagine this bird-bat-dragon creature undressing and changing into jeans and a T-shirt, looking like a human, eating human cereal for breakfast, drinking human water from a cup, reading to its human children, living in a human house. It's a real monster, somehow arrived here from Monsterland. Maybe it has stepped out of a tear in the world, or has come up out of a well, or through a mirror, or has been conjured by jinn. Maybe it *is* a jinn. Maybe it's been living in a bottle and comes out once a year for the Monster Parade. Or maybe it flew high over the clouds and landed here in our town, squawking and cawing.

The monster is not as delicate as a bird. It sways as it walks and nearly stumbles. It catches me staring and opens its mouth, baring pointy, golden teeth. It cocks its head to one side and flaps its wings, dispersing the people and monsters around it and creating a circle of empty asphalt. It turns away from me and flaps its wings again. A dragon-like tail floats behind.

Rana and I move into the parade's current. Monsters walk alongside us and past us. Their weird features blend into each other. Horns and large yellow eyes, feathered wings and scaled wings, long furry tails, talons, serpent heads, scorpion claws, mer-people being pushed along in wheeled water tanks. There is a man who has somehow attached himself to a horse in a way that makes him looks like a real centaur. I try to find the horse's head, the man's legs, and I can't; I can't figure out how the costume works.

"Amazing," Rana says, and I want to scream at her—it's not amazing. It's clearly dark magic. This horse-man is real, just like the bat-bird. It galloped through the mountains to arrive at the parade, its flanks shiny with sweat. As it trots, its tail flicks and dung drops like magic.

The parade turns a corner. Spectators line the street. Some sit on folding chairs on the sidewalks, or sit right on the curb, eating biscuits and drinking tea and banging drums and holding up their children to see the monsters go by. One man plays a flute, a snake charmer without a snake. As we walk with the crowd in the street, I'm clutching Rana's hand, afraid of getting lost.

I take in the revelers, the watchers, the ways the parade spills off the street, how it's a part of the town's geography for these few hours, like a road or a creek.

Part of its architecture, a moving monument to fear and resilience.

Later, I'll analyze my memories of the parade, look at the two photos Rana asked a stranger to take, of me and her looking small and normal with the dressed-up monsters around us.

There's a guy all in white standing in the middle of the street with a posterboard with scrawled-on handwriting in black marker: "Beware jinn! Ask me about exorcisms!"

Police officers stand at regular intervals along the parade route.

Rana points up. People lean from balconies and windows of flats, some holding masks to their faces, some with sculpted dark red nails like claws. They look half-human, half-monster, not as scary as the people on the ground. Stuck between worlds, a predicament that is scary in its own way. I look up and back down, trying not to smash into someone, trying not to lose my footing as I walk or get distracted by the people up there.

"They had the right idea," Rana says. "To watch but not get stuck in this chaos. I love it though, these crazy, dressed-up people. Where'd they get all these great ideas?"

There's joy on her face, something I haven't seen in a while. She's talked for months about hating our town, wanting to leave. How our parents have gotten more and more strict, how they won't let her and Lajwa go anywhere after school, how it's the parents in our neighborhood who keep us all inside. I haven't understood why she's complaining. It seems to me she has more freedom than me. She's allowed to go to the store after school if we run out of milk or fruit. She has to call Mama before she leaves and when she gets home, and she has to go with Lajwa. But she's allowed to go. She's allowed to come to the Monster Parade; she didn't have to plead and beg. She says there's nothing to do here, no jobs for people who don't want to work in the factory or teach or take care of people or animals. I ask what she wants to do; she doesn't know. Travel, she says. Eat foods she's never tried before. Paint murals. How do you get to be seventeen and not know what you want to do? I've wanted to be a perfumer since the days of sneaking out with Susu. I think I can be a perfumer anywhere, but Rana's rants wriggle into my chest and unlock something. I need to smell the smells of the world, go somewhere else. It doesn't occur to me that I could change my mind about perfuming, that at thirteen I don't have to know what I want to do with my life. I'm certain about perfuming. That won't change.

Ahead, there's an empty circle with someone at its center. Monsters and people have stopped to look. Rana grabs my hand and we push our way forward. I'm a cocktail of feelings: thrilled, excited, frightened, worried, anxious, giddy. As we move along, I smell roasting meat coming from somewhere, vinegary stewed chickpeas, sugar being spun into cotton floss, popcorn. I smell the sweat of the people we pass and the cheap floral deodorant they used to cover up the odor of perspiration. I smell the thick pancake make-up on the face of a man in costume as a wolf-man creature, his face painted pale as milk, lips red as apples. He wears a ruff of fur around his head, pointy ears, a thick furry suit that must be steaming hot inside. He bares his sharp canines joyfully, as though about to sink his teeth into tasty flesh. I smell his stale breath. I edge away from him, and he looks straight at me, then my sister, his eyes twinkling with malice. He growls like a wolf, and I step back in fear.

"She's caught something," he says.

"Who?" asks Rana calmly. He doesn't seem to scare her.

"The Monstress."

We squeeze to the front, and Rana tells me to climb on her shoulders. I say I'll crush her. She laughs. "I'm strong," she says. "I want you to see everything."

Above the crowd, before I see, I smell. It's a bright perfume, roses or gardenias or a blend. It's all her—the Monstress. No other scent pierces my nose in her presence. In the middle of a sea of bodies, the Monstress is alone but not alone. There is a corpse at her feet, its arms and legs splayed in a caricature of running, a pool of blood around it. Fear builds in my throat. The corpse twitches and twitches and stops. Lies completely still. The woman, the Monstress, has huge yellow eyes and purple-black hair that falls to her knees. When our eyes reach her legs, Rana and I gasp audibly in unison. We can't help it. We've never seen anything like her, never seen a costume so real—all the other costumes seem shoddy in comparison now. I believed in them only because I was a newbie. But the long-haired woman is truly otherworldly. Her thighs are donkey's thighs, her knees are donkeys' knees, her feet donkeys' hooves. She rotates, her eyes on the crowd, swinging her hair to one side to reveal her donkey rump, her donkey tail. Now that we're closer, I smell something different. She's surrounded by an odor of orchids, that bitter yet beautiful perfume. I imagine white and purple flowers growing from the backs of her knees and the insides of her elbows, her armpits, exuding a powerful yet subtle smell. Now I smell sandalwood, smoky and earthy.

Not only blossoms and greenery are beautiful to the nose. Dead things can smell beautiful too.

Does she change scent at will, or is it impossible for my nose to pinpoint her? For my memory to pinpoint her? She confounds in every way. Others might think the donkey legs and rear are beastly, ghastly, but she wins my heart with her unique beauty. I love the way she defies all expectation for what a female should be. Beautiful, ugly, young, old, fragrant, malodorous, alluring, horrific. I have these thoughts even before I see her hands, how long they extend, how she holds them up and out, as though in supplication. They are curved blades growing from her wrists. They shine and glint. They drip with blood. Fake blood that appears incredibly real.

Do her sharp hands make her want to stab? Make her want to hurt someone simply because she can?

"She killed that person," I say, in awe and scared of what I'm feeling. Admiration, affection. For the Monstress. "He must have hurt her and she fought back."

I think about Susu. This is the first time I have truly understood her wish for revenge for her father's murder. To crave violence is to make yourself feared, instead of fearing—it seems like a powerful thing. But I don't have this thought in words. I simply feel the power of the Monstress because I am in her vicinity. I savor it.

My sister must realize the Monstress is a bad influence on a younger sister. She's responsible for me, and she let me see the Monstress and her victim. Rana makes me get down and puts her hands over my eyes, but it's far too late. I saw.

The mass chants, "Monstress! Monstress! Monstress!"

The creature opens her mouth, like she's inhaling their voices, taking the sound in like sustenance.

I wriggle away from my sister. I want to be closer to the woman. I break through the front row, so that it's me and the Monstress, eye to eye. Rana calls me, telling me to come back, yelling, "Mama and Baba are going to kill me!"

My eyes don't move from the Monstress. She seems familiar. She seems to recognize me, the way her eyes open and then narrow.

"Welcome," she says.

Who is she? Do I know her? I can't recall anyone with hair so long. The black stream obscures her face. She steps back and whips her hair to the side, the flat of her right sickle against the side of her face. She could be a dozen women I know. Women with honey eyes, lush eyebrows thick as a thumb, skin like amber. My math teacher or her sister who teaches first grade, the mother of my brother's friend, my father's co-worker's wife, the woman who sells roasted peanuts on the corner across from my school, a nurse who lives in our building.

Now the crowd is chanting something new: "Mother of Sickles! Mother of Sickles! She's the one who killed our brothers! She's the one who killed our fathers!"

"I killed him," the Monstress says, her voice plump as a beating heart. "I killed *them*."

I can't place her voice.

"Mother of Sickles! Mother of Sickles! You're the one who tempted them! You're the one who tempted them!"

I chant with them: "Mother of Sickles! You're the one!"

She hisses and laughs and claws the air, the pointy ends of her sickles centimeters from my face. I stumble back, straight into Rana. My stomach contorts. I smell donkey musk, just like Bumbo. Her hooves nearly stomp on my feet. She's real! She's real!

"Little one," the Monstress says. "Little one! Come with me."

People throw objects at us: aluminum cans, sandwich wrappers, plastic shopping bags, wadded-up Kleenexes, chewed-up gum, pebbles, sticks, apple cores, banana peels. I duck, and my back is pelted. Nothing hurts, it's just demeaning, and it makes me mad. I'm a kid. And I'm not dressed up as a monster. Why are they throwing stuff at me?

"Monstress, Monstress," they chant.

The street is strewn with trash. The parade moves, swirling around the Monstress and her prey like rapids around a boulder.

I had forgotten about the dead man at my feet.

The Monstress reaches one of her sickle hands to the corpse, who grabs her wrist. He gets up, dusts himself off, smacks the side of her blade, not at all afraid. I realize they're high-fiving each other, pleased with their performance.

Where are her hands hidden? Does she have hands?

"See?" Rana says. "It's not real. It's make-believe. It's a skit. They'll walk a bit farther and do it again."

I'm devastated and ashamed at being duped, for believing the Monstress was real, not a woman who spent months gluing real hair to a pair of very realistic plaster-cast donkey's legs. Rana mistakes my embarrassment for terror.

"I shouldn't have brought you. I'm sorry. Let's go home."

The wave of shame ebbs and I'm intrigued. I don't want to go home. I want to watch the Monstress and her victim playacting. I get a thrill imagining them treading a thin line between real and not-real. How are they able to make us believe?

Maybe the characters are real. Maybe this woman *is* possessed by a jinn.

"More," I say. "Can we watch again?"

The roasting meat smell has returned, and now there's the aroma of peanuts too. I ignore my burgeoning hunger and beg Rana to hurry up. When we arrive at the Monstress's new location, in the middle of the park, in the shade of a tree, her victim is standing. We climb onto a low-hanging limb to see better. This time, we see the skit from the beginning. She pretends to stab him twenty times—I count them as her arm violently gashes at him. The stabs are slow, dramatic—choreographed, though I don't think of them that way until much later, thinking back on the scene. The victim's stomach pulls farther and farther inward with each jab, and he goes, "Uh, uh, uh, uh," and collapses. He squeezes something at his stomach. Does anyone else see it? The trick he does? And yet, even though I see him make it happen, I believe in the blood gushing from his body as he falls to his knees. He writhes. This death is better than the first. More satisfying an ending, maybe because I witness all of it.

I take pleasure in witnessing her power in killing, his power in dying. She makes him a victim. He makes her a monster.

I want to watch another performance, but Rana is tired and ready to go home.

"Have you seen her before?" I ask as we leave the crowds behind.

"Last year."

As we walk on a quieter side street, Rana tells me the woman with sickle hands and donkey legs is a story made up to scare little children, to make men seem more innocent than they are, to shame women and turn them into villains when really they're victims—of abuse, violence, oppression, of men's jealousy, of other women's suspicions, of the "strictures" of our society, of rules that make no sense. I'm impressed with my sister's analysis; I'd never have thought of things that way.

The character at the parade was new last year, Rana says, but the story has been around since before our family came to town.

In those drawings of my classmates when we were younger, after Susu's father died, I'd thought the sickle woman was from their imaginations, but maybe they'd heard these stories. Maybe they hadn't made her up out of nothing.

"I love the costumes," Rana says, "but not how the stories are used to scare people, as though the made-up stories are real.

They should only be told for entertainment, for a momentary shock. I can't wait to get away from all this superstition."

I want to sound smart to my sister, so I disagree with her, just a little. "Not everyone's like that. Not everyone believes all women are evil, like the monster-lady with sickle hands. She's just one person. One monster." I stop to pick up a rock the shape of an ear and put it in my pocket.

Rana taps her foot to hurry me up. I must be hungry, she says, and promises to buy me a sandwich and soda.

"I think she's real," I say. I believe it.

"Who?"

"The sickle woman."

"It's a costume, Layla. A skit."

"How do you explain the murders? Who killed all those men?"

"Don't you think the police would arrest her, if she were the one?"

The parade has gone on without us, and we've entered an oddly quiet stretch of road. A shady patch with birds whistling above. Across the street, I see two boys from our neighborhood eating vanilla ice cream out of cups. One of them, Layth, waves at me. I half-wave back. We used to be in class together, but now we're at the separate boys' and girls' schools. He's cute, and maybe that's why I've never talked to him much.

Today, I feel brave. I tell Rana we should get ice cream.

"Like them?" she says slyly, pointing at the boys. There's a long line at the ice-cream truck. She tells me to hang out with my "friends"—she says the word with a funny little emphasis— while I wait for her.

Layth and his friend Na'el wear similar outfits: loose T-shirts, track pants, slides with socks. Layth's clothes look natural, organic. Na'el looks like he's trying too hard. His T-shirt is pilled and his socks have a hole in the toe. I try not to judge him, but I'm drawn to Layth. They came to the parade by themselves, they tell me, and next year they're going to dress up.

"My sister is in the parade," Layth says.

Next year, Na'el will be an animal with an elephant's trunk and a tiger's teeth. Layth wants to be a dead man, he says, a victim.

"Spurting blood and writhing on the floor looks fun," he says.

"And everyone feels sorry for you," Na'el says.

"Right, but I'll be a corpse who fights back. With a machete. My dad has one that hangs on the wall. I'll rise up like a zombie, and kill the killer."

Susu's father was a real corpse; his death was not funny or entertaining. It blasted a missile-sized hole in Susu's life. She'd wished him alive many times, but a zombie father would not have been what she wanted. An undead father. Skin like paste, eyes like rotting hard-boiled eggs, limbs twisted.

"That would be really scary," I say. "Scarier even than the sickle woman."

They crumple up their cups and stick their spoons in their pockets. Spoons make great catapults, Na'el says.

We're awkwardly quiet, and then Layth says, "She's real."

"That's what I thought! That can't be a costume."

"No, that's not what I mean. The lady you saw today is wearing a costume. Best one in the parade. But there's a real sickle woman. She lives in the well. We've seen her."

"When?" I don't believe them, but I hope they're telling the truth. If she's real, I want to see her in the flesh.

"We'll show you," Na'el says.

I ask when they saw her. A few weeks ago, they say. At first, it sounds like they're making things up as they go along. Then they pick up steam and the story flows out of them. They wanted to see for themselves where those guys died. So, they went to the well after school. And they saw—

Layth shuts Na'el up. "It'll gross her out, if you tell her."

"What do you mean?" I say. Even though I suspect they're pulling my leg, I'm angry that he thinks I'm delicate, easily grossed out. I begin to second-guess. Maybe they really saw something. Lots of people have stories about that well, about what's hidden there. I've seen a video online of a religious man tossing holy water into the well to cleanse it. Clearly that hasn't worked.

"Let us show you." Na'el tosses his trash into the gutter and stands up. His toe wiggles around in its hole. I'm changing my mind about him. He's funny and he doesn't care what anyone thinks. But Layth is cuter and I want to touch his soft, dark, wavy hair.

I peek at my sister. The line has hardly moved. We can go to the well and back before she gets to the front and buys our ice creams. It's stupid to risk my sister panicking if I'm not where she left me. She'll call my parents on her phone and tell them I've gone missing. But I don't think it through. I'm thinking about cute boys and pretending I have the freedom to go wherever I want, without asking anyone's permission. The freedom I've longed for.

The well is nearby. Down an alley, around a bend, past a smelly dumpster that forces us to breathe through our mouths. Most of the route smells like garbage and motor oil. I stare up at the backs of buildings where people have hung their laundry across their balconies, like ragged curtains. I walk behind the boys, watching how they move, enjoying the curve of their bums, the wave of their hair against their necks, the shape of their shoulders, pretending I'm not checking them out, until Layth stops and waits for me to catch up.

He walks next to me and tells me a ghost story. Before the murders, when the town and neighborhood were young, a man and his wife fought. Right on the street, next to a tall palm tree. He grabbed her throat. She kneed him in the stomach. He stabbed her in the eye. She stabbed him in the groin. They died before their families or doctors could find them and save them. Their blood seeped into the ground and fed the roots of the tree, and their spirits got caught in there, in the thorny trunk and the whispery leaves.

"So, if you hear a groan in the night as you walk these streets, it's not the wind, it's those violent fucks," Layth says.

"Booooo," Na'el moans, trying to sound spooky and creepy, but instead sounding like a thirteen-year-old creep.

I stop to listen. They stop in their tracks, looking antsy for me to catch up. I do hear something. A woman's voice, muffled, like it's tucked in an envelope, or behind a curtain. Words indecipherable, as though in a language I don't speak.

"Well?" says Na'el.

"Nothing," I say. Did I really hear her? Or did I trick myself into hearing her?

We arrive at the well. I'm jumpy. My skin prickles. The barrier between my body and the dangerous world is more liminal than ever.

"The husband in the story, he probably beat the wife," I say.

"She probably beat him, too," Na'el says.

Na'el is leaning over the lip of the well, yelling into it. *Too, too, too,* it echoes. The well is ancient and crumbling, and it smells like people have treated it like a dumpster, tossing trash in there. In another town or neighborhood, people would take care of it, restore it to its original beauty as a place that provided water, the stuff of life. They might restore its function, so that people could pull water out of it. They would put a plaque on the side of it that told its history. They would exorcise it, say prayers over it to keep bad jinn away and leave offerings for good jinn: fragrant woods and dried petals. They'd plant a lemon tree to keep the well company, and children would read under the tree with their parents. People would come here for beauty and sustenance.

I regret coming here with these two boys, regret thinking they're cute. This place feels cursed, abandoned, ghostly.

"What do you think?" Layth says.

"It's creepy."

"That's where she was." Along our route, Layth has picked up a stick. He points it at Na'el and the well.

"Inside the well?"

The boys nod.

What kind of idiot do they think I am? "Then how did you see her? Is she ten feet tall—or does she float?"

"Listen, we can go back if you don't take this seriously."

"You promised to tell me what you saw."

"Tentacles."

"Talons."

"A whoosh of light."

"A clap of thunder."

"None of that makes sense. You said you saw the sickle woman." It's like they planned to play a trick on me, and forgot the trick they meant to play.

I start to walk back the way we came.

"Wait." Layth trembles, and starts to sob, rubbing his fists into his eyes.

"You're such a baby," Na'el says.

"It scared the shit out of you, too."

"What? What did you see?"

"Look!" Na'el says.

A figure rises out of the well. Its arms are spread to the sides, gauzy wings of black. I look closer: not wings, but hair. I see hands, fingers, and grasped in them, large, curved knives. She is wearing tall, hairy boots. At first, I don't recognize her.

I am looking at the woman from the parade. The Mother of Sickles.

"Where's the dead man?" I say.

"Come find him," she says, gesturing with her blades.

"How did you kill him?"

"Come closer, and I'll tell you."

I take a deep breath, inhale a whiff of garbage, and obey. I step closer, kicking an empty soda can out of my way, weaving around a rotting banana peel. How is she rising out of the well? I hold my breath and go closer. So close we could touch each other.

I peer over the edge.

She's standing on a ladder.

The veneer of fantasy disappears. I see what she really is: A human in a cobbled-together costume.

They've tricked me.

The woman steps out of the well, and I recognize her as Layth's older sister, Mayyadah.

She tucks her sickles, which look sharp but must be fake, into her belt and takes off her long wig. Her hair is short and spiky underneath. She laughs, and I remember what Rana has told me about her: she's got a mean streak as deep as a well. She played tricks on her schoolmates and on her teachers, even on the headmistress. Once, she left a sheep's heart in the teachers' lounge. She's a piece of work.

She wouldn't hurt me. Would she?

Rana is going to be so mad when she finds out where I've gone.

Mayyadah is taller than me, and stronger, and so are the boys, but they're closer to my size. I step up to Layth, smiling. His teeth are crooked in an endearing way. His irises shine like marbles. He smells like corn chips, cheap antiperspirant, and sweat. He's cute even when he's being mean. Maybe cuter, because he's being mean, because I want him to like me as much as I want him to stop being a dick.

They're not expecting what I do next. I put my hands around his thick, solid, beautiful neck. I don't mean to hurt him, or strangle him. I want to warn him. I want him to stop playing with me, like he's a cat and I'm a poor little mouse. I want to be the powerful one, the winner in whatever game we're playing.

He tries to move, and I squeeze. Mayyadah and Na'el have stopped laughing at me. I squeeze harder, and his knees bend a little. He's probably stronger than me, but I have him in my grip. I stare at Mayyadah and Na'el over my shoulder while my hands remain on Layth's soft neck. All of this is an instance; I like the feeling of power that's rushing through me, and I'm scared of it, too. Scared of becoming the kind of person who likes to hurt others. Who gets a thrill from it, an electricity through my core. I feel it now, tingling from my navel up to my neck and down to my crotch.

"Layla, what are you doing?"

It's Rana calling me, carrying two cups of ice cream. She gasps, and drops the cups. Mayyadah has picked up her sharp blades and is threatening me with them.

"Let go of my brother," she says.

I drop my hands and step away.

"Don't be stupid, Mayyadah," Rana says. "I'll call the cops on all of you, and they'll link you to the murders."

"That's a silly threat," Mayyadah says. "You wouldn't do that. They won't believe you."

"Leave her alone, you bullies."

My sister has accused the other three of bullying me, even though I was just strangling a boy. I'm overcome with love for her. Later she will tell me anyone could see threatening a girl with knives is worse than threatening a boy with bare hands. And Layth's sister is grown up; she should know better. Still, Rana's furious at me. I should never have touched Layth or put my hands round his neck, she will tell me.

Rana holds up her phone. "I'm dialing the emergency line."

Too fast for me to duck or hop away, Layth winds up his arm and punches me in the face, right on my cheekbone. He calls to his friend and sister, and they scramble and run.

I'm on my butt. My face is on fire.

Rana is laughing hilariously, bent over and cackling. "Oh Lord," she says. "Mama and Baba are going to kill me. What will we tell them?"

"Stop laughing. It hurts." I take her outstretched hand, and she lifts me up. We lean against the well, and Rana hugs me from the side.

"Have you had enough of the goddamn parade?" she says. "I've got to get you home and get you some ice."

"I'm OK," I say. "Our ice cream is ruined."

"You've got a shiner, Layla."

I'm not done with this place. I need to make peace with it.

"This is the well where those men died," I say. I wriggle out of her embrace and climb onto the lip of the well. I clamber onto the ladder inside.

"Oh my God, get out of there. Are you trying to get me killed? If you knock your head, Mama and Baba will kill me *and* lock me in the flat forever."

I climb down, breathing through my mouth again. The bottom is muddy and strewn with trash. Water drips loudly. Though I can't see proof of anyone dying here, I feel the presence of something undead, something from the other side. I hear the spirits of the dead men griping, asking why they deserved their fate, saying they didn't deserve it, saying they want another chance. They want to come back.

Now I breathe in, and I smell the dead, too. Do ghosts smell? It's that funky wet dust odor that follows rain.

If a monstress lived here, where did she come from?

When I climb out, Rana is holding the wig Layth's sister left behind.

"This is what convinced you she was a real monster?"

The wig looks sad and fake.

I say I saw something real during the parade. I had a glimpse of a being that must exist in some other plane. I believe that with all my heart. We can only mimic her. We can only pretend to be her. And when we do, we start to become her; we gain some of her horrific, monstrous power.

"You're delirious."

Rana's still fingering the dark wig. She takes a picture of me with her phone and shows it to me, so I can see what Layth did to my face. The sky has darkened, purple and plum streaks like the bruises blooming around my eye. It's nearly sunset. We should be getting home.

I sense something foreign in the air, brushing my skin. Spirits gathering.

"How do you feel?"

"I'm hungry," I say. "I don't care if you don't believe me. I feel the proof of the Monstress." I shouldn't be feeling joyful, high, when I've just gotten a black eye and otherworldly whisperings are coming out of the well. But I do.

"It does feel real," she says, shaking the wig. "Like real human hair."

"Try it."

She makes that monkey face of hers. "I need to get you home."

We'll be in so much trouble when we get home. We'll have to concoct a story about what happened. We have to prepare for my mother's glares of concern and my father's haste to call the cops on the perpetrators. We'll have to pretend a stranger hit me. In less than an hour, I'll be sitting in front of the television with a bag of frozen peas on my face, and Rana will be pretending to listen to an extended lecture on responsibility, getting all her freedom taken away for the next year—because of me.

We face each other, postponing the inevitable.

"You'll make a better monster than Mayyadah," I say.

"For sure, I will." Rana smooths her hair flat and swings the wig up and over her head. She pulls it over her skull and adjusts the edges. She stands with her fists on her waist, like a superhero, curls her lips, and bares her canines. She lifts her arms, holds her hands like sickles, and stands on her tiptoes as though she's on hooves.

It's funny and exaggerated, but also amazingly beautiful to see my sister as a dangerous, powerful, deadly creature. I close my eyes and see, etched in black, the image of my sister in a black wig, pretending to be something other than she is.

Rana the Monstress. Mother of Sickles.

I squeeze my eyes tighter and the Monstress's face changes. She's me.

CHAPTER 9

Mindless

A murder-suicide.

Then a child was murdered in the neighborhood.

Her grandfather found her. Her father had shot her. Then shot himself. The grandfather found the child's body embraced by the father's body, sitting close, as though the father were reading his child a bedtime story.

The shock of what the grandfather saw that day nearly killed him. He sank to his knees, heart twisting in his chest, head throbbing, fingers digging into the pads of his palms as though a prick of nail against skin could be enough to erase the awful tragedy of a bloodied child's body, a child dead at the hands of a parent.

So many things humans did to each other should never happen, the grandfather thought, but this more than anything.

This more than anything.

He prostrated himself on the floor and asked the god of whatever good remained in the world what they were thinking when they let this happen. Why did they let evil slide and slink its way into his son's heart? Why did they not stop him?

Why did they curse his family with a stain that might never wash away?

Most people in town didn't hear the true story. They heard a different truth, fabricated by the child's extended family, on both sides, who dubbed the two deaths a double-murder, the work of the serial killer. The woman who cut men's hearts out. She was jealous.

Of a child? Why?

Most families faced with a horrific tragedy that stole two of its members, one a child, and implicated a son of their blood—most families would not have reacted with obfuscation and deception. Most would embrace the truth. Most would hold each other and comfort each other and refuse to blame anyone but the murderer. Some would forgive and some would not, but all would grapple with the truth.

But *this family* was a family that couldn't see itself clearly, couldn't admit that a father among them had killed his own child. Couldn't mar their image of themselves as one body that stuck together. A murder-suicide confounded their collective self-image. They had no choice but to lie. They convinced the child's weeping mother that lying was for the best, that their brother, son, uncle, nephew, father of her children was gone and couldn't hurt her or her children. Why bother with the truth, when the truth was more complicated and horrifying than fiction?

The police gleefully aided their cover-up. The murderer had eradicated himself, went the officers' thinking. Why sully the family's name?

*   *   *

The lie spread fear, as lies often do. A monstress who had murdered one child might murder others. Keep your children close, neighbors said. Protect them from evil.

The dead child had lived in a part of town with uncracked sidewalks and unblinking streetlights, small villas tucked behind white walls with green-painted steel gates, fragrant gardenias that carpeted the sidewalk with their petals. She died in the next neighborhood over. Her mother reluctantly sent her once a week to spend time with her father in his two-room flat, just above her grandparents' flat. The building's entrance reeked of garbage the municipality had failed to pick up. The girl had never heard the word *Horrorville*, but her mother had.

No one comprehended how erratic the father had become. Except for his parents, people rarely saw him; no one suspected the depths to which he'd sunk. All his life, he'd excelled at pretending: to be good, to be kind, to be moral, to care, to love, to be happy, to be content, to be gentle. Pretending so he could get away with a little cheating, a bit of lying, a smattering of backstabbing, a smidge of fisticuffs on a weekend night, a bit of wife-slapping and bullying. You know the kind of man. We know he's pretending, but not how much he's hiding. We give him a pass, put up with his self-delusions. We believe he might one day see the light, rehabilitate, become a better person. We're not wrong. Redemption happens. Monstrosity is, we tell ourselves, an aberration of the human condition and we rarely see it coming, though it's as common as kindness.

On the fateful weekend visit, the father collected the child from her mother's place. She was eight, and he was her father, and he lived above his parents, and she missed him.

As she followed him down the steps of her building and out into the blinding sunlight, they squabbled, the way parents and little children do. She wanted to take her scooter and go to the park. He said no, she insisted, and he seemed angry, but he agreed. The scooter was parked in the lobby of the flat. She carried it to the sidewalk and balanced herself on it, ready to go.

It was a beautiful day, though a little hot. Prickly heat that made perspiration bloom on her nose. As she pushed along, she said she was thirsty. He had no water. She asked if they could stop at the corner store and buy a soda. He said no. She insisted, like she had with the scooter, in that way of persisting and getting what they want that some little girls are very good at. He didn't give in. He was in a hurry to do something. But what?

She was wearing her favorite yellow T-shirt with her name on it and her favorite purple sneakers. She sported a little bead bracelet her father had given her for her birthday. He didn't notice.

She said, "See, Baba, I'm wearing the bracelet."

He grunted. She kept scootering.

An adult observing them might have said he was agitated and she was feeling his agitation, trying to appease him. It's true, the little girl felt something was different about him, or if not different, something was *more* about him. She didn't know the word *agitated*, and she didn't really comprehend the words *violent* or *violence*. An adult observer might have hesitated to suggest her baba had violence in him; one wouldn't want to slander. Later, after the news came out, if the news had come out, they might have second-guessed themselves. Blamed themselves. Shamed themselves. They might have said, "Yes, he did seem as though he were capable of hurting her." They might have wished they'd asked if he was OK, or asked her if she were OK. Wasn't that what a bystander was supposed to do? Step in for the victim?

He rushed her along, and the rushing confused her. She said she was hungry and thirsty, and he snapped, which made her jump, and the jumpiness made him angry. A flush of red darkened his face like a cloud. He told her to shut up, and she wondered whether, if she waited a few minutes and said she was hungry again, maybe he'd understand she wasn't exaggerating, wasn't begging. Maybe he'd pull something out of his pocket, like dried fruit or candy, like he used to do. His pocket was weighed down and he kept stuffing his hand in, like he was making sure the thing he'd put in there hadn't fallen out.

She sobbed once and he raised his hand.

She swallowed her hunger.

She was right. He did have something weighing down his pocket. She didn't know it was a gun.

No one, least of all his child, had ever suspected he could do such a thing. Kill his own child. Why would he? Wasn't it enough to end his own life?

You could barely call the stuff in his mind thoughts, because his consciousness had become so jumbled and jangled, full of shit and pain and nothingness and despair and hate. Empty of love or empathy or kindness or compassion. His mind had gone AWOL, had gone missing. But if you could call the stuff in his head thoughts, then he was thinking he would take her with him. If he had to die, because this life was so much pain, he would take her with him. Spare her? Not exactly. Take her, as a symbolic gesture. Of what? Well, that was a stupid question.

He had seen the monster.

He had seen her in his dreams.

She told him what to do.

She told him to buy the gun.

She stood next to him when he shot his own daughter. She guided his hand.

Her warm touch on his fingers, leading him to the trigger, showing him how to do it.

He'd never shot a gun before. He'd never killed before.

If he had survived his own bullet to the head, he would have begged forgiveness, would have explained that without the Monstress, without her black hair and her thick voice, he couldn't have killed his child.

He tried to tell the Monstress no. No, I won't do it.

Her hands transformed into blades and she threatened him. She would slice him to pieces.

He wanted to shoot himself; she would not let him aim the gun at his own head until he'd shot his daughter.

"If you don't take her with you, she'll spend the rest of her life in pain because you're gone. She'll never understand why you killed yourself and robbed her of your presence."

The monstrous words made sense. He could save his daughter from a life of grief and emptiness.

They'd gone to the playground, stood at its outskirts. The sun scorching his neck, his child's hand warm and clammy in his.

The scooter fallen aside. As though blinkered, he saw the cone of sidewalk ahead of him, not the bright world, the achingly deep sky, the serenely dappled trees.

Children's voices mingling with the voices of birds. Mothers laughing, and one yelling at her child to get down from the monkey bars before he broke his neck. The child stood with his feet on two bars and said, "See, Mama." He walked from one end of the structure to the other, and jumped off and landed with one hand in front and one behind, like a superhero.

She swept him up, saying, "Never do that, you're giving me a heart attack."

The daughter said, "Baba, can I climb up there, too?"

People saw them, a father and child who came to the playground and didn't play. They heard her question, but not his response.

When the child didn't come home in the evening, the mother called the father, then the father's father. The grandfather asked around. His son hadn't responded to a knock on the door. A neighbor had happened to be at the playground, had retrieved the fallen scooter, wanting to return it. No one had answered the door. The grandfather sighed in unjustified relief. She'd been seen alive. She was with her father. They hadn't responded to knocking. Had they fallen asleep? Forgotten the time? He hadn't heard them come home. He knocked on his son's door over and over, tried the key. It was barricaded from inside. He asked the tenant in the flat next door to let him climb over the balcony, help him smash through the sliding glass door to the living room.

The room was dark, the sun setting bloodily outside the

broken glass door. His son's cat, Beauty, mewed from the next room, as though calling for help.

The two men froze in front of a blood-red message spray-painted on a wall.

"No one is safe."

The words entered the grandfather through his eyes, settled in the back of his throat, stuck in his craw.

Mew, mew, mew. Why didn't the cat come to them? What did she need them to witness?

Without a doubt, the sight in the next room would be awful, but love and fear and hope and desperation compelled the grandfather to move toward it. He had to open the door and see.

The scene was a horror. Grandfather and neighbor crumpled to their knees, felled by the blood, the death, the gun, and the desperate new sound emanating from the cat: a ferocious lapping.

Beauty the cat licked the little girl's limp fingers as though a life depended on it, as though the girl's hand were a kitten just delivered from the womb, and a creature's love could wake a girl from the dead.

CHAPTER 10

The Balancers

Refuge on the rooftops.
Mayyadah reenters the scene. An escape.

When I am fifteen, the neighborhood becomes a prison.

At the start of the school year, the town government closes the playground, cordoning its perimeters with yellow tape. Police officers tape up the slides and swings too. Soon, yellow strips hang limp and sad from the trees at the corners of the park and from the quiet, sad play structures—evidence that people have been trespassing. Candy wrappers, empty cigarette packs, and spent vape canisters appear. One time, a twisted condom. To stop trespassing, the mayor signs an order and the town builds a fence around the park. My brothers and I peek through the slats at the abandoned monkey bars and slides. Empty swings sway gently in the breeze.

Soon enough, someone's mother notices a lone single man loitering on street corners during times when kids are going to and from school. I never see him. I hear later from my friends that this man, this bogeyman, wore baggy clothing and smelled like booze or weed or a combination of both. The gossip machine cannot pin him down. He is young, he is old, he is someone's uncle or grandpa or a complete stranger or someone from the next neighborhood over or the former mayor who has recently been down and out or a migrant who crossed over at the border town four hours away or a panhandler or a vagrant or a thief. Whoever he is, the man is apprehended and hauled to jail, or so the whispers go. Parents should feel we are safe now, but then someone's grown-up older brother, barely into his twenties, spots a gaggle of older teens smoking and vaping after school. He argues he has seen a street gang or the start of one or the threat of one. Something must be done. To protect The Children, the neighborhood council outlaws balls and jumping, sidewalk chalk and hula-hoops. They might as well outlaw Children's Laughter. Emails and texts using phrases like "community safety," "neighborhood resilience," "operational safety plans," "concerning incident," "teachable moment," and "collectively reinforce" land in parents' inboxes. My mother reads hers out loud to my brothers so they'll understand what's going on. Fadi, eleven years old, looks like he's going to jump out of his skin. After my mother leaves the room, he and I play video games. I ask what's worrying him. He says he doesn't want to be stolen by a creature from the other world. What are you talking about, I say. His friends have told him all about fanged jinn and real bogeymen—they swear!—who swallow you into their bodies like a black hole. I wonder if these ridiculous fears keep him and his friends from worrying about evil humans—pedophiles, kidnappers, actual murderers. I can't tell if he believes me when I say monsters aren't real. He vengefully bangs his controller with his thumbs, as though his warrior protagonist is fighting real-world bad guys, keeping my brother and his friends safe.

What I believe is this: The adults cannot keep us safe. They pretend they can protect us so they won't have to face the truth. Children die, get hurt, are left behind, get lost every day. We see the fear in our parents' eyes when they walk in the door and gaze at us scrolling through news sites or watching TV. We see from the corner of our eyes. I speak for myself and other children. I can't be the only one who senses my parents' horror at what might happen to me in the world, who smells the salt of their fear. We're not stupid. The world is full of danger. And there are kids my age who love to talk about danger, to scare each other. The day after that little girl died, my classmates talked about nothing else, unless the teachers were in earshot. Over the months, we tell each other the story, what we know of it, again and again, embellish with details we've picked up by eavesdropping on adult phone conversations and things they say in our presence when they think we aren't listening. Even little children talk about the horrible killing of a girl their age. An innocent victim, not a flawed man who may or may not have deserved his violent end. Some kids say the serial killer got her, and the serial killer—the monster—could get us, too. They say the flat where the bodies were found smelled like rosewater, like Chanel No. 5, like lavender-oil hair tonic, like a woman.

A few brave children who're not afraid to say terrible truths out loud tell us the killer might have been her father. The father who died next to her—he killed himself too, they say.

Others argue. It couldn't have been her father. He loved her. Parents don't kill their children.

Do they?

*   *   *

Mid-year, the mayor sends police officers in neon yellow vests to prowl the streets and make sure no one violates the new regulations. I'm in charge one afternoon when my brothers and I sit on our balcony and watch the police chatting with each other at the borders of their assigned blocks. Bassam says he's glad they're there; he wants to be a policeman when he grows up. That's cool, I say, but I don't feel safer. I feel penned in by the irrational fears of others. I resent how the mayor and the council keep using gobbledygook to explain their rules, how their actions don't have to make sense or be consistent with what they say matters: neighborhood safety. I believe my skepticism is factual and true, and the council reinforces my conviction when it takes its next drastic action: for absolutely no good reason, they shutter all the after-school clubs and sports. Students are to go straight home, where their families will keep them safe, the mayor says. The council is considering raising the driving age to eighteen.

No more soccer or karate for my brothers. No more art club or book club for me.

I overhear my parents one evening after work as they come into the flat. They're talking about the council's decision. They sound resigned, and also like they don't know what to think. I'm in my room doing homework, door ajar. My brothers are playing video games in their rooms with their headphones on. My mother's voice is louder than it should be. She mentions a woman at work who called the council tyrants. A teacher at Fadi's school who whispered to her about child abuse and family violence; not all homes are as safe as they seem. My father says the council took its action on the advice of heads of school. That's good enough for him. For most kids, home is safer.

"And most parents are too busy to do more than follow the new rules," Mama says. "Who has time to fight bureaucracy?"

That evening, while I'm helping my parents cook dinner, my mother says I must watch my brothers like a hawk, no, like a mama bear. Which is ridiculous, because at thirteen, Bassam is taller than me now. Whenever she talks about safety, Mama goes on and on, and every opening for me to talk back or question is unexpected and fleeting. So, I stop talking back or questioning, even when her advice makes no sense. Mama says not to talk to *anyone*, not even the children we've known for years, not even the neighbors. *Don't go to the store for candy and soda. Come home straight away. Don't linger on the corner. Don't complain. This is for your good, for your brothers' good.*

My brothers don't hear the lecture. Mama says all they need to know is I'm in charge because I'm older. In our overheated and muggy kitchen, my father fries onions, pungent and caramelizing. My eyes sting. I'm soaking rice, rinsing off the milky starch.

Baba shakes the pan with one hand. "Maybe we should move somewhere the children don't have to be so protected."

"Where? The city?" Mama asks, as though he's said the stupidest thing possible.

She chops vegetables for salad, slices a lemon in half and squeezes it into the bowl, using her fingers to hold back the seeds. She's mechanical, efficient. Over the past few months, or year, and especially since the little girl's murder—which we never, ever talk about—Mama's temper has shortened, like a fuse burning down to its end. She reminds me of a petty toddler. She used to be calm. She hugged us when we came home from school. Now she barely touches us, as though even grazing our skin with hers would be too painful. As though we are fragile bone porcelain that must be kept from cracking and hardly ever used, packed away in a cupboard in quilted storage containers.

Baba nods and blinks as though he's agreeing with Mama—he's smart to make her think so—then he slyly disagrees, using words that sound like concurrence, like he's simply building on her thoughts.

"Or the country," he says, spreading dark brown, crispy onions on a paper-towel-lined plate. "Live on a farm."

"Uncle's farm," I say nonchalantly.

"This is our home," Mama says. "We'll make the best of it."

She can say that. She's a grown-up. For us children and teenagers, there's no *best of it* when adults yank our freedom away. When there are rumors of a parent murdering his child. Who could blame us if we look at our parents askance if they raise their voices, if they tell us to behave, if they raise a finger? Where can we be safe, if we are not safe at home?

I shove that awful, unthinkable thought away. With all my might, I grab on to the idea of the serial killer, a killer outside the home. A stranger.

I have my fears, my existential dread, but I don't understand the deep communal fear my parents swim in—I don't think any of my friends get it, either. The whirlpools of dread parents are caught in. As though a tentacled ocean creature has them by the ankles, threatens to pull them down, down, into a place where even existing is dangerous, where the pressure of the depths could explode their lungs. The dead child's mother lives in that undersea deep, and no one wants to float there with her. Every other parent worries another child—their child, their sister's child, their best friend's child—might die. Not just die—be murdered. The definition of senselessness.

We children don't know that when we become parents, if we become parents, the dread will sink into our bones; the dread will threaten to sink us.

At night in bed, with the shadows mingling with passing cars' headlights; walking my brothers home; eating meals with my family; in the shower; in class—with each heartbeat, each breath, I think about the Monstress, the picture I've created in my mind of a single killer, responsible for every murder in our neighborhood. She refuses to leave my mind. She pulses through my veins. She is the donkey chimera from the Monster Parade—a mix of woman, beast, and weapon—except she's not a woman in costume, she's a real creature, and in my fantasies, she lives on the outskirts of the neighborhood, in a tin shack with walls that lean inward, and a small flower garden with a little chain-link fence. She smells like clover and carrots, sugar and cardamom, dung and sunshine. I picture her tenderly, peacefully tending her garden. Her hands are hands, not blades. Calmly, she waters the soil like she's adding moisture to bread dough. She gently pets leaves and petals like they're the soft ears of bunnies. Her tail shoos flies, nudges bees toward flowers' pollen-laden stamens. What happened to her? What made her kill? I can't face her past, can't fabricate one for her. I avoid thinking about what she may have experienced. I only want to imagine an idyllic present. I don't make up reasons or excuses for why she is the way she is. In my head, she's a part of the garden, an organic, growing thing. Her eyelashes are antennae, turned toward the world.

THE NIGHT IS NOT FOR YOU

I imagine her to forget the questions that haunt me: *What if we die? What if I die? What is death, anyway? What is life?*

The week after the after-school activities close, my friend and neighbor Leena knocks on my apartment door and tells me a bunch of older kids who live in the building are going up to the roof. I ask if I can bring my brothers with me, and she says yes. When I pop my head in their rooms, they tell me they'd rather play video games.

I'm not supposed to leave them alone, I tell Leena. She begs me to come.

I'm afraid that if I don't go now, she'll never ask me to hang out with her again.

"I'll be back soon," I tell my brothers. My parents won't be home for a few hours.

The stairwell leading up to the roof is clammy and humid. Greenish, lit by fluorescent bulbs. Geckos cling to the walls, upside down, flicking their tails and tasting the air with their tongues.

"It's so creepy," Leena says. "Clearly no one ever cleans up here."

It's a warm spring afternoon, with a pleasant breeze kissing the rooftop. Clouds speckle the sun-bright sky. A couple of pigeon cotes stand in one corner. A pair of sisters, Aya and Maya, sit on the tile floor, scrolling on their phones and taking selfies. Three boys are balancing on skateboards and playing music from a wireless speaker. Our neighbor Sami, who I have a faint crush on, vapes and looks sheepish. He has wire-rim glasses and a gap in his teeth, a waterfall of hair that reaches his shoulders. I don't know the other boys' names. Usually, I keep to myself.

"Look," Leena says. Standing on tiptoes and peering across the wall, we see other kids on the building next to ours.

"I bet I could jump over there," Sami says.

"No way," I say.

Leena wants to do it. "I'm already bored out of my mind," she says.

"We haven't even been up here five minutes."

Sami and Leena argue about how best to get to the other side. They climb up onto the wall, sit with their butts drooping, their feet hanging above the street. We're five stories up. Aren't they scared of falling?

Just over there is the other rooftop. A group of children stares at us from across their wall.

Aya looks up from her phone and says, "If anyone sees you, we'll all get in trouble, you asses."

Maya holds up her phone to take a selfie. "And we won't be able to come up to the roof anymore," she says. She smiles, snaps the picture, and goes back to scrolling.

"Help me up." Leena turns and reaches for my hand. I steady her as she gets to her feet, balanced on the wall.

If I let go of her, she might fall, and her death will be my fault.

"I'm going to jump," she says.

Aya snorts. "You're going to fall."

"I'm not afraid of falling."

"You should be."

Aya is right, but as scared as I am for Leena, I want her to land on the other rooftop, because now that it looks possible to get from here to there, I want to do it. I want to escape where I am. I'm afraid of falling, but I'm even more afraid of staying in one place.

"Don't jump," Sami says. Across his shoulder he's holding a rickety aluminum ladder he found on the other side of the roof. He swings the ladder over the wall, next to where Leena is balancing, and it clangs onto the wall of the next roof. Leena places her feet just in front of the first rung. She points the toes of one foot and carefully places them on the rung, feeling how solid it is. She flattens her foot, adjusts. The left foot stays flat on the wall. She's going to do it! Leena holds her hands out from her sides to balance, daintily places a foot on the next rung and tests its steadiness. Sami holds the end of the ladder to keep it from budging.

I hold my breath. Leena adjusts her front foot and lifts up the rear foot. As gracefully as a gymnast, she swings it forward onto the next rung. She shifts her weight, standing one foot in front of the other, like a figure in Egyptian art. Maya claps. Leena loses the tiniest bit of balance, rights herself. Aya says, "Shut up, you'll make her fall." Sami raises his hand for silence. Leena stands still as a statue.

Sami says, "Stop looking down. Choose a spot on the other side to focus on." Leena lifts her head, straightens her neck, and dips her shoulder blades down. Her arms are cushioned on the air like wings, her knees softly bent, her torso pillar-straight. She lifts and swings her back leg, lifts and swings, toes pointed like a ballerina. If I imagine the ladder isn't beneath her, it's like she's float-walking from one roof to the other. She looks free. And brave. Unafraid of gravity, parents, a stray gust of wind, mean girls and boys. I'm angled to the side of her, and I see her face. It's serious, lips pursed, forehead bunched like Kleenex—and then her forehead and cheeks and eyes relax. She has a ghost of a smile, and her chin tilts slightly upward.

She's unworried. Enjoying herself. Rung by rung, she makes her way to the other side. The length she walks is short, but the journey is fraught. It sucks my breath away over seconds that pass as slowly as an hour.

Leena hops down and her feet thud forcefully on the ground. The others behind me erupt in applause. My breastbone twinges with jealousy because the next performances—Sami's, mine— will not seem as groundbreaking. We have been able to study Leena's technique, which will seem like an advantage, like cheating.

Sami pinches the back of my hand, like children do playing a silly game. My skin tugs minutely away from my bones. An exquisite feeling of pain.

"You next, beautiful," he says, holding his hand toward me, palm up, like a gentleman.

I want to walk across, and at the same time I don't. What I want is to *be* on the other side. My stomach clenches. It wants to punch something. But I don't want to miss the chance to touch Sami's long fingers and almond-shaped fingernails.

I take Sami's smooth, dry hand. He winks at me. Leena's calling me.

"You go first," I say.

He squeezes my hand and pulls me up. One of the skateboard boys holds the end of the ladder.

There's a sweet breeze, and the air up here smells like food cooking, onions and garlic, then a whiff of warm dryer lint, wafting from below us, as comforting as baking bread. The scents of home. I shield my eyes from the sun with my hand.

Leena's standing on the other side, arms folded on the top of the wall, next to the ladder, the bridge from one world to another. She's egging us on. "Come on, do it," she says. "Do it, do it."

"Hold the thing down on your side," Sami says.

"No one held it for me," she says.

Sami flips two fingers at her, then takes the first rung. He wobbles a bit, nearly trips on the last two rungs, throws himself over the wall on the other rooftop. What if he had fallen, splat? Another dead body in our neighborhood.

I wait till he's stood up and brushed himself off, then take my first step. I pretend I didn't witness his near tumble from the bridge. I tell myself I can balance, I can make it across. The stink of garbage rises up from the alley. I'm alone up here.

"Don't look down," says Leena. "Keep your eyes ahead of you."

My eyes immediately fall to the ground, and beneath me in the alley, I see a cat. She howls. I freeze. I want to turn around. Panic takes over my brain, looks out through my eyes. It sees danger everywhere. It tells me, *You will not do this.* It says, *What are you doing? Why are you standing here, with the rungs of a ladder pressing into your feet and the hard, garbage-strewn ground meters below you?*

Leena recognizes the terror and confusion in my face. "Don't turn around. Keep coming or you'll fall."

"I need to go back," I say. I'm not exaggerating. Going back *is* a need, something my body is convinced it has to do. I want someone to take care of me and tell me it's OK to give up. If Lajwa were here, she would have stopped me from being so risky. Rana would tell me I'm as stupid and brave as they come.

I turn slightly, and the ladder shudders as though it's alive.

"Layla, if you fall, they'll put us all in jail for murdering you," Sami says.

"If you go back, I *will* murder you," Leena says. "Come here!"
I tell myself, *Layla, don't be stupid. Keep going.*

For a long moment, the rooftop is quiet except for a quiet murmur from the pigeon cote. *Coo, coo.* The pigeons belong to a grandmother on the top floor whose name I can never remember. I hear a scream in the sky, maybe a hawk.

Go, I tell myself. This panic is a wave; it will leave me. Or I can leave it behind me, on this ladder. *How did I get here, anyway? Why did I listen to Leena?* I start with my feet, my foundation. Where my feet are in contact with the rung, I send all the power of my body, then I let it bounce back, up through my body. I put my arms out like Leena did. I start slowly, slowly, and when I'm at the final few rungs, I rush.

I'm over the ladder and on the other side. The others clap and yell.

I'm a different person here. A more mature person. I raise my arms in the air, as though I just won a race. Leena hugs me, and Sami pats my shoulder. I have never felt so happy.

Then I fall to the earth. I look around me, and as quickly as I triumphed, I acknowledge there's nothing to do here I couldn't do on my own roof. What's the point? This roof is just like our roof, black-and-white mottled tile and the apple smell of vapes and some children huddled around an older child's phone, watching him play video games.

I've leapt to somewhere exactly the same as where I was before. I've left one jail for another.

I catch Sami looking at me, head cocked like a pigeon's and eyes squinty with questioning, like he's asking, "Whatcha thinking?"

The tiny crush I've had on him blooms. Inside me, a moon

glows. I would like to touch his hair, gaze at the space between his shoulder blades forever.

"That was fun," he says. He touches the back of my hand, pinches the skin again. I swallow a yowl of pleasure. I pinch· him back.

Leena shakes her head and sticks a lit cigarette in my mouth. I suck, cough, suck again and feel the heady hit of tobacco. It tastes terrible. It tastes like courage.

We sit cross-legged on the floor and smoke, passing between us Leena's cigarette, the only one we have.

Over the next week, Sami and his friend Mish'al build a network of ladder-bridges connecting four or five roofs, and we make our way around the circuit. Sami gives our quartet a name: The Balancers.

I demurely extinguish my smile when Sami looks at me, keep quiet in his presence, avoid taking cigarettes or vapes directly from him. I don't want anyone to know that he lives in my mind, holding my hand, running away to the city with me. Leena is not so shy with the boy she likes. She sits next to Mish'al with her thigh touching his, removes cigarettes from his mouth and sucks on them, touches his hair.

We don't find much freedom going from roof to roof. Each rooftop looks the same, and when I stand at a wall and look down to the street, every block of the neighborhood looks the same. Gum-splotched sidewalks, spindly trees, bobbing pigeons foraging for fallen French fries. I nearly lose my crush on Sami when I learn that Layth, who lives three buildings down from us, is his best friend. How did I miss that fact? I've lived in this tiny neighborhood, on this same block, my whole life. How could Sami be friends with such a terrible person?

I stay away from Layth as much as I can, not just because of how he treated me at the well two years ago, but also because of how I've seen him treat other girls. He's handsy. Before the parks and clubs closed, I saw him on the walk to and from school. He'd put his arm around girls, like they were his possessions. He'd drape his forearm over their shoulders, hook his elbow around the backs of their necks. One girl at a time, a different girl every week. Like he was marking his property. The looks on the girls' faces: confused, or proud, or disgusted. Some girls pushed him away. He called them sluts. Others let him possess them till he discarded them, and he called them bitchy if they complained.

The good guys, the nice guys, wanted to know why girls let this sleazy guy touch them, let him lead them around like a barn animal or, well, a dog.

Now, I want to know why Sami hangs around with him, but because I like Sami, I don't ask.

There's a string of hot days, and I stay inside with my brothers, and then one day near the end of the school year, Leena begs me to come up to the roof again. It's so hot, and the sky is blue as an ocean on one side, roiling with clouds on the other. The air is clammy. And there's Layth on my roof, sucking on an ice pop. He offers one to me. I shake my head no and then wish I'd taken it. It's going to melt in its plastic casing now. Sami puts his hand on my arm, and his fingers are cool and soothing. We find a shady spot and Mish'al deals a game of cards. Sami goes off to smoke; he doesn't want to play.

Layth sits next to me. I don't want him to touch me. I want him to drop dead. The closer he gets to me, the more my fingers ache with violent intent. I squeeze them into my palm. I wrap my arms around myself. I'm afraid I will put my hands around his neck again.

"I'm bored," I say. "Can't we do something else?"

We're a few weeks away from summer vacation. What will happen when school is out? Will the parents keep up this incarceration? The thought intensifies my boredom.

Layth says, "Let's go downstairs to my flat. It's cool down there."

"So is mine. I could just go home."

Sami has wandered back. "But you want to hang out with us, right?" he says.

I say I have homework to do, though I do want to hang out with Sami, and I'm sure they can tell I'm lying. What teen would rather do homework?

"We just can't smoke down there," Layth says.

"I'm tired of smoking," Leena says. "It's boring."

Layth says there are sodas in his refrigerator, and that seems to decide it.

I wonder if we'll see Mayyadah. Although she tricked me, tried to frighten me, threatened me with her blades, I think often about Layth's sister, about her power and her ability to transform herself into another being. Rana wanted to throw away her wig, but I convinced my sister to keep it. It's in the back of Rana's closet, and when no one's around, I take it out, brush it, smooth it with my hands. I put it on and look in the mirror. I don't transform the way Layth's sister and Rana did. Why? Is it because I'm less dangerous than they are, because I lack some spark they both have? Because I'm too young, because I don't believe enough that the Monstress could be me?

Because I'm looking at myself? Between my fingers, the hair of the wig feels fake, inhuman. I don't know where Layth's sister got the wig, how much she spent on it, why it looked so real and alive when she wore it. I would like Layth to introduce me to her. I would like to learn more about her costume, about the rage she channeled at the Monster Parade, about where she got the knives that looked like they were growing out of her hands, how she made her legs look like donkey legs, how she walked so gracefully on her fake hooves. A donkey isn't graceful, but she was.

I thought Leena was going to come, but now she says she and Mish'al have to talk about something.

"It's going to rain," I say. Leena promises to come in a few minutes.

I follow the boys to Layth's roof. No children are playing here. The three of us go down the stairwell. Someone's cooking dinner—lamb stew, something tomatoey, something with onions and garlic. The smells remind me of my parents.

Layth's flat smells clean and lemony. The windowless entry hall is dark. Faint, old-timey music, the kind of song my parents listen to, emanates from a back room. Layth grabs cold sodas from the refrigerator and tosses them to us. I hold mine against my forehead. Layth leads Sami and me down the corridor between the front room and the bedrooms. He wants to show me his sister's room.

"That doesn't seem right," Sami says.

Layth says, "Layla knows why." As though he knows I'm obsessed with his sister.

Layth opens the door. The room is bathed in pink light coming through the fuchsia drapes. There are signs of her:

photos, blades hanging on the wall, a dark curtain that reminds me of her hair. I smell her, floral with a hint of funk. The walls are a deep pink, almost red, like they're bathed in blood, darkening the already-dark furniture. The dresser is littered with perfume bottles.

Layth says his sister is going to move out soon and go to the city. He opens her wardrobe. Inside is her costume. The robes are draped over a dressmaker's dummy, the donkey's legs stand beneath. The wardrobe's shadows inhabit the costume.

"She lost her wig." He glares at me.

"Too bad. Is she getting a new one?"

"She hasn't gone the past two years, and now they've canceled it indefinitely."

A voice behind us says, "Caught you! Trespassers!"

Mayyadah stands in the doorway, not much taller than I am, hair grown to her shoulders and dripping. She pulls her bathrobe tight. For the first time, I notice the constellations of freckles on her cheeks.

"Where did these children come from?" she asks her brother.

Sami averts his eyes at first, but soon they're drawn up to her as if pulled by a puppeteer's strings.

The boys tell her about the ladder-bridges. She promises not to rat on us. I can tell Sami's a bit in love with her, which makes me want to steal something from her. I wonder if she remembers me from the well. Has she forgotten that I nearly strangled her brother? Does she suspect my sister and I took her wig? I look at her long fingers, the trimmed nails. She doesn't wear nail polish or acrylics. Her fingers look utilitarian, not dangerous. Fresh from the shower, she wears no make-up.

There's a flash in her eyes and her smile that reminds me of her character, a ruthlessness in every word she says. Like her sentences could cut.

"I'm sure Layth was the mastermind," she says.

Layth doesn't tell her otherwise. I want to say her brother's not as smart as Sami, but I keep quiet because I don't want her to see the good qualities I see in him. I don't want her to like him.

I say, "We should probably go now."

"No problem," she says.

She sits on her bed and her robe sags at the front, revealing one half of one boob. Her wet hair leaves a dark mark on her shoulders. The thought of sitting half naked like that in front of boys makes my ears buzz.

Sami asks Mayyadah all sort of questions. She tells us she finished college, but there are no jobs around here except in the factory, at corner stores, or making knickknacks at home and selling them online. She prefers none of those options, though maybe she'll take a job at the factory if she has to. To save money. She's going to move to the city.

"We heard." I tell her Susu lives there.

"You talked about me," she says flatly. "That's another problem with town. People talk about you. They want you to follow their ridiculous rules. There are no rules in the city. You could disappear into the crowd. That's probably what your friend Susu did. How often do you hear from her?"

The question stabs me in the gut, though I'm pleased she knows enough about me to know I was friends with Susu.

"Never," I say. And now I can't stop thinking about how Susu and I are never in touch and she will never be my best friend again. Maybe we'll never see each other again. The thought hadn't occurred to me before.

"I'm going to be a perfume maker," I say, my eyes on her bottle collection on the dresser. I've never voiced my aspiration out loud till now.

"I love perfume. I collect it."

Layth yawns loudly. His sister reties the sash on her bathrobe and walks to her dresser, winking at Sami, who looks stricken with fear now that she's paid attention to him. She picks up a beautiful bottle, square and solid, filled with gold liquid. She lets me hold the bottle. It's like holding gold in my palm. Expensive and precious. What if I drop it, ruin it, spill it? She has other bottles, different colors of gold or pink or copper or pale yellow. I beg her to open them, to let me smell them. The glass keeps the scent inside, like bottling a jinn. I imagine the perfume as something alive, confined and wishing to be free.

When she opens the first bottle, I catch a strong whiff. I cough a little, and she asks if I have asthma.

"No," I say. I don't want her to think I'm weak or ill.

She lets me tap a few droplets on my wrist and tells me to breathe in deep. I do, and the fragrance is rich and velvety in my nostrils. She explains how the scent will mingle with the scent of my skin and change character over time, each level of the perfume taking a turn on the stage of my nose. She puts a drop on her own wrist and lets me bring my nose to her skin. Then back to my skin. The perfume smells slightly different in each place, and less antagonistic than it did straight from the bottle. She puts a little at the back of her ear. I ask if it smells different there.

"I don't know," she says. "I can't smell behind my own ear."

She lifts her hair and I try not to get too close, try not to tickle her, but I want to smell, to see if the scent really morphs itself at different locations on her body.

On her wrist, the scent is salty and pungent. Behind her ear, it's mixed with her shampoo, conditioner and the oily smell of her scalp.

"Which perfume do you want to try now?" she says.

The boys are sitting on the bed, bouncing on their bums with their feet on the floor. We ignore them, and I choose an emerald-green bottle. The drop of scented oil comes out clear. I breathe. Its deep rosiness pierces me.

"What do you wear when you're the Monstress?"

"That's a secret," she says. "My most intoxicating scent."

"Are those the blades from your costume?" I ask, pointing at the wall.

"Maybe."

"Have you ever cut a man?"

There's a crack of thunder. The boys and I startle; Mayyadah doesn't flinch. Against the sound of deep rumbling, she starts to tell stories she's heard, about men who beat their wives and men who impregnate their girlfriends then disown the babies, men who drink too much, men who touch women in lifts and alleys, men who harass women on the factory floor. She never names names.

Fifteen minutes later, when she stops, the boys have left the room. Rain is crashing down. We're stuck here until it stops. Going back over the ladder-bridges would be too dangerous. Mayyadah says she's going to change, and I wander into the living room. While I have been in Mayyadah's room, Leena has made good on her promise. She and Mish'al are in the living room with Sami and Layth, drinking sodas. After a few minutes, Mayyadah joins us, dressed all in black and smelling strongly of rose essence. Her parents will be home soon. She says we need to leave or we'll all be caught. She's an adult, technically; she could talk her way out of it. Still, she insists we have to go.

"It's raining," I say.

"You can hide on the roof, then go home when it stops."

"It'll be slippery."

Leena tells me to stop being a wuss. She grabs my wrist, pulls me out of my inertia, and we leave the flat and take the stairs two at a time. We open the door to the roof and watch the rain fall. It whips into us. I choke on the smell of wet dust.

The boys follow us, including Layth, who could stay home but seems to want to risk his neck for no reason. Ahead are obstacles: the rain making everything slick, the walls around the rooftop, the distance between buildings, the fact of our humanness—that we aren't birds or other flying creatures.

We aren't half-human, half-bat.

I don't expect what's next, even though I've seen how Layth treats girls, like soulless pieces of meat. Fingers encroach on my body, and Layth and Sami are touching my boobs and my butt, pulling my hair. Mish'al has pushed Leena against the wall.

"Get off me, you ass," Leena says. She stomps on Mish'al's foot and kicks him in the groin. "Go to hell! What's gotten into you?"

"Come on," Mish'al says. "It's going to rain for a while."

Leena's courage inspires me. I elbow Layth and punch him in the eye. I've wanted to feel the crack of his bones since he punched me the day of the masquerade.

The boys could grab me now, hold me down and keep me from running. I yell, "Leena!" and rush out the door, into the rain. She's right behind me. I'm immediately drenched, heading for the closest ladder.

Maybe, with good boys, we wouldn't be in this situation. They wouldn't have led us astray.

I tell Leena we have to scream. I don't care if anyone blames me for being here. At least they'll save me, get me away from these boys.

"Get us down from here!" Leena yells.

No one is out in the rain.

The ladder is gone.

The boys have come up behind us, and Layth is holding a gun while the other two look at him in horror and surprise. He's not aiming the gun at us, he's just holding it, like it's a banana or a screwdriver, something harmless.

"Where the hell did you get that?" I say. "Put it away."

He stuffs the wet gun in his pants. "I carry it for protection. If she ever came after me, I'd shoot her," he says.

Leena is intent on escaping. She's leaning precariously over the waist-high wall that encloses the roof and supposedly keeps us from falling. She turns to him, one arm looped over the top of the wall, her clothes sopping wet, her body partially extended over air. Like she's having a little chat in the midst of taking flight.

"Who do you mean?" she says.

"I mean the murder lady. The one who kills only men."

"And a little girl." It makes me livid that people forget her.

He waves a hand like, *Of course. Yeah, yeah.* Like I should realize that *not mentioning* someone is not the same as *forgetting them.* He's wrong. There's no difference between omission and oblivion. If you don't name her—her name was Sara—she never existed.

"Almost all the people she's killed were men."

Does he think we'll forget he and his friends just had their hands all over us?

"Why the hell are we talking about the murderer lady?" Leena's standing on the wall now, at the corner, where there's room for a running start. She's making me nervous, bouncing at the knees, as though she's coiled and ready to jump. With or without me.

When she runs and jumps, I panic. She's left me alone with three monstrous boys. She's done something stupid that might kill her.

Now, she's landed safely on the next roof. She calls me to follow her.

I can't float or fly. I'm not Leena.

Layth, Mish'al, and Sami swagger toward me, a wall of boyness, a forcefield that pushes toward me. I turn, scramble up the wall and go for it. I hurtle toward the wall of the neighboring rooftop. I am a meteor hurtling through space. I am not a girl but an object, a stone flung by a giant from a giant slingshot, or maybe a beast that is half-girl and half-bird, my talons grasping for something to alight on. Instead of flying, I hit the wet ground with my stomach, and all the air slams out of me. Leena grabs me, lifts me up to make sure I'm OK. I'm barely OK. The rain is letting up, and the sky's eyeshadow is bleeding purple and pink with the coming of evening. The air is warm, tinted with coolness. Night is coming soon.

We run. We're going to have to jump again, several times,

to get home. But now we've gone from roof to roof on our own, without the help of boys or ladders, so we can do it again, as though we are super creatures, or galloping animals. It doesn't sound plausible, but it's true; we leap all the way home.

This will be the last time I hang out with Leena on the roof. It's not safe there anymore. I never want to see the boys, but it will be hard to avoid them, even harder to accuse them of trying to hurt us. We're stuck in this neighborhood together. Our parents know their parents. Our brothers are friends with their brothers. Their aunt teaches at the girls' upper school; we see her in the hallways. And what will we say if we tell someone what happened and they ask why we were alone with three boys? Maybe they would be right to question our judgment. To say whatever happened wasn't right, but. But we followed those boys across the rooftops. We went into one of their homes. We got close to them.

CHAPTER 11

Labor

Death at the factory.

Years later, Mayyadah would wish she, and not the mousy girl, had been the one to find Saleh.

Saleh was Mayyadah's fiancé. For the love of him, she gave up her dreams of the city. Then, he was murdered in the factory break room.

On that summer night, the mousy girl had left her station, opened the break-room door. And then as quickly shut it, screaming, loud and high-pitched.

Later, someone remembered the glass door to the foreman's office shattering. Others said that was impossible, no matter how powerful the scream.

What the mousy girl saw: A man so soaked in blood he appeared to be wearing a sweater.

Most people had hardly heard the mousy girl's voice before. She gestured, mostly: thumbs-up for "Yes," downward glance for "No," index finger pointing toward the WC when she needed to pee, a barely noticeable nudge at the end of her shift for "Get out of my way."

Now she yowled, bent over as though overtaken with painful cramps, or about to give birth. All the women and the best of the men went running from their positions on the line, a gush of hair-netted heads and aproned bodies. Concerned faces, a dozen women muttering, "Why is she screaming?" A dozen other women thinking, *How stupid a question.* A man saying, "I'll get her some water." Was she hurt? Or had she been groped by a member of that category of men at the factory who could not be trusted to keep their hands to themselves?

Mousy Girl screamed more, twisting her hairnet in her hands, her eyes wild from the sight of something they could never unsee.

Everyone thought of the string of murders. How gruesome each had been. A decade had passed since the first, almost two years since the last.

The women sat Mouse down on the floor, kneeled at her side as though praying with her. The supervisor arrived with the bottle of water, and two women held it to her mouth, hoping she'd drink and that would stop the screaming. She pushed the bottle aside. They tried to coax out of her what had happened, what she had seen, but the questions brought out the screams. She couldn't even point or mime.

The door stayed closed. The workers had been avoiding opening it. They had been taking care of her, putting their arms around her, so they wouldn't see what she had seen. Everyone had turned their backs on the room. Now, all at once, convinced the only thing that would stop Mousy Girl's screaming was sharing her horror, they opened the door.

He was upright in a chair—*sitting*, if you could say that of a corpse—with his hands flat on the bloody table in front of him. As though there were life in him. As though he were about to eat a sandwich, drink a soda, play a game of cards on his break. He was naked—waist up, and waist down below the table. They couldn't see his blood-stained legs, one crossed over the other, like he was sitting in a meeting. They swore he was smiling, as though he'd enjoyed the violence done to him. How and why the killer had created such a mundanely horrifying tableau, no one could fathom. The floor slick with blood. And in the blood...Were those? They couldn't be...Hoofprints? Had the killer ridden into the factory on a horse or a donkey? A goddamn pony? Wouldn't someone have seen it?

Then again, the hoofprints were neither here nor there. The horror of what they saw superseded all theories about what had happened.

They stared. They gagged. Several people screamed at once, as though they'd practiced for this moment. Mousy Girl screamed the loudest. Some people didn't want to compete. Instead of screaming, they cursed the goddamn, fucking, sucking ridiculous gods or fate or human malevolence that made this happen in the place where they worked, where they usually felt safe except from the threat of a tongue-lashing, a finger severed by a machine, a broken wrist, a hernia from lugging heavy boxes, a man who went too far with his attentions, a boss who had it in for them.

This was something else. The weight of knowing this kind of awful death could happen here, inside their factory, sent them to the ground. The foreman, when he arrived after several minutes of ignoring the screaming because nothing should keep him from doing his job, found a gaggle of lolling, sitting, hurting people, and the door to the break room wide open.

He pulled it shut. Not even the loud slam stopped his workers from rolling on the ground in pain. The day was a bust. Wages would be garnished.

Someone would have to tell Mayyadah, who, as usual, was here but not here.

Through the screaming chaos, Mayyadah stayed on the periphery with a few others who kept their heads down, never got involved with anything. Her real life existed outside the factory. She did not want to know what was in that room. She did not like to see other people's pain or feel a responsibility to heal them from whatever hurt them. She did not like to help. She didn't know the emergency concerned her. She didn't worry that her Saleh wasn't in the crowd because he'd had the night off. She thought him safe at home.

After she'd dawdled a few minutes, digging around in her tote for yarn and needles, she began to think there was no use staying. She thought to call Saleh and ask him to pick her up and drive her home. She knitted a baby blanket and waited till the screaming died down. Which took forever. It was nice to have a break. She thought about going outside, away from the screaming. A few men straggled toward the door, tapping cigarettes out of their packs.

Then the foreman called her.

She arrived at the crowd which had gathered by the now-closed break-room door. A bony hand pushed her into a chair and told her not to move till the police and medics came.

She asked for her knitting. She asked, "Why do I have to sit here? What's in there?"

When no one answered, she made up excuses, none of them compatible with the level of horrified noise in the room: They knew she hated rats, they knew she hated bad smells; something had invaded the trash can, something had gone bad in the refrigerator.

The police took twenty minutes to arrive. They asked her when she'd last seen Saleh and whether he'd been cheating on her, and she got up from the chair, made her way to the breakroom door, and entered hell. Not a burning place, but a place devoid of hope, devoid of human kindness, a place from which she could never return.

Saleh had been devilish since childhood, his grin full of impish possibility, his hair thick as fur, his eyelashes so long they brushed the ridge above his eyes when he blinked. He wore red. He wanted to be recognized from a mile away. Never cared about being spotted, being caught. Mayyadah met him on the night shift, where a lot of girls from the neighborhood worked and met their husbands. After the other girls got married, they moved to the day shift or opened up tailoring businesses or took care of their babies and the working girls' babies, the neighbors' children.

One side of the factory bottled soda. The other side packaged candy. The neighborhood smelled stale-sweet. Dozens of people from Mayyadah's neighborhood worked here, the boys and girls funneled from their separate high schools after graduation. Saleh was one of the ones going to college during the day, working at night.

Some of the girls told Mayyadah, "Be careful. That one's trouble."

She didn't ask what kind of trouble. Most of the men were trouble. Better not to know Saleh's history, or the gossip that posed as history, because the trouble in his smile, in his wink, in his fingers holding a cigarette, the knuckles bent like tiny hills—those were the kinds of trouble she wanted to get into. He had a reputation as a joker. One time, his friends said, he'd spiked the foreman's coffee with salt. The foreman never again asked Saleh to make the thick coffee they drank all night.

He'd gotten someone pregnant, maybe. "Can't be true," one of the prudish, proud girls said. "Would never happen here." Meaning in our town, in our neighborhood. Girls getting knocked up happened other places, like the city or the slums.

Mayyadah didn't care if some girl had been ruined by his love. He couldn't do that to her. She was tough as a turtle's shell, sharp as a blade.

Yet she fell so hard for him she could count the bruises on her elbows and knees, her thighs, her chin.

He told her he'd had a crush on her since he saw her in the Monster Parade.

"A beastly woman turns me on." He touched her thigh. Was he imagining a donkey's leg—hoof and muscle and rough hair?

"They've banned the parade," she said. "I'll never wear my costume again."

After they got engaged, he drove her to and from work. Evening and morning, with roosters crowing from the rooftops, confused about night and day. In every conversation, he dared her to wear the costume for him.

On a night off, she asked him to drive her outside town, to a little valley. She changed in the back of the car while he waited under the spilt-milk stars.

She'd lost her wig, and hadn't replaced it. She stood before him, arms spread, sharp blades bared, legs transformed. She loved the clop of her hooves. She pawed at the earth, then licked his lips. She wore a new perfume that kicked him in the gut with its bitter, resiny, garbage base notes.

He'd left the car's headlights on; outside the V of light, the pitch-black night went on and on. Crickets shrieked. Everything living in the valley was invisible to the girl and boy standing there.

He told her she looked real.

"I am real."

He lunged forward face-first, arms reaching.

She twisted to the side. She was laughing. She wanted him to kiss her.

She held her blades above her head and nodded. He kissed her neck, her earlobe, her chin, her lips.

When she sucked in his breath, she felt beastly. Monstrous. More powerful than a human woman.

She took off her blades, her donkey legs, and lay on the hard dirt in her costume dress, Saleh fully clothed on top of her, like they were two stacked mattresses. Her blade-hands, her hooves, waited next to them. The night sounds echoed in her head, painfully loud. She wished the crickets would shut up. She imagined she heard a train whistle, although no railway had ever come through this part of the country.

He kissed other women. He smoked with her friends in the parking lot on his breaks. He could be cagey about what he'd done on his days off. She burned to know. Once she asked him, innocently, expecting only a modest response, like, "Slept in," "Helped my father," or "Ate lunch at my sister's."

He raised his hand, flat and dangerous-looking, as though to slap her. She was wearing a long skirt and T-shirt that day and smelled like shampoo and face cream, clean and girl-like. Her hands ended in fingers, the nails cut short and filed blunt. Nothing sharp about her. Nothing half-and-half. All Mayyadah.

She flinched. He lowered his hand, an apology blooming on his lips like a nasty-smelling flower.

She never asked again. But she watched, counted the number of times he talked to Lara, Ruwaida, Deena, Lama, Hanna, Seema. The number of times he smiled at a girl, touched her arm, winked at her, told her she looked nice today.

Her envy ate her from within like a tapeworm. The evil eye, the eye of envy. She was guilty of it. She considered breaking off the engagement, but she couldn't bring herself to do it.

Yes, she had wished him dead, but more often she had wished him gone from her heart. More often she had wished the other girls dead. Or herself. Not because she wanted to die, but because she wanted to stop loving him, and death seemed like the only way. He knew she wanted to call off the engagement. He told her no. He told her please don't leave me.

As much as the sight of him dead haunted her, the killer's message, scrawled on the wall near the door, burned itself into her heart. Simple yet terrifying words that, in future years, people in town would repeat when they rehashed the murders, debated Mayyadah's innocence or guilt, or remembered the lives of Saleh and the other murdered men.

Mayyadah left town soon after Saleh died. She didn't hear the gossip. Some nights, she murmured the killer's words to herself as she was falling asleep, as though she could reclaim Saleh's love even in death.

"He's mine."

CHAPTER 12

Beasts and Roses

Farewell to Bumbo. A father–daughter story.
Perfumery lessons.

My name is Layla, and here is how I come to be: I grow up in a neighborhood on the edge of town, in a town on the edge of the hilly countryside, on the edge of change, on the edge of time.

When I'm nearly a woman, I dream of leaving. But my family tethers me.

My father and I visit Bumbo for the last time just before I graduate high school. We've gone to the farm once or twice a year for the past decade or so; we like to go when the roses are blooming. This year for my birthday, I want to smell Bumbo's donkey smell; I want to breathe in the perfume of roses. I don't know I'll never see Bumbo again. I'll never recapture the innocence of the first day I met him.

I have another motive for this visit: I want to learn to be a perfumer, and I'm going to ask the farmer's wife, Auntie Wardah, to teach me. She's been making and selling scents for years. I'll learn from Auntie Wardah, sell scents to raise money, sock it away in my closet, and one day soon I'll leave for the city.

I dream of being a perfumer. It's the only job I want. My attraction to odors, fragrances, scents, smells, and aromas is intense, and I crave not only fragrances from flowers and incense and perfumes, but also pungent foods and drinks: bread-infused water thick with grated cinnamon, stinky moldy cheeses, fermented yogurt, and honey-sweet, orange-blossom flavored desserts that attract ants from miles away. I press my nose to the cutting board after my mother has swept garlic or onion into a pan. I rub into my palms the crunchy-frilly black-and-white lichen from her spice cabinet, bring my hands to my face, and inhale the scent of the underside of a stone. I wear cheap perfume from the corner store, with the fakest seaside smell you can imagine, because the essential oils the Attar family sells at the weekly market are too expensive. Whenever my father splurges on expensive incense, I light it up without asking his permission. With a few waves of my hand, I get the smoke to waft over my body. I drift about the flat, smelling mysterious and smoky.

My brothers say I smell like ashes.

"That makes me Cinderella," I tell them.

"Poor and dirty," Bassam says.

Bumbo's mulish, hairy, musty, fecal, halitosis odor is one of my favorites. Smelling it, I'm seven, meeting Bumbo for the first time, believing with all my heart that I can ride him away from here. But I'm so much older than that now. That's why I love the roses, every variety. Their scents suggest adulthood, true freedom. When I sniff them, I'm confident I'm going to leave home. When I'm away from the roses, I worry I'll never be free of my town.

Today, the farmer's face is fallen with sadness when he greets us. Bumbo is on his last legs. He's been tired and sad, not eating as usual, not whinnying at visitors. The poor donkey wants to lie down and sleep for the last time.

I've witnessed Bumbo's aging over the past year or so. He wobbles on his arthritic knees; his muzzle and mane have become tinged with gray. I'm not prepared to say goodbye, though.

Auntie Wardah tries to comfort Uncle. When she comes near him with care in her eyes, he tenses like a rubber band. He snaps. I flinch in sympathy for her. She doesn't crumble or simper. Her face is stone. She goes ahead of us to the garden. I wonder what's wrong. Uncle is mourning in preparation for mourning, but is there more to it than that?

I go to the barn on my own, enter Bumbo's stall, and press my face against his smelly side. I lead him by a rope to graze in the small enclosed grassy area behind his barn. He kisses my fingers and pushes his head into my hand, asking me to pet him. He tires quickly. I lead him back to the barn. He nods off. I love the smell of manure because it's the smell of Bumbo, but now, it's almost too powerful. It stops me in my tracks.

Auntie Wardah waits for me in the rose garden, where bumblebees buzz loudly and bump against our faces and bodies. They can't be bothered to fly around us. Auntie is happy and relaxed as she leads me through the garden. When I ask where my father and Uncle are, she tenses and pretends not to hear. I let the question go. The garden smells like dirt and leaves until I get closer to the bushes and put my nose right into the petals of a rose. Some smell stronger than others and they all smell rose-y, but each rose has a unique scent. Auntie

Wardah is named after roses. She plants bushes of every kind and color and scent, pink and tiny as my pinky and sweet as cotton candy; yellow like a lemon with thick floppy petals; orange, and red-orange and orange-red with petals fine and stiff as chiffon; coral and climbing a trellis like flames; red as cherry jam and red as blood; purple and lush as velvet; lavender like the end of sunset. I touch the blossoms as though they are kittens, and as usual, Auntie Wardah warns me to be careful of the thorns, but I don't care. My hand grazes a thorn as I reach for a crimson rose. I suck the blood from my thumb. Years ago, Auntie Wardah taught me how to snip the blooms, and she usually insists I wear gloves. Today, I want to touch the roses with my bare fingers. I'm not a child to be protected anymore. With gloves on, I feel deprived. I bury my nose in the petals and breathe. My body revives. I want to bring the roses home with me, but of course, that would kill them. I want them to live.

Taking the petals for fragrance is a different matter. Less cruel, more like the flower is gifting me its scent.

Auntie Wardah wears big black sunglasses and a black scarf with a colorful fringe and little crochet roses knotted at the back of her neck, the end tucked in to conceal her hair. Her gold chandelier earrings dangle almost to her shoulders, and around her hips, over her black shift dress, she wears a gold coin belt. She's old-fashioned, younger than my mama by a few years, or older by a few years. When she places her sunglasses on her head, I see that the fine lines at the corners of her eyes and around her lips are not etched too deeply, despite her hours in the sun. When she slides off her gardening gloves, her hands look soft as rose petals.

My father calls, and I wave, glancing at Auntie Wardah. She

has brought out a pair of clippers to give some love to the roses. Baba and Uncle lean against the barn and talk while we putter. Uncle has loosened up a little, but I can't help but wonder what he's really thinking when he laughs at my father's jokes. Is he storing up some insult for his wife, to mete out to her when we're gone?

Maybe not. Maybe he's enjoying a distraction from his beloved donkey's deterioration. Baba tells me to come and listen to the story Uncle is about to tell. I stand between two rose bushes on the border of the rose garden. Auntie Wardah prunes. She has heard his stories a million times. This one is about a tribe that wears roses in their hair and harvests petals every year. Piles of rose petals, which they dry, and from which they make rosewater and tinctures. Auntie Wardah bought her first plants from them, up in the mountains. They taught her to tend and fertilize roses, to prune them properly so more blossoms would grow. Then she ordered more bushes from all over the world.

Uncle looks at me and says, "We stopped buying their roses because we found out they make poisons that smell like perfume. The mayor of the city who was assassinated years ago? He smelled like rose oil. That tribe killed him."

"Lies," says Auntie Wardah. "Conspiracy theories."

"It's the truth. Everyone says so."

Their exchange feels portentous, like they might start to yell at any moment. I scowl at my father. I don't want to be caught in their spat. Baba says maybe he and I should go.

"No, no, you must stay for lunch," Uncle says. "The table's already set."

We never say no to his generosity. I'm on edge as we sit at a wooden table at the perimeter of the rose garden. There's food set out under mesh, a pot of tea in a cozy embroidered with roses, and four tea glasses. We eat candied rose petals, dates that stick to my fingers, and little pistachio biscuits that crumble into my lap. I start to forget about the argument earlier. Auntie Wardah tells me about the tinctures she's made lately, the scents she's designing. She's an artist whose material is fragrance. I want to be like her. She says it takes years of experimenting to make the perfect scent. I tell her I want to come back and learn from her, get a real lesson in perfumery.

I expect her to say yes immediately. Instead, she nibbles a biscuit and stares at her roses.

"Perfumery is a dangerous, dark art," Uncle says. He asks if we'd like to hear proof in the form of a story about a merchant, his daughter, a rose, a beast.

"Beauty and the Beast," my father says. The classic French story—which, my father points out, has nothing to do with perfumes.

The farmer looks confused. No, he says. His father passed this story down to him. A merchant arrives from the far-away city. He wants to extract the knowledge of the local people. Specifically, he wants to learn to grow the perfect rose. To draw from it the perfect scent. A scent that, when worn on the skin or breathed into the lungs, lengthens a person's life. He visits a tribe of rose-growing people who have lived longer than anyone in this part of the world.

My father cocks his head and squints, like he's trying to make sense of the farmer's words. "Is this a folktale or a true story?"

The farmer says whether the story is fiction or fact doesn't matter. "Listen before you question," he says, focusing a glaring eye on his wife. She tops off the rose-infused tea in my glass.

"Truth matters," my father says. "Facts matter."

Uncle picks his teeth while Baba goes on about lies versus facts, truth versus fiction, science versus fairy tales, gossip versus news. He's been talking this way since the last murder, of the man who was going to be Layth's brother-in-law, Saleh. People have relentlessly, brutally gossiped and conjectured about Mayyadah, while the police have insisted they cannot solve the mystery, with no sense of shame for shirking their duty to protect the public.

According to the cops, Mayyadah's innocent, for now.

Innocent and gone. Living some kind of life in the city. Just like Susu. Do people from our town gravitate toward one another when they migrate to the city? If I go there, will I find them? Will I want to? The boy I've been secretly dating, Habeeb, has an uncle who works at a department store in the city that has an internship program. Since Saleh's death, Habeeb has dreaded going to his job at the factory. He's applying for a position at the department store, making plans to leave our town. He lives in the next neighborhood over from mine, where everyone seems a little happier, where there have been no murders, and yet he wants to leave. He's been to the city a few times to visit his uncle. He even finds the horrific traffic to be wonderful. Traffic means people, life, things happening, places to go. In our town, the streets are empty and quiet, because no one goes anywhere and there's nothing to do. Whenever Habeeb and I talk, I disappear into the mole on the edge of his chin. I imagine the taste of that mole, salty and earthy. The smell of a young man, musky and tart at first, then tobacco-y and mellow.

While Baba rants, I eat another candied rose petal. It tastes like I'm eating the fragrance of a rose, a fragrance that stops my body in time, in a moment I never want to end. A bee buzzes raucously in my ear. It's loud enough to be at least the size of my hand. I hold still till it flies away.

Bumblebees don't sting, but danger can come from anywhere, even here, in my paradise, in proximity to Auntie's roses, the sweetest things I've ever smelled. What smells did they have in the Garden of Eden? Mint and rosemary and sage and leek? Lichen and cinnamon bark and nutmeg and peppercorns? Animal scat? Sticky tree sap? And every flower God invented: Jasmine, lavender, honeysuckle, gardenia, and on forever.

Uncle has interrupted my father to continue his story. He goes back to the beginning and starts it like a fairy tale, to tease my father, I think: Once there was, or there was not, a merchant who had a beautiful daughter who loved the smell of roses.

Is he talking about my father and me? Odd, maybe even creepy, if he is, to describe me as *beautiful*. The fictional father seeks the finest luxuries to sell to others. He arrives in a rose-filled valley. Butterflies land on his shoulders. Birds serenade him. A stream gurgles past. He crosses a bridge. He thinks he's found paradise. In the shade of a fruit tree, he plucks a peach from the low boughs. When he bites the fruit, juice runs down his chin.

What he wants most is to please his daughter, who is his eyes and his moon.

He strolls among the roses, searching for the perfect bloom. Will she want red or white, purple or orange? Will she want a rose with a bright or deep smell? He wanders the garden, hunched and giddy, intoxicated and distracted by the roses, bent over to breathe in their scent.

Unbeknownst to the merchant, a beast watches. He is hulking and furry, walks on two legs like a man, and wears a turban and a vest like a prince or a wealthy merchant. The beast's fangs measure longer than a girl's pinky finger. The heady perfume of roses conceals the beast's stench of garlic, raw meat, and vinegar.

The beast clears his throat, like a teacher announcing himself to chatty schoolchildren.

"Thief!" he growls.

The man jumps, falls onto his rump, sees the beast, and begins to sob.

The beast locks the man in a tower. The man's daughter dies of sadness.

"That's not how it ends," my father says.

"He changes the ending every time." Auntie Wardah sounds not amused but exasperated.

"It's not your story," Uncle snarls. She sighs and starts to tidy up.

"How does it really end?" I ask.

"The man's youngest daughter searches for him for years. She cannot get him out of the tower, but under cover of night, she plucks all the roses' petals and makes perfume out of them so no one will ever again be caught stealing and fall under the beast's spell."

"No, no," says Auntie Wardah. "That's not it either. The man's daughter saves him."

"And marries the beast," my father says. "Don't forget that part of the story. That's what makes it fiction. What beastly father wants his daughter to marry a beast?"

At home, I tell my parents I want to learn perfumery from

Auntie Wardah. They say they'll discuss the idea, and the next day my father says he doesn't want me to go to the farm alone.

He won't say why. I yell. He follows me to my room to apologize, but he still doesn't explain. "Because I'm your father," he says. He's never said such things to me before. I slam my bedroom door in his face.

When Bumbo dies a few weeks later, a day or two after my graduation, I drive myself to the farm without asking permission from my parents. I'm an adult, after all. From Bumbo's empty stall, I grab a handful of straw and bring it to my nose. I smell the dry sandiness of straw, the acid of Bumbo sweat, and something sweet, like a hint of apple or plum, his favorite fruits. I stuff the straw into my pocket. I'm bawling in his shitty stall.

Rana would say I'm overreacting. Bumbo was just an animal: a beast of burden and then, when he aged, a pet—not even my pet. But an animal's death is not different from a human's death. A life exists and then it doesn't. A body exists and then it doesn't. A consciousness leaves the earth. Death is existential subtraction. I would like to believe Bumbo can be reincarnated, come back as a younger donkey or a gazelle. Or that some part of Bumbo can be merged with me, that I can carry on his animal legacy in the world.

I wipe the snot and tears off my face and join Auntie Wardah in the rose garden. She says a few words about Bumbo before she starts my first perfumery lesson.

"He was a good donkey. He lived a good life. He would want his favorite young lady to remember him well."

My lesson begins. Auntie Wardah tells me to journal the things I smell, to catalog and collect them. I tell her I've been doing that. I have a stash of labeled plastic containers in my closet, each of them containing a precious and fragrant memento: the rose petals from the day of the masquerade, a pinecone from a hike I once took with Baba, sticks of cinnamon, cloves, sandalwood I stole from my grandma's house, musk, ambergris, that smelly lichen I love.

Auntie Wardah teaches me to tell the difference between roses by smell. She ties a scarf over my eyes and holds my hand as she leads us down the aisles of prickly bushes. I smell each flower, and Auntie Wardah tells me which variety it is. The blooms' scents are physical things, smothering my face, punching me, caressing me, tickling me—all depending on the particular rose bush. When a scent overpowers me, Auntie Wardah steadies me. Bees buzz. Birds chirp a passionate conversation in the orchard. We go through the garden three times. On the fourth walk, I repeat the names of the roses from memory. Then Auntie Wardah spins me five times, and lets me go. I wobble forward. Auntie Wardah catches me. We walk a new route. Auntie Wardah keeps me from touching the plants, so I won't cheat based on a tactile clue. The scents are like old friends. When I breathe each one in and let the notes of the perfume rise through my nasal passages into my brain, I see in my mind the rose that made this unique smell.

I identify all but two, which I mistake for each other.

I pull the scarf down to my neck. Auntie Wardah has set out lemonade and little thyme-flavored biscuits. Bees try to dip their feet in our drinks. I've brought a sketchpad with me, and I sketch Bumbo's legs and hooves from memory. I cover the page with my hand so Auntie Wardah won't see I'm not drawing the whole donkey, just a part of it, limbs that could be mixed and matched with a human body, human limbs and head, or with the body of a beast of imaginary proportions.

I miss Bumbo with my heart, lungs, mind, and soul.

Auntie Wardah tells me she's proud of my ability to detect scents. I have a natural gift few people have. Hearing her compliment me makes me blush.

"I'm not as good as you," I say.

She laughs. "You're not as experienced as me. You'll do great."

After our snacks, we go inside the farmhouse, to a little green room with shelves and shelves of vials. Auntie Wardah shows me how to mix my first perfume: rose petals she's soaked in alcohol, as well as cinnamon essence, orange essence, basil essence, clove. She explains head, heart, and base—the layers of an aroma, from flightiest to longest-lasting. I hold the dropper, so delicate in my hand, the droplets of essence entering the coconut oil like doll's tears. I'm overwhelmed by the barky bite of cinnamon. It mellows in my nose within moments. I follow cinnamon with basil, its licorice depth like a bass note in a musical composition. When I release too much clove, Auntie flips the ramekin over and tosses everything down the drain. I panic. She swipes her index finger inside the ramekin and lets me smell the stinging, awful results of my mixing.

"You can't save a bad perfume. Start from the beginning."

My shoulders tense with concentration as I count the drops. Auntie Wardah demonstrates how to test on my skin after each drop, how to jot notes about each step of my creation, so I can retrace if things go wrong.

"Add one more," she says.

I choose rose essence. I expect the final scent to be more perfect than perfect, but now it's off.

"Your first attempt can't be your best," Auntie Wardah says. "This way, next time can be better."

For the next two years, I secretly visit the farm several times a month to learn from Auntie Wardah, and side by side we mix fragrances. After my first few lessons, she deep-cleans the barn and moves her perfume organ there: shelves of vials, dozens of aromatics, some she distills herself, others she orders from far, far away, places I've never heard of.

Being in Bumbo's barn is a way of remembering him, staying close to his spirit, but the farm smells different now. The roses dominate the air, as they have long wanted to do, and the orange trees send out their citrus notes. Closer to the earth, I smell chicken shit on Auntie Wardah's clothes, hay on her skin. When we mix perfumes, she wears a white jacket, almost like a chef's jacket, and she holds her fingers steady and calm as she drops tiny amounts of this and that into beakers. She laughs when I say "this and that," warns me that I must remember the names of my materials. I must treasure them.

Bergamot, I say. Rose, of course. Ambergris. Aloe. Lavender. Tuberose. Oud. Fig. Frankincense. Sandalwood. Sage. Birch. Cardamom. Cedar. Grass. Cinnamon leaf. Civet. Clove. Lychee. Raspberry. Geranium. Lemon. Lime. Musk. Neroli. Oakmoss. Orange. Peach. Black pepper. Peppermint. Rosemary. Pine. Ylang ylang. Grapeseed. Gardenia. Foxglove. Vetiver. Magnolia. Coconut. Cucumber. Grapefruit. Honey. Balsam. Patchouli. Myrrh. Cassis. Carnation. Seaweed. The list goes on and on. I fall into the scents, and never want to come out.

I help Auntie Wardah carefully wrap tiny sample vials and bottles the size of a fist to send to people all over the world. We fill little boxes with shredded paper. If we've done our job right, the scents are hidden inside their bottles, and the boxes and packages smell like nothing, or maybe a little like paper and cardboard.

When I become good enough at mixing to sell my own fragrances, I'm going to leave.

CHAPTER 13

Poisons and Thorns

Death in the park.

The four men choked on thorns, the site of their pain invisible to each other as they writhed, the damage confined to their bleeding interiors. She'd lured them to the park with her scent—rose, ginger, cloves, orange peel, jasmine—and kissed them each on the lips, the oldest first, then his son, then his son, then the youngest. Each man watched, believing she wanted him more than the man before. Tasting her before he tasted her, getting harder as he watched and wondering how much longer till it was his turn. She pushed her fingers into their hungry mouths. Her smell grew headier the longer each man waited. The youngest had never kissed a woman, but he knew he would be the best. He disappeared into the shadow of her hair, which had its own smell: coconut and the bite of olive oil. Her mouth tasted waxy, like lipstick.

The jogger who discovered the four bodies in the park thought they were passed out.

They were dead. They sprawled over two benches next to the

new playground, which later in the day would be full of children and their parents.

The man didn't slow down for a better look or stop to take their pulses or hover his hand over their mouths, searching for warm breath. He kept going, jogged by at a distance, and called the police, panting into his phone. *Public nuisance, can't you do something?* The cops said they'd come, no need for him to wait there. Something nagged at him. He circled back and jogged past again, this time noticing what he hadn't before: a thick carpet of rose petals on the ground, a muddy, cloying fragrance that stuck in his throat and nose. The scent reminded him of his deceased grandmother, the rosewater she dabbed on her wrists and behind her ears and baked into desserts and spritzed onto the damask of her formal sitting-room furniture. It dislodged memories of bussing her on the cheek and playing cards on her sofa.

Uneasiness washed over him and he wanted to get away from the scene. He jogged straight to the police department just around the corner.

"A family of drunks," they said.

He banged on the desk. "She's back!"

The police did not ask who *she* was. When they arrived at the scene, they recognized the family. Men of different ages; four generations. Teenager, father, grandfather, great-grandfather. A family known for their longevity. One might normally say what a blessing for four generations to know each other—but this was not that sort of family.

Froth had gathered on the lips of the youngest. The oldest man smiled stonily. The air was warming, and the tree above the bench was lousy with chattering, anxious birds. Their droppings covered the ground like snow in a Scandinavian procedural drama.

The jogger had babbled on about rose petals and a smell like a dozen dying grandmothers doused in rosewater.

How or why he'd mistaken guano for roses, the cops couldn't say. They simply noted what they saw.

At first, the police suspected alcohol poisoning, but they found no bottles, and forensics detected something else in the men's bloodstreams: a cocktail of toxins. Determining how this entered the bodies stumped the police. Even stranger: From each of the dead men's throats, the coroner removed a handful of rose thorns, which had sliced their throats from the inside.

This was the cleanest murder the cops had seen—the cleanest *murders*. Foul play for sure.

There had been rumors about this family for years, the meanness of the men, from the moment they were born, over and above the meanness one saw in any family from time to time. They slapped their children's hands with rulers when the teachers at school no longer would. They smoked cigarettes mostly to have something with which to burn misbehaving children. Doors in their homes were locked for days at a time, unspeakable secrets hidden inside. Girls left school to be married off at too young an age. The women of the family never talked to their neighbors.

People made other accusations. Too dire to believe, too shocking not to share.

Possibly, the police officers assigned to solve the mystery of the four deaths theorized, the women had, after years of silent suffering, conspired to kill their torturers. When the officers knocked on the women's doors, they looked adequately bereaved, heads draped in white, not a speck of make-up, even on the woman with a black eye like a bat flying across her face. The police detected a puzzling absence of scent. They sniffed the air for the smell of snot crumpled in tissue, tearful onions, antiseptic cleaning agents, incense to greet mourning guests, or glutinous lamb bones boiling for the soup of the dead, a local tradition. Nothing. As though the women weren't living. As though they had morphed into spirits, swapping their odorous bodies for wispy nothingness.

One officer swore there was a jinn in the house, a woman she'd never seen before, with skin lit from within, the silhouette of bones visible.

The captain sent the officer home to recover from her delusions.

When the police brought the women in for questioning one by one, each woman cried buckets and blamed herself for the men being out at night. No, she hadn't argued with any of the men that night. They never argued; it was just that in the men's eyes, the women were never right.

In the interrogation room, the cops' noses detected something new: an animal smell, glandular and urinous. It brought acid to their throats. One of the women wore a locket that she removed from her neck during the interview.

"Did your husband ever strike you? Did you want to strike back? Did you want him dead?"

She popped open the locket and rubbed her finger in the solid cake of something. Applied it to her temples. A waft of ginger, musk. The younger cop wanted to close his eyes and drift to sleep. His partner kicked him in the leg to rouse him, but the interview never got any more insightful.

In their interrogations, the remaining men of the family smelled like fear. They spilled their hearts out, scared out of their minds.

They admitted to being wife-beaters, child-terrorizers, adulterers. "I've been awful," they said. "Lock me up."

"Did you kill these men?" the police asked.

"No, of course not, it wasn't me. Lock me up, though, or my wife will do something drastic. Protect me, please."

Having no evidence beyond the men's confessions that the admitted-to crimes had truly occurred—and no interest in investigating further—the police refused to throw the men in jail.

They had a quadruple murder to solve. They interrogated business partners, coworkers, neighbors, and in the end, couldn't pin the crime on anyone.

Look the other way, the police told themselves. Look away, as they always did.

They told the women of the family to get out of town, go start a new life in the city.

There was something the cops had seen in the park, a hoof-print in the guano, and they'd smelled sandalwood and a note of fertilizer in the men's clothes. Maybe a whiff of roses; maybe the jogger had been right. And written in permanent marker on the bench where the men had slumped:

"Don't doubt her."

Whether the message came from the night murderer or a copycat, evil never slept, the police concluded. And neither could they.

CHAPTER 14

Gone

A sudden loss. Susu returns. Doomed love.
An encounter in the city.

At twenty, I have been a secret perfumer for two years. And for
the past year, I have sold the perfumes I handcraft with Auntie
Wardah to my friends, my mother's and sisters' friends, my
aunties, the neighbors, the teachers and students at the small
local college I attend in the evening. Everyone understands
that I have to keep my parents in the dark because I don't want
them to know I'm saving up to leave for the city. My customers
protect me.

I've learned it's not hard to keep secrets. It doesn't eat your
soul the way people claim it does. Secrets can be freeing.

If my father knew my plans, as good as he is and as much
as he loves me, he would argue with me and try to stop me. He
has come to believe relocation is the scourge of modern life. He
has come to believe there's no reason to leave.

And it's true, since the appointment of a new mayor a year
or so ago, our town has slowly become a better place to grow up
in than it used to be, though it's too late for me. Low-rise flats

have risen where the old playground stood; the mayor commissions a new one in the shape of a pirate ship, with a sandbox to the side, and tells parents again and again that this must be a town where it's safe for their kids to play. I'm glad for the younger kids; sad for me and a whole generation that grew up with this town's mania for controlling us and our movements and activities. That pirate ship can't replace our stunted childhoods. When I see kids playing and having fun, with no fear etched on their faces, I see how stunted my childhood was, how fearful I was. Instead of playing on a playground, I summoned the ghost of my best friend's brutally murdered father. What seemed exciting to me at the time, now seems sad. Tragic, even.

I still want to leave my town. I think about leaving all the time. So why haven't I? I tell myself I'm saving money to be able to afford an apartment, maybe a car. I don't want to disappoint my father, or grieve my mother, but scents are my rebellion, and maybe they can be my ticket away from here. My escape. Still, I second-guess myself. Maybe this town is all right. It's all I know. Does not having moved yet mean I'm placid, compliant? I want to be a hellraiser, a rebel. In my heart, I want to go, but am I ready to leave my family?

Habeeb has one foot here and one foot in the city. He drives there every week for his job at the department store, stays with his uncle, comes home for the weekend. I borrow my dad's truck, pretend I'm going to a weekend study club, meet Habeeb in the parking lot, and kiss him in the back of his car. The dark tinted glass windows protect us from prying eyes. But we can't spend much time together. His parents are divorced and his mother needs him.

I want him to take me with him to the city—I ask him to

help me find a job there. Even though I've never been there, and I don't really know what it's like. I imagine it's a place full of freedoms.

"Are you sure?" he says. "You keep waffling, and if I land you a job, you'll have to take it or embarrass me."

He acts calm, but his fear smells ripe, acidic.

When four men are found dead on a park bench in my neighborhood, I worry there will be a backlash against the new laxity. There is discussion in the paper of a curfew for everyone, adults and children. I stop worrying and start hoping; the return of strictures and rules would be more reason for me to leave.

The mayor and police are surprisingly moderate in their reaction. They declare the crime a quadruple suicide and quash rumors about our neighborhood's serial murderer now resorting to "gentler" means. They fine anyone who repeats such drivel. Though tragic and worrisome, the four-generation death will not deter us from taking our town back, the mayor says in a televised speech. She vows to launch a mental health campaign.

My parents and brothers and I watch the speech together as it's airing live after dinner. My father says the mayor speaks the truth. There's no reason for people to leave our town. Things have improved. And why leave a place filled with family and friends and neighbors for the loneliness of the city, as so many have done over the years. My brothers ignore him, get up from the couch, and go to their room. My mother straightens things on the coffee table: the Kleenex box, stray bits of mail, pens, coasters.

I'm burning with the need to convince him that moving away wouldn't mean I'm abandoning my family and history.

"You can't mean everyone who leaves ends up lonely and alone. People have good lives in the city. Susu, her mom."

"You don't know their lives. You don't know their hearts," he says.

"Right, exactly. Neither do you."

My mother taps a pen against the table. It's distracting.

"Mama, stop that."

"Stop fighting with your father."

"I'm not."

"You're so obstinate."

Baba comes to my aid. "We raised her that way. To speak her mind."

But I'm not speaking my mind, not really. I'm not telling them I want to leave. I'm ashamed of myself for not being who my father thinks I am. For not being able to go. For not claiming my freedom. I thought I would, the minute I got the chance, and here I am, at home, unfree.

And then, a week later, tragedy visits my family in the most mundane and yet surprising way.

My father dies in his geography classroom at the college. He's young, not even fifty, and his collapse from a blood clot in his brain shocks everyone: his students, who rush to give him CPR and call the emergency line; his colleagues, who have known my mother all her life and must now tell her Baba is gone, dead before the ambulance sirens even sound across campus; his children, who never expected to lose him before old age; his mother, who never expected to outlive him; his neighbors, who show up at our door with platters of fruit and pastries and just-off-the-stove pots of rice and meat swaddled in potholders and tea towels. Auntie Wardah comes the first day, with rose jelly and fresh bread. Our flat smells like a banquet, a wedding, a time and place of celebration.

Maybe I'm wrong to think that way. Food is for sadness, too.

Baba's death shocks my mother the most. Even when Rana and Lajwa, who is pregnant with her first child, tell her to sit and not to lift a finger, they'll handle everything, she goes to the door herself when it rings, holds the pots and Pyrex containers as though she's holding the weight of my father's loss, says thank you to every well-meaning neighbor, smiles at them, wanly, gratefully.

"She's holding up so well," people say.

They ask me and my siblings how we're doing. Saying, "Terrible," though it's the truth, seems like a betrayal of my mother's stoic nature. What is her brave face worth if I tell everyone her face lies? And I have a new secret: With my father gone, my biggest mental obstacle to leaving town is gone, too. I am overcome by terrible, nauseating relief.

Our neighbors, family, and friends insist we keep the pots and the plates they bring so we won't feel obligated to return the favor by filling the containers with food for them. We can't eat all the food; we freeze a lot of it. Still, the counters are covered with extra pots and dishes.

When everyone but me and my siblings has left, Mama stands in the middle of the kitchen and says, "Get these goddamn things out of here. I can't stand to look at them."

I hide everything in the highest cupboards.

My mother insists that we, the dead man's wife and four children, clean Baba's body ourselves. In a back room of the five-story family building where my father grew up, she starts alone with her husband's nakedness while my sisters and brothers and I wait outside, drinking sodas our grandmother thrust into our hands as though she can't help but force hospitality onto us, even when we're devastated by grief for the loss of her son. She's lost her child; she can't help but treat us like children.

My mother opens the door slightly and calls us in. The room smells clean as lemons. Not what I expect death to smell like: rotting flesh and sadness.

Underneath the white cotton in which Mama has wrapped his body, our baba is naked except for a strip of fabric across the groin. He lies on a large double bed, as though he's an overnight guest. He's a body now, not a person. Lumpy nose, purple lips, closed eyelids, flabby arms, hands that lifted me when I was small. Hairy legs, hammer toes, which he let me pull while he yowled, "Oww, oww!" exaggeratedly, dramatically, and knowing he wasn't hurt, I pulled harder. I would never really hurt him. I can't look at him now. Rana, Lajwa, and I hold each other and bury our faces in each other's shoulders while my mother steadily instructs my brothers on how to clean the body with camphor. She could be teaching them how to boil rice or cook an egg. She lifts the cloth, and their hands disappear beneath it, preserving my father's dignity. The room smells like mothballs, as though my father were an old carpet we're rolling up and stowing away.

My father was the only good man, and now he's gone.

To counteract the camphor, I set up my father's incense burner on a nightstand. I have brought sandalwood I bought in the market, which stained my hands with scent when I picked it up to put it in the bag, and deep red dried rose petals from the farm, which I've kept in my dresser for months; I don't know why. And oud, its scent as strong and pungent and un-avoidable as dung. I plug in the burner. Slowly, smoke appears then intensifies, like a storm brewing. Our clothes and skin become infused with the scent we are sending Baba to the grave with. This ritual of scent is a way of carrying his spirit on our bodies. We wave the smoke onto his body and onto our bodies, into our clothes. The spirit scent of Baba. I smell a corner of the shroud. Rana and Lajwa stare at me like I'm crazy. I want to forever smell like Baba.

With everyone cooking for us and even tidying up the flat, my mother and sisters and I are left with nothing to do but grieve. I'm thankful he died in a place he loved, with people he loved—he adored his students, year after year—and not terrorized by our neighborhood killer. During the day, Mama naps or we take her for walks. In the evening, for a week after Baba's collapse, more people and the same people come to give their condolences.

The seventh night, a surprise: Susu and her mother arrive at our door. She's taller than me, as tall as her mother. They have matching pixie haircuts. Susu's clothes are flowy and black. Her mother wears white, the older, more traditional color of mourning. Their faces are sallow, as though they relive their grief over the death of Susu's father. Still, they smile when they see me and Rana, the first to greet them. They seem glad to see us yet tentative, cautious, and carved in their faces are expressions that show what it costs them to be here, in the place where her father so brutally died. Their eyes dart back and forth, searching for ghosts.

Crying women fill the formal living room's sofas and its

floorspace. My aunts and my grandmother and all my mother's friends, every last one. My classmates, my sisters' classmates. Everyone stops sobbing and gabbing when they see Susu and her mother. I'm wearing a perfume Auntie Wardah made for me, to remind me of Baba, and delivered the day after my father's death. Sandalwood and oud, roses and orange blossom, a hint of wild thyme and rosemary, the tiniest note of eucalyptus. When Susu kisses me on both cheeks, she says, "You smell like him." No one has ever understood me like Susu did when we were little. I'm flooded with memories of Baba's Place, where we built a small world and tried to communicate with her deceased father. Would it be possible to hear from my father from his place in the beyond? Since we buried him, I have not stopped picking up my phone to call him. Every time, I am devastated by his absence from a world where soundwaves can reach.

Susu hugs me, and I am overcome by an urge to apologize to her and her mother for not understanding in the past what grief was really like. All the times I followed Susu to Baba's Place, I thought of our actions as a real-life game. I didn't know what I know now: How violently she must have wanted to hear his voice. How it feels to cry yourself to sleep, to cry till you choke on your own snot, to not be able to stop, and then to have to stand in front of other people and smile, and pretend that grief is only the scent on your skin, not the deep rotting in your body and soul. How the only person who can understand your grief is you. No one else, not even the grievers closest to you.

When people say they can't imagine what it's like to lose someone, it's because they don't want to. Because it would be stupid to feel a loss we don't have to feel.

Susu sits next to me on the floor. The conversation is banal, everyday. My sisters ask her questions about the city. Where do she and her mother live? Do they like the city? Isn't the traffic awful? Doesn't it take a million years to go anywhere? Susu offers one-word answers, like little round mints. My mother sits nearby, too tired to chat, most likely lost in a memory of my father.

Susu says, "Auntie, do you need anything? You should sleep if you're tired."

I'm jealous that she's the one tending to my mother's needs, rather than me or my sisters. Because she already understands; she has done this before.

"She's alright," I say. "I'll get her water."

Susu follows me to the kitchen. She's crowding me. She smells like simple lemon water splash and scorched rayon. I'm glad she came, but I wish she'd stay with the mourners. Alone in the kitchen with her, I could apologize, just as I told myself I would, a moment ago. But now I'm thinking we haven't been close in years. I'm not sad about our faded friendship anymore, not the way I was when I was younger and her abandonment of me and our town was a fresh, throbbing wound. I should forgive her for leaving, of course. But I can't. Not yet, anyway.

And then she goes and reads my mind. I don't appreciate it.

"It'll get better," she says. "But you'll never be the same."

"I know. You don't have to tell me."

She pulls herself onto the counter, points her socked toes toward the floor. "You think you know, but you don't."

After a moment, she says, "When are you moving to the city?" as though we've been talking about me wanting to move for years. No one but Habeeb knows I want to leave.

"I can't move now. Mama needs me." And with those words, I have hit upon a way to erase my relief at Baba's death and my guilt over feeling it. I have just erected a new barrier for myself: Mama.

"You want to, though."

"I'll visit."

"Spend the night with me. Your mother doesn't have to know you're looking for an escape hatch."

The idea of controlling something, going somewhere, appeals to me more than ever. I can't bring my father back, but I can go to Susu.

"Just a sleepover," she says. "Ask your mother."

At sunset, Susu and her mother leave our flat and head back to the city. Susu texts me from the road: *Come stay with us.*

I tell her I will. For months, when she sends me nudging texts, I pretend I'm looking for the perfect time to go. I'm relieved when the texts stop.

Grief keeps me tethered, and the first year after my father's death passes quickly. This will sound odd, maybe wrong: My grief for my father brings back my grief for Bumbo. The two people I loved the most. Not everyone think animals are people. Many might think it's wrong to love a donkey more than I love my mother, my siblings. I love them a lot, but they have flaws Bumbo didn't have. I stop going to the barn. I focus on my studies. I stop selling perfume, stop saving money. Auntie Wardah calls me to check on me. She tells me the essences on her shelves will never run out, her love and care for me will never run out, not to worry about calling ahead. When I'm ready, I should return to the barn. Put the scents on my wrist. Get back to making and selling. Mix a fragrance of joy to counteract my mourning.

One weekend night, with the first anniversary of my father's death only a few weeks away, I ask Habeeb to come with me to the farm, for moral support and to distract me from thinking about Bumbo and Baba. I walk to my old grade school, where no prying eyes will see him pick me up. We leave town at sunset, and by the time we arrive at the farm, it's dark. Sleepy chickens are lazily pecking at the dirt. I'm not sure how they got out of the henhouse. Habeeb's a bit of a scaredy cat, hates spiders and snakes, crickets, even lady bugs. He's afraid of the farmer's chickens. He won't walk to the barn until I carry the chickens like cats into the henhouse. I pet their feathers and rub their heads to taunt him.

"They're as tame as cats," I tell him.

"I hate cats," he says.

"Well, that's a red flag," I say.

"What do you mean?"

"If you hate cats, we can't be together." He looks hurt, so I say, "It's a joke," but I'm lying. The clarity the lie represents surprises me. *He hates cats. I can't love a man who hates any kind of animal.*

But I do love him, I tell myself. And I convince myself for the rest of the night.

I have a key, and I let us into the barn. On the neat and tidy worktable, there's a notepad turned to a new page, a sheathed pen lying next to it, as though Auntie Wardah knew I was coming tonight. I want to recreate the fragrance she made for me, the comfort it gave me.

I dab sandalwood essence on my wrist. The scent reminds

me of Baba's corpse, of washing and wrapping him, burying him.

Habeeb sees my face. He says, "It smells like him."

I put my wrist near his nostrils. His breath warms my skin. I step away and cover my face with my wrists, breathe in the unadulterated scent of Baba.

"You bury me," I tell Habeeb, words mothers usually say to their children to express the unbearable possibility of a future without them.

"We'll bury each other." He touches my cheek. His tenderness is almost too much to bear.

The opposite of sandalwood is something floral. I mix all the florals I find on the shelves, one drop of each. I create a cloying, overpowering mess. Habeeb winces and pinches his nose when he smells the scent strip.

I pour the contents of the beaker down the sink and flush it with hot water to eradicate the smell.

Chickens snore in the coop next door; the wind moans; the barn creaks.

I lock up the barn while Habeeb shines the flashlight on his phone. The farmyard is dark. The smell of roses wafts by on a breeze. I look up at the sky full of stars, a bright round moon, low in the sky.

We hear a crack, and a thump, then the sound of hooves. Habeeb jolts, puts his arms around me. A wave of deep affinity for whatever is out there rushes through me. Some sixth sense, a pins-and-needles tingling through my body, tells me what we heard is not an animal, but a jinn or spirit or half-human thing. This is knowledge I keep to myself, not because I'm afraid of what Habeeb will think, but because I want to savor it, hold it for myself like something precious.

"It's nothing," I say, pushing him away.

"Is it an animal that's gotten loose?"

We're walking quickly to the car. "Could be a sheep," I say. I'm lying, as though I'm covering up for a girlfriend, or myself. If a sheep were loose, we would have heard it baaing.

"I smell something," he says. "Do you smell it?"

I inhale, and a scent settles in my nostrils: licorice or anise, a hint of chocolate, a bit of frankincense. Other notes I can't place.

Now we hear moaning. We grab each other's hands and don't move an inch.

"It's her," Habeeb whispers. "The Monstress."

I shiver. He might be right. Her story is imprinted on all of us in town. Our childhoods shaped and stunted by an imaginary figure. The murderess is known to change her fragrance. She's known to leave hoofprints behind.

If it's her, I want to protect her. I don't know why. She's a murderer. But I want her to be free.

"That smell is the ghost of Bumbo." I'm disturbed by how easy it is for me to lie to Habeeb. "I miss him so much I've manifested him. Or maybe it's the chickens come to get you."

A twig cracks, and we both startle and put our arms around each other. Then we pull apart, run to the car, lock the doors.

The wind has picked up and it's whistling. Maybe there's nothing in the dark farmyard but the wind. What will give me courage is to kiss Habeeb. When our lips touch, the energy between us crackles more than usual. When we move apart, he sighs deeply, like he misses my touch already. I sigh in sympathy.

"It's you," he says. "The smell. It's you."

"Me? You think I'm the Monstress?" At first, I'm panicked, and then I'm flattered. She's so powerful and dangerous. Of course I'd never kill an innocent man. But the men she kills are probably not innocent.

I'm the Monstress, I'm the Monstress. I like how the words sound echoing in my head.

"No, of course not!" He sounds scared, uncertain. Like he's convincing both of us. "The smell is on your neck, in your hair."

"The smell made you kiss me?"

"You kissed me."

My brain fogs. I don't know who kissed who.

"You think I'm her," I say.

"Did you just hear me? I don't, I really don't," he says.

Whether he does or doesn't, whether he lies to me or tells the truth, the mood has changed between us. It's tense and awkward. He drives me home and doesn't kiss me again that night.

Our relationship is doomed to end—or fizzle. For the next month, Habeeb isn't able to see me on the weekends. On the weekend he is free, I drive Baba's truck to the town center, where we're less likely to be seen by someone from my neighborhood, someone who knows me. He says he's moving to the city for good. He doesn't ask me to come with him. We pass a man selling roses in the new park at the center of town, where the mayor has chased away beggars and encouraged families to picnic. Leggy rose bushes ring the park. At their peak, they are the rosiest of pinks, with fluffy petals and blooms the size of a small child's fist, and a scent like freshness after a bath. Now they've dropped most of their petals and smell fetid, verging on rotting.

I wonder where the peddler got his bright-red Valentine's roses. He's wearing gardenia garlands around his neck.

"Flowers for your wife!" he calls to Habeeb.

Habeeb talks to the man out of my earshot, hands over a bill, and returns to me carrying a single rose. I thank him, smell the rose deeply. It smells refrigerated and weakly fragrant; it feels cool. It brings to my mind the story of the father and his daughter, the rose, the beast.

I don't want the rose.

As the man passes us, heading toward a family on a blanket, I catch the high scent of gardenia. Is he a good man? Does he treat his wife and children well?

"Would you mind?" I ask Habeeb. "Will you return this rose and trade it for gardenias?"

I've surprised and offended him, and I nearly apologize and retract my request. But Habeeb has already gone and returned with the gardenia garland. He puts it over my head. All evening, till he takes me home, I'm flooded with perfume and regret.

Habeeb and I text from time to time. We're not officially broken up. Susu gets engaged and invites me to her engagement party, the weekend after my twenty-second birthday.

I can't decide whether to go. I don't even know the name of her fiancé. I wait for a sign.

The night before my birthday, I dream of smells and the city. City smells as real and concrete as an object. Rubber and bus exhaust, sewage and smoldering garbage, wild dogs and stray cats, roasting meat and baking bread, excrement, pigeon feathers, night jasmine. And the multilayered fragrance of a perfumery, beckoning me every night with a different scent. In my dream I witness darkness—not a true, black darkness, not the darkness of a night sky lit by stars, but what I will later know is the washed-out darkness of a city. I hear footsteps. Someone's following me, and it's not Habeeb. He smells like dusty rain, mouthwash, and green olive oil soap. My stalker wears a spicy, musky, anti-floral, masculine cologne.

In the morning, I tell my sisters about the dream. They've known about Habeeb since the beginning, have helped me keep him secret from my mother.

"What if dream Habeeb smells different than real Habeeb?" Lajwa says.

I've spent the night at Lajwa's house, and Rana's there too. Lajwa's baby, Kareem, is a toddler now. He's perfumed by milk and bananas with hints of mud and chocolate and new sneaker, not the fresh little baby smell he used to have, not the ripe little boy odor he'll wear by the time he's eight. Something in between, uniquely Kareem. When I wave scent strips under his nose to let him sniff my perfumes, he wrinkles his nose. He'd rather bury his face in a hibiscus on one of our walks, letting the petals tickle his cheeks. He'd rather smell the world around him than a concoction I've made.

My sisters feed me flourless chocolate birthday cake with raspberries for breakfast. The kitchen smells like a cup of cocoa. Lajwa snips mint growing in a pot, and the scent of it floats in the air. She stuffs the leaves into a teapot, pours hot water, and the scent blooms into something sea-weedy, spinachy. I take another bite of cake.

Rana says very few people dream smells. A smell in a dream means death, she says.

"That can't be true. Every smell means something different in waking, why not in dreams?"

I tell Rana about my interpretations of bergamot and lavender, cinnamon and basil, musk and sandalwood. *Contentment, love, home, journeys, lust, hospitality.*

"You made those things up," she says.

She's right. Those are none of the scents from my dream. The smells of my dream say *adventure, into the unknown, what are you thinking, stop dreaming of the city.*

As I'm eating my cake, Susu texts me, asking me to make her a perfume to wear at her engagement party. *You say you'll come visit, but you never do,* she writes. *Make me a perfume, and come to my party.*

I text: *OK.*

The next day, I help Auntie Wardah harvest rose petals and make essential oils out of cinnamon, thyme that grows wild at the edges of her farm, jasmine, gardenia, date palm leaves, and resins collected in the desert. I say I want to concoct something skunky for Susu, a scent that will hint at the complexity of our relationship, the deaths that have punctuated it, the losses.

Auntie Wardah suggests another way. "Make a perfume for the friendship you wish you had, the one you want."

I want a friendship that lasts through anything and combines the best of everything. I mix gardenia and anise, orange blossom and a hint of almond, the tiniest bit of mint. Clove, carnation, musk, and grapefruit. Auntie Wardah brings out a crystal bottle she ordered from the Czech Republic and has saved for a special occasion. It fractures the light, paints a rainbow on the wood of the barn. We funnel in the perfume, carefully package the bottle, and wrap it in tissue paper.

After some back and forth, Habeeb agrees to go to the party with me. I'm excited to go and see the city for myself, but I'm afraid to drive alone. So, Habeeb suggests he can drive to our town to pick me up, and then drive all the way back to the city. OK, I say. We have a plan.

We haven't seen each other in several months. I dress in a gold silk top and pants with no jewelry or make-up, and no perfume other than sandalwood smoke from my father's incense burner. As I'm burning it, waving the scent onto my body, clothes, and hair, the smoke transports me to another place. I'm standing in another room, in another building, in another plane. There is a woman in front of me who looks like Mayyadah, or Susu, or me. She is all of us: Mayyadah's hair and freckles, Susu's eyes, my hands. Her eyes glint like light on a blade.

When my phone buzzes because Habeeb is around the corner from my mother's apartment, waiting, my mind and body do not want to return to the present day. The smell of that other place is the smell of the smoke. It's all over me. It will be with me for several hours.

I make sure there are no other cars or people around before getting into Habeeb's car and kissing him awkwardly on the cheek; he smells like cheap aftershave. Before we head to the city, we go to our favorite roadside restaurant, a place far enough from town that we don't ever see anyone we know. It's shabby and perfect, with plastic tables outside and a small pond bordered with fake-looking rocks. Three bored turtles swim and sun and climb on top of each other; the pond smells like scum and turtle pee. We order a whole chicken and roast potatoes to share. Our meal smells like home, or like the little storefront rotisserie chicken places all over our town. We're outside with turtles, but to me we feel domestic, like we already belong to each other. Habeeb says, "This is nice." He tells me about his roommates in the city, and how one day he'll open his own import shop and sell women's lingerie.

Impulsively, I say, "I think I'm ready to come to the city. To live." I ask if he can get me a job at the department store. They've got an opening in kitchenware, he says, but I want cosmetics, perfumes. He says the only way to get to the city is bit by bit. Dip in a toe, don't wait for the perfect opportunity.

"This is your first visit. You'll see what it's like. Then you'll get an in at the store. Then you'll be a city girl."

"What if the pond is full of turtle crap?" I ask.

"Selling microwaves and toaster ovens is not like swimming with turtles," he says.

When we leave for the city after lunch, I'm still chewing on our conversation. Why won't he arrange for me the perfect job that I want? I think he could, with the people he knows.

I hold Susu's gift-wrapped present on my lap. Habeeb says I look amazing. I'm surprised when he brings up the future. One day we'll live in the city together, have an engagement party like Susu, where we will serve lamb and small fried appetizers.

"I thought you were going to break up with me," I say.

"Why?"

"Because you left."

"I'm making a place for us."

"A place for you."

I'm intent on our talk and I don't notice the scenery; all I see is Habeeb's face. All I feel is a low-level anger—at him for being confusing, at me for being confused and for not being independent enough to drive myself. A part of me wants him to disappear from my life. Maybe even to die. I'm so afraid of that thought I stare at his face and try to love it. I don't notice how the countryside becomes more and more urban, nor do I see the sea straight ahead of us as we turn into the city down a long avenue before turning into a neighborhood of sprawling walled villas.

We're in my dream place and I'm immersed in the city scents and odors, and everything smells the way I dreamed it.

We park around the corner from Susu's flat, in a new neighborhood where sand-colored flats are going up all around. I get out of the car first, clutching Susu's perfume. We are going to Susu's party together, but we will pretend we arrived separately, that I drove with my sister who is visiting relatives in town. We've concocted this ruse because Susu's older relatives might disapprove of an unmarried couple having spent several hours alone together in a car.

Habeeb will wait till I've gone inside before he leaves the car. I'm to text him when I'm inside the party.

All this subterfuge is so stupid, but we do it because we feel we must.

The sidewalk and street are clean and litter-free, but there's a man on the corner winking at me and whistling. Middle-aged, nice-looking but not handsome. He's chewing fragrant luban gum, like my father did.

"Hello darling," he says. "Won't you smile at me? You'll be prettier that way."

My fingers curve into talons. I want to scratch his eyes out.

When I flip him an obscene gesture, he seems to lunge toward me, and I drop the package onto the pavement. The tissue paper doesn't protect the crystal, and it shatters, the smell of the perfume infusing the air. It's skunky and foul; in the barn, it smelled muscular and warm. The lech cusses at me. The smell is all over me now.

"Come on, honey, calm down! I wasn't going to touch you."

"You son of a bitch! My gift is ruined."

Later, remembering what happened, I will wonder if he meant to help clean up the mess I had made. Was he trying to come to my aid? Maybe he truly meant me no harm. But you can never know what's in a man's mind. And all I know is he's standing too close to me now, standing between me and Susu's flat.

I shove him away. I reach for a shard of glass, but before I can pick it up, he groans, "Goddamn you bitch" and lurches forward.

I run. My strappy party sandals pinch, and I'm sure the man is faster than me. He'll grab me, hurt me.

Habeeb's listening to a loud song on his car's stereo, a wedding song about love. I didn't know he liked that sort of old-timey music. He looks enraptured. I hustle into the car, looking to see if the man followed me. I lock the doors. Habeeb smiles and wiggles his shoulders to the music. He mouths, "Why are you back?"

"Take me home," I say. "A man attacked me."

Habeeb turns down the music, asks me to tell him what happened. He listens, and I think he's going to say he's sorry about what the man did, sorry I was scared.

"It sounds like a misunderstanding," he says. "That bastard was being cheeky, but he didn't touch you. He didn't hurt you."

"Because I shoved him."

"You didn't have to do that. You could have walked away."

Habeeb says we should go to the party after I calm down.

"I want to go home."

"We just got here."

I will never forgive him. He drives me back to town. I forget to tell Susu I'm not coming after all, and for years, she doesn't forgive me.

CHAPTER 15

"My Love, My Moon, My Eyes"

Death at a wedding.

At the only wedding hall on this side of town, jasmine bloomed, exuberant and sweet, climbing up the building's corners as though searching for a lover. The honey scent of the blossoms invited you to lick the air with passion and abandon. White lightbulbs strung zig-zagged across the hall's façade; joyful music blared and infiltrated the quiet nighttime streets.

My love, my eyes, my moon, my night.
My love, my moon, my eyes, oh night.
Oh night, oh night, oh night, ohhhh.

You loved that song. You never expected screams to rise above the love lyrics, above the stirring strings of the ballad, in a place of joy and celebration.

Through the screaming, the music went on. No one saw the DJ fall to his knees. Blood everywhere. Her signature.

What kind of animal, what kind of monster, murders at a wedding?

Moments before the chaos, people arrived in ordinary fashion. Cars pulled up and dropped off women in bright dresses, shoulders bare and baby-oiled, others covered in black robes and scarves with a strip of silk or taffeta peeking from underneath. You closed your eyes: The skunk of knock-off perfumes hovered along the guests' path from car door to entryway. Just inside, lamb roasting, rice steaming. The music, louder and louder as you entered, eyes still shut, as though blindfolded by a lover you could follow by scent. Now, you smelled roses; it seemed you were walking over a carpet of them. Every footstep released their scent. *This is the smell of pink*, you thought.

Then the screaming, and a crush of people buffeting you; everyone trying to escape, the hard-sugar smell of candied almonds on their breaths. Now, sweat and fear. More screams and shouts, the brush of fabric against fabric, the music stuck on one phrase: *My eyes, my eyes, my eyes.*

You realized you had not opened your eyes. They wanted to stay shut. You pried your eyelids open, and then wished you hadn't, because they burned, they teared up. You stampeded with the crowd, blinded not by a lover but by a killer.

Later, like the other women who escaped, you would not be able to reveal this: chemicals assaulted you, stung like hot peppers rubbed on your eyes, stung the soft tissue inside your nose, down your nasal passages into your throat and lungs. You—all—rushed to get out into the fresh night air, thinking maybe that would help, and there were too many, the crush of women pulled the oxygen out of the air, squeezed it out of fragile lungs.

Squeezed the life out. At least a dozen women crushed to death.

Incidental deaths, because the true and intended victims were the groom in his wedding robes, dead in his chair, and the tuxedoed DJ at his turntable. The men's eyes gouged, black-rimmed, sockets empty. Mouths open like cyphers. The smell of charred oud. A silver amphora of kohl tipped onto the carpet, its long, thick rod sticky with blood.

The bride hiding beneath the bridal stage, her white dress pouffed around her like meringue or a giant white bin bag, crying till her eyes were nothing but red, kohl paving roads down her face, snot dripping down her décolletage.

"What did you see?" the police asked, her family asked, the whole town wanted to know.

"Nothing," she said, blinded by the gas, not to see again till tomorrow, on her hospital bed, with her family all around her and the beeping of machines. Severe dehydration, the least of her problems. She did not see what happened, but she would have nightmares, dreams her imagination would fill with new horrors every night. The loss of a life with her groom even before she had the chance to live it. She'd fallen in love with him at college; he was engaged at the time, to someone else. She trusted him with her life. Cursed with allergies, she never smelled gardenia on his collar, another woman's perfume. She never wondered where he was at night.

She should have wondered, but in the end, he saved her, though he would die. He told her to hide, shoved her under the stage, both of them going blind with the gas, and he faced the killer without her. Did he know who it was? Was he making amends for secrets he'd never told the bride, things he'd done that he regretted but could hardly admit, even to himself? Truths he would now never have to admit?

And the DJ?

He died for playing love songs in a world that makes love impossible.

"My eyes, my eyes, my eyes."

He died with his hands on the turntable, headset on his ears, hearing only the song he was playing as she appeared from out of the fog to murder him.

CHAPTER 16

Scents and the City

Layla moves to the city and sells perfume.
Terrible news arrives.

I move to the city, finally, at twenty-three. Why has it taken
me so long? Why is leaving the known so hard, even when
I so badly want to leave and never return? I don't know the
answer—maybe I'll never know myself well enough to say.
But here is how the time has gone: It has taken me nearly two
years to decide my father's absence and my fear of strange men
can no longer keep me in town. Then six months to decide I
deserve to move to the city even though I want to avoid running
into Habeeb at all costs; three months to get my perfumers'
certificate online; a month to find a job at a rival department
store to the one where Habeeb works; and an hour to convince
Lajwa to drive me to the city with all my stuff.

I spend no time convincing Mama I should leave. Expecting
her to understand why I'm going would be like explaining the
smell of the underside of a geranium leaf to someone with an
interminable cold. It would be like trying to talk to the dead,
which I once naively believed possible—but no longer do.

I call her from Lajwa's flat, where I've lived for the past year, and tell her, "I'm moving to the city."

She says, "OK. But I won't say goodbye, and I won't visit you there."

She refuses to discuss the issue further. She doesn't believe she can sway me. I don't want her to keep me from leaving, and I should be grateful she doesn't try. But her concession of defeat hurts me. Mama can't bear to see me go, refuses to go to the city, refuses to leave my father's ghost even for a few days, even three years after his passing. She sits in a cloud of sandalwood incense, a scent she made fun of in the past: too old-fashioned, too woodsy, too musty, not clean enough. Now, the stink of sandalwood is all over her house, her clothes, even after she washes them. I can't stand the scent anymore. It no longer brings back memories; it haunts me. I walk into Mama's flat and expect my father to be there. Sandalwood incense is bodily, it lives and breathes and walks through the house in his form. A human smoke-creature. A chimera. It doesn't look like my father; it smells like him. It has horns, hooves, a tail, glaring eyes, a face like the worst man I know. I blink my eyes, and the chimera holds out its hand. It reaches for mine, forces me to greet it with a shake and a kiss to the cheek. When I return to Lajwa's flat, I shower to remove the fatherly scent.

My mother's attachment to the past is not the only, or even main, reason I'm leaving home. Neither is the break with Habeeb, our slow pulling apart that I can finally see as an end. He never returns to town anymore, not even to see me. When did we stop texting, calling, leaving each other voice memos? When did we stop telling each other about our days? Why did he think that after six months of silence between us, he needed to text me when he became engaged to his mother's best friend's daughter, who'd grown up in the city and loved to ride motorcycles with him? Why did he think I cared for so much detail, any detail at all?

I refuse to linger on my grief or his betrayal. I don't want them to become a smoky chimera like Mama's. I want to let my grief over Habeeb dissipate, like a bad scent I wore too much of. Mama's grief and Habeeb's stupidity are incentives. I need new smells, new people, a new life. A new love. A new outlook. After a few years of breathing, our neighborhood has gone back to suffocating. The deaths at the wedding of one of Rana's best friends have pushed the mood to the brink. The situation is direr than ever before. People feel hopeless, helpless, and dozens have left, for the city, for farms, for other countries, for a life at sea. My mother is one of the ones who stay. My sisters have their children and husbands and lives here; my brothers are in college. I tell the boys they can transfer to one of the city's universities and live with me if they want. They don't want to leave my mother, and their determination to be near her fills me with guilt.

When I go to Mama's flat to say goodbye the night before my departure, she says, "I told you I wouldn't say goodbye," then keeps her lips firmly planted together and won't stop shaking her head. She does not seem well. I'm filled with shame.

I look for the chimera. The windows are open. The smoke-creature seems to be gone.

I don't want to leave like this. I hug Mama, and she nearly suffocates me. Now she's holding me at arms' length, looking into my face, sniffling and tutting as she smooths my hair.

She lets me embrace her again; her head shudders against my chest. I ask if I can make us tea.

She peels herself away from me, and I follow her to the kitchen, like a hungry cat at mealtime. She puts the kettle on, fills a large pot with teabags and fragrant mint, even though it's just the two of us. When I try to step in and make the tea for her, she pushes me to the side and hands me a packet of hard, sugary biscuits. I open the packet and put four biscuits on a plate. I carry Mama's silver tea tray, with the teapot and the plate on it, into the living room. We sit, waiting for the tea to steep. When it's done, she pours. Steam rises between us. There is an empty seat next to Mama on the loveseat. She starts to talk about Baba, an alternate version of him, who supported my leaving, who would have wanted me to promise Mama that I will visit her and my siblings often, who wants to be sure I have people in the city to take care of me. Who would have regretted how this town has robbed me of my childhood and any kind of future.

My mother fishes sodden mint out of her tea. I don't know why my mother can't say these things herself. She can only pretend my father would say them.

"You don't know," I say. "You don't know he'd really say those things."

She smiles and rests one hand on the cushion next to her.

"He'd be proud of you. He'd want you to go. He's brought alive when we remember him. Keep him with you."

From a metal bowl on the coffee table, she takes a piece of sandalwood and presses it into my hand. I rub its ridges, bring it to my nostrils, and breathe.

Auntie Wardah tells me that between our town and the city lie large fields of wild lavender and basil. I don't remember them from the time Habeeb drove me to Susu's party. Auntie says I must stop and gather herbs to hang in my new flat, for cleansing good luck. My flat will have the scent of goodness.

So, I pack a pair of shears in my purse, and midway on the drive to the city, I ask Lajwa to stop at a rippling lavender field.

Lajwa rolls her eyes at my preparedness when I take the shears out of my purse. She follows me sheepishly into the brush, holding Kareem's hand. The air is intoxicatingly fragrant, a wild, herby, heady, calming smell. I want to roll in it like a dog. I push Lajwa into the field of lavender and she calls me a bitch, and then I fall next to her and roll. The smell and the breeze must get to her, because she copies me. Our clothes are full of lavender scent, our hair, our skin. My body vibrates with happiness.

I haven't been this joyful in a long time, since before Baba died. Since before Bumbo died.

Kareem watches us like we're crazy. It's a craziness he wants to join.

"Can I do it?" he asks.

In general, he's tentative, has trouble playing on the playground without holding his mother's hand, hates going to school, cries every day when she takes him. Lajwa blames his behavior on the string of murders, on our town's backward reaction. I doubt her interpretation; he's the only child of his generation I know who's become so averse to the outside world. The playgrounds aren't empty; they're full of overbearing parents. Most children don't balk at going to school; they dash out of their parents' arms toward their friends.

The lavender scent brings out Kareem's wildness. He runs

in circles and whoops, falls on his butt and back and rolls. He rubs his face with flowers and sneezes. He radiates joy.

I sit amidst clumps of lavender and breathe. I clip a full bouquet and wrap the stems in tissue from the car, place it on the seat next to Kareem, and tell him not to touch it. He'll listen. He's a good boy.

The rest of the ride, I can't stop smelling myself, lifting my collar to my nose, pulling my hair across my face. I'm as pungent as the bouquet riding in the backseat, maybe more so. The smell of lavender is the best cure for heartache. If Habeeb were here, the mix of my body scent and the scent of the blooms would drive him crazy. I smell my blouse, my forearm, my wrist, the hard edge of my palm.

Lajwa laughs at me. "Those flowers are making you hot for yourself."

I punch her arm. She keeps her eyes on the road.

"You're so weird," she says.

"Try it," I say. "Smell yourself. We smell amazing."

Kareem sniffs loudly. "The flowers smell amazing on us, Auntie," he says, like he's discovered something new about himself. Like his own fragrance has opened a portal to a new world of understanding.

Before we reach the foothills, we see a young guy standing by the side of the road holding a sign that says, "Take me to the city."

"Why is he standing there?" Kareem says.

"I don't know." Lajwa half-turns her head toward her son, keeping her eyes on the road and her hands on the wheel. "I hope he stays safe."

I peer into the side-view mirror and watch the man get

smaller and smaller. From the glimpse I got as we passed, he had a handsome face, strong shoulders. In that moment, I swallowed an urge to roll down the window and holler at him. Something about his ass, or his eyes. To ask my sister to stop the car, pick him up. He's going to the city and so am I. He might be the love I want to meet.

But my sister and I have a child with us, and anyway, it's dangerous to pick up strangers. Even men I know are dangerous.

We go up and through the mountains, wind back down onto the coastal plain, the flat empty desert. I roll down the window and stick my head into a breeze carrying a smell that I hope is oud. Dusk falls like a translucent curtain. Slowly, homes and strip malls appear, and then multiply. I keep my window rolled down. We're inundated with city odors.

I've rented a one-bedroom flat from my friend's uncle, who lives upstairs, a fact that soothes my mother—and me too, I admit. I want to be on my own, but not alone. It's a three-story building on a quiet street near a huge main artery. There are few cars on my street, but the traffic a few blocks away is loud and incessant, all times of day. The building has mirrored windows and balconies all around. Bougainvillea bushes flame with dark pink flowers out front. A couple of flowering trees fan out over the sidewalk. The first floor has a small convenience store and a tailor shop. The foyer welcomes us with onion and garlic aromas.

My flat smells like fresh white paint. The landlord has furnished the place with dark wood and white leather. I brought two suitcases, a laundry basket of books, a box of kitchen items, and four plastic grocery bags of food my mother insisted on sending. I fish out rice, lentils, two onions, a tomato, garlic, cilantro, a hot pepper. Lajwa jabbers about how small the place is, and how tiny the kitchen, and how I should plan to move to a nicer neighborhood next year.

This flat seems fine to me. I'll be spending most of my time at work, or with newfound friends, I tell her.

"I already can't wait to get home," she says. I'm not sure what she hates so much about the city.

Kareem says, "I like it here. I hear trucks."

We dig a saucepan and a knife out of the moving box. Chop onions right on the counter because we can't find a chopping board. Make lentils and rice, browning the onions crisp just like our father used to do. We make hot sauce by hand because we can't find the blender. We rummage for plates and forks, eat on a cloth on the floor. I savor these moments with my sister and her son.

Kareem won't touch his food, so we walk down the street to the main boulevard where green neon winks at us, five kabob shops side by side. Kareem drags his feet and yawns. We should have just tucked him into bed and fed him in the morning, but Lajwa insists he must be fortified now.

My city neighborhood is not only bigger and noisier than my town neighborhood, but also more anonymous. We can disappear into the crowd. No one knows us. I could run naked here and no one would do a thing.

"Bullshit—I mean pish-posh," my sister says, putting her hands over Kareem's ears. "They'd lock you up, and Mama would cry and waste away."

"I'm exaggerating. I'm talking about the freedom not to be gossiped about, watched."

"You can't convince me you should really leave us."

"In six months, if I tell you I'm happy, will you be convinced?"

"Live your life. Stop worrying what I think and asking for my approval."

In the humid and meat-scented night, we are the only women standing in any of the lines. I wish I'd brought a headscarf to drape over my hair, though I don't usually wear one. There are men in flip-flops and rolled-up pant legs, a few men in suits or traditional robes—we can see that rich and poor eat the same food, line up for the same sustenance. Rich and poor stare at us, and a few wink.

"Why are men so unrespectable and disrespectful in public?" Lajwa says loudly.

We choose between the longest line—presumably the most popular and best sandwiches—and the shortest, which represents the fastest way to feed Kareem. I vote for the longest line and try to convince Kareem he wants the yummier choice. I don't believe men's rudeness should keep us from enjoying food. Lajwa drags Kareem and I to the short line, with only one person ahead of us. I order fries and eat most of them on the way home, sharing with Kareem, who also can't wait.

Just before we turn the corner to my building, some men I recognize from the line overtake us. One of them makes a lewd noise and Lajwa explodes.

"How dare you assault me while I'm with my son," she says.

"Go away," Kareem says quietly.

"We love children," one of the men says. "You're a lovely young man."

Drugs are forbidden in the city, and alcohol is only allowed in hotels. I smell something on their clothes and breath. I wonder where they've been.

Lajwa has her fists up, like she wants to fight. I want to believe the men are just annoying and harmless, but what do I know? How can we tell if someone intends to hurt us, or might hurt us incidentally, accidentally, or without forethought?

"Ignore them," I say—to my sister about the men, to the men about my sister and nephew. I never told her about the man who accosted me and prevented me from going to Susu's engagement party. I want this feeling of threat building in my gut to disappear. I want to run, but we're better off walking calmly. I lead my sister and nephew past our turn, intending to loop around the long way. The men don't follow us. The dark of the night is dulled by streetlamps, and crickets' voices clamor from somewhere. How are they loud and yet invisible in their hordes? The sound of music and laughter drifts from an open balcony door. Incautiously, I do a little dance as I walk, and Kareem skips a little, and my sister watches us with affection. Her love for us is as fragrant as roses at the height of summer.

My flat is a refuge, but also cut off from the beauty of the night. We settle Kareem into a sleeping bag next to the sofa where Lajwa will sleep.

My sister says, "I worry about you, here alone. Walking around the neighborhood with scum like that lurking in corners."

"I'll be fine," I say. "If you're worried about me, stay a few days."

She won't stay longer. She hates everything I love about the city.

"There's no local culture here," she says, feet on the couch's armrest, drinking a cup of warm milk with turmeric before bed. "No community feeling. Everyone in their separate flats. No one knows each other."

"You're judging based on only having met those skeezy men."

"That's my point," she says. "I've seen enough."

After Lajwa and Kareem leave the next morning, I revel in my independence and solitude. I sit on the balcony, on my one plastic chair, which I've lugged out from the living room, and do nothing. Bougainvillea climb the walls and spill over the edges of the balconies. The fiery blooms have no scent, unlike the bushy gardenia and creeping jasmine vines that adorn the building across the way. I will learn over the next few days that if I keep my windows open, the scent of jasmines and gardenias will wake me in the morning.

I drive to work in the small white coupe with the broken headlight that my landlord lends me because he thinks it's safer than taking the bus alone as a woman in the city. It takes me one day to learn he's dead wrong. Driving here is not like driving at home, whizzing down empty streets, passing your neighbors, everyone on their best behavior because the person you cut off knows your mother. Here, I'm dodging through traffic, stuck in jams, bumper-to-bumper, getting honked at constantly, cussed out, fingers and fists waving at me out the windows of cars, their owners invisible. The whole city hates me.

I try not to hate it back. I want to love it here. In the beginning, I do. In the beginning, I feel more alive here than I ever did at home. When does that change? When do I start to hide in the shadows?

On my first day, I arrive at work frazzled. The store is on a quiet street fringed with trees. Women with expensive handbags stroll in and out of little boutiques. They don't need perfume; they smell like money. I've forgotten to wear lipstick, which makes me self-conscious in front of the assistant perfumery manager, a woman in a headscarf with a thin strip of hennaed hair exposed. She has bright-red lips, eyes kohled like a Nabatean goddess. She wears a sophisticated scent I can't place. Notes of honey, cardamom, orange blossom, sandalwood, and oud. She's young, unmarried, lives with her parents, and has quickly been promoted at the store. She doesn't think I'm a bumpkin, she promises me, but I'm certainly not urban. People in the city lie to you about lying to you; they say to your face what they think and instantly deny it. I will encounter this truthful dissembling not only with the Nabatean Goddess, but also taxi drivers who say I remind them of their daughters and then hit on me, the store manager who says we are free to do as we like outside the store and then asks us if we have boyfriends, inquires about our menstrual cycles, and tells us to eat less bread and rice. A grocery clerk who says I shop like a country girl, but there's nothing wrong with that. My landlord, who says I will never be safe here and pretends to care for my safety.

During my training, Nabatean Goddess spritzes the air and says, "This is how we hook customers." She likes to get them with something gaudy, and then introduce them to better, more sophisticated, less hackneyed smells. She says we have to sell at a range of price points to make the best commission. The most popular, populist scents are not necessarily the most expensive, she explains. The most expensive shit smells like . . . She grins.

"A lot of the good stuff has more than a hint of fecal, of sweat gland, of plastic," she says. "Like jasmine."

She grimaces when I show her my perfumer's certificate.

"You're that kind of girl," she says. "You think you're an artist."

I don't think, I know. I say, "I've made perfumes for years with my auntie."

"Your *auntie*," she says, emphasizing the word. "You haven't trained with a real perfumer."

Over the next few weeks, my mantra becomes, "Stop caring what Nabatean Goddess thinks." I like others who work the counter better.

There is Nur, a young man with a slim mustache and a collection of beautiful leather loafers. He's a former soccer player who couldn't make it as a model because of his temper, but has the humility to walk the floor. We wear similar clothes on purpose and spritz ourselves with the same scent. We're friends, and he might be gay, something he can't talk about at the store.

Umaymah brings her cat to work in a backpack and feeds her bits of tuna all day. Mysteriously, the Goddess never hears the cat's mews.

Najma wears kohl drawn all the way to her hairline. She upsells every customer, selling them the most expensive perfumes: mixes of dozens of essences, top-quality ambergris and oud in one bottle, packaging made of Baccarat crystal. Even people who can't really afford the price tags want one luxurious thing to take home, she says. Like driving an opulent car.

I like to sell simple scents. Rose and orange, strongly piney fragrances, the most basic frankincense. Many scents can be cheap or expensive: jasmine and rose, even amber and oud. People with undeveloped noses can't tell the difference.

Nur and I try to guess what customers might like: candy

sweet or woodsy, acidic or animalic, bitter or soft, flat or sharp. There is not one clothing style or body type or age or gender that likes one type of fragrance or the other. We have to look at the whole package of the person, how they walk, the way they're talking to their companions, whether they're friendly to department store staff or haughty or shy, the way they carry their purses, the squeak or clack of their shoes on the marble floor. All these things suggest to me what someone will like, and determine what I put on their wrists or under their noses first. The first scent is a ruse to get closer to the customer. I want to smell them, get as close to their skin, their neck, their armpits as I can without being creepy, without them stepping aside because I'm too close. Each person's individual funk tells me what they should be wearing, as opposed to what they like to smell. I have to think fast, imagine quickly what special scent I would mix for them, and then find the brand and bottle that is closest to my perfect match.

Some customers want the fragrance they've worn since they were twelve. I'll sell it to them, but I'll talk about my vision for a perfect scent for every person, every moment of their day, every fluctuation of their natural odor.

Most customers aren't listening.

My manager, a foreigner named Lloyd who wears a different quirkily patterned bowtie every day, tells me to tone it down. Sell the perfumes we carry, not the ideal philosophy of perfume, he says. He says fragrance is a luxury available at any price point. Whatever perfume is almost more than the customer can afford is luxurious to them.

He doesn't understand that fragrance is freedom.

I tell him, "If the people who come into the store every day were to wear the right perfume, they'd be liberated from their daily mundanity."

He laughs at me. "Right," he says, pulling at the one lock of hair that seems to have escaped his overabundance of hair gel. "Their 'daily mundanity' having nothing to do with having money or not, with the government, with world politics."

"Don't you believe in art?" I say.

"Perfume's not art, it's commerce," he says. "We sell lipstick too, and mascara, and cold cream. No one really needs any of it, but they want it. Our job is to make them want it."

You don't need any of this. Lloyd would fire us if we expressed such a blatant truth to a customer. He's manager because he was once top seller.

Despite the pressures of selling, I find small moments of joy in smelling the perfumes. I aim to smell every single perfume we carry and be able to name every one of its notes. I keep a notepad in my pocket. During slow times, I inhale a scent and write about it. My favorite perfumes are woodsy and floral, or strong and leathery, or sweaty and pure.

At first, I never say no to Nur and Najma's pleas for me to go with them to dinner or a coffee shop or a poetry reading or a movie. When Nur and Najma's friends ask where I'm from, I pretend I grew up here. Nur and Najma know it's not true, but I keep lying, and the more I lie, the more I believe I'm an urban girl who's used to traffic and smog and crowds and anonymity. Then we go to a rooftop party, and the sight of the lift floods me with panic. My heart races and I want to run. I grip Nur's hand, squeeze his knuckles like pebbles in my fist. As the lift rises, I close my eyes and imagine I'm—

I can't return home. That's where a father was murdered in a lift.

"Are you OK?" Nur says. "Is it claustrophobia?"

"Not used to heights," I say. I visualize the hitchhiker my sister and I passed on the way to the city. I convince myself I have a little crush on him. We only saw him for a moment, but maybe I'll run into him on the streets of the city. Stranger things have happened.

After several months of going out every night, I'm exhausted. I say no till my coworkers stop asking. Alone in my flat, I eat rice, boiled chicken, and a quartered tomato. I watch stray cats from my balcony and dream about rescuing one. I have my eye on a little white scruffy kitty with an orange patch over the right side of her face, green eyes that glow brighter than any of the other cats' eyes, and a habit of attacking the biggest toms. If they try to steal her food in their goofy, entitled way, she smacks them across the eyes and keeps eating. She would be a perfect companion, but she's too feral to rescue.

I need something to do in my spare time.

I turn my bedroom into a perfumer's workshop and sleep on the couch. I salvage a door from the curb and lay it across the bed to make a worktable. Nur and Najma help me carry home an abandoned bookshelf, which I use to store the vials of essences I use every bit of my savings to buy online. I name the green-eyed cat Bal, for the ancient queen Balqees, and I make a fragrance inspired by her. It is built on an amber aroma—which too many people confuse with ambergris—made up of labdanum and benzoin resin, for her ginger marks, and mossy hints for her eyes. I want it to be fierce yet playful. I give a vial each to Nur and Najma. After that, they sample all my creations. They want me to start my own business, sell my perfumes online, but I don't want to lose the fun of creating fragrances for myself and my friends. I send vials to my sisters, to show how much I miss them. When I'm not perfuming, I'm falling into a deep hole of aloneness. Some days, that's all I have energy for.

There have been no murders at home since I left. I'm grateful. My brothers are old enough now to be potential victims. I invite them to live with me in the city, but they don't want to leave Mama. They're right to want to protect her, I say, but my sisters are in town, and aren't two siblings enough to take care of our mother? What about me? Don't my brothers want to keep me company?

"Come home," they say.

Life continues. A couple of years pass. Bassam gets married to his college sweetheart, and I miss the wedding because I have to work that weekend. I pretend to be mad about it, but I'm glad not to have to face aunties wishing for me to be the next to marry.

As fate would have it, that weekend a woman comes into the store.

I've seen her here before, but never waited on her. She's the type of rich who doesn't need expensive things; her affluence is broadcast by the perfection of her skin and hair and her exquisitely fresh but neutral scent. She's not beautiful or even very compelling or charismatic. But she clearly doesn't struggle against the world. She coasts, she floats. Today, her teen daughter is with her.

"Your turn," Nabatean Goddess says. "They never buy anything." Every time they come to the store, they sample six, ten, a dozen fragrances. She suspects they smell our wares and then order them more cheaply online.

"That's not fair," I say.

"It's brilliant," says Nabatean Goddess.

I greet the mother and daughter, and the mother tells me the daughter is getting married. The young woman is either older than I thought, or marrying extremely young.

"May you be next," the mother says, a sweet and condescending sentiment.

The daughter wears pure-gold chandelier earrings and a thick gold bracelet, a golden chain-link belt. These are traditional things that have recently come back in vogue. I show them a perfume that is flecked with gold and combines the fragrances of citrus, geranium, ylang ylang, fig, jasmine, and mandarin. I tell them we're stingy with samples of such a rich perfume and put the tiniest amount on the daughter's wrist. The moist millimeter of skin sparkles. They decide to buy a bottle for the bride-to-be and tiny spray bottles for her closest friends.

The girl says that for the groom, they want something rosy and masculine at the same time. I tell her about the roses Auntie Wardah grows, about her perfect rose amber perfume.

"Her name is Wardah? That can't be real."

Why have I never thought of selling Auntie Wardah's scents here? People like this mother and daughter might pay a lot of money for authentic, natural perfumes, for perfumes connected to the traditions of our country, for a rose nurtured by our soil and our air, even if that soil and air belongs not to the *country*, really, but to the people who have farmed the villages and the *countryside*. I tell the mother and daughter to come back, promising I'll have a sample next week.

When Lloyd hears I sold them one of our most expensive perfumes and smells Auntie Wardah's amber rose, he agrees to carry her perfumes—with a large mark-up. Within two months, Lloyd announces that Wardah's Notes have become our top sellers. Nur and Najma want to take me to celebrate at a late-night concert by a local punk-folk-lute band, in a dark concert space that smells like sweat and apple tobacco. It's the first time I've gone out with them in over a year, and I'm anxious. At least a half dozen times, I decide to tell my friends I'm staying home, and then change my mind. I should go. I'll have fun. I don't want to have fun. I don't know who I am anymore in this city. I'm a perfumer and nothing else. Not a daughter or sister. An inconsistent friend. I drive to the club. Nur and Najma wait outside, beaming when they see me.

"We thought you wouldn't come," Nur says.

The crowd glows with light-stick necklaces and bracelets, and people wave their arms in a trance. Strangers lay their heads on my shoulders and pet my hair. I lock arms with my friends and sway. I have never set foot in a place so humanly beautiful. I'm joyful, content. I've been here forever, surrounded by people with love-filled bodies. No one here would ever hurt me or each other.

Back in my apartment, the feeling doesn't last. I have dreams in which I forget my name, in which I drive home and my town is gone.

The next day, Lloyd suggests I go home to tell Wardah the good news and give her an advance from the store, so she can make new fragrances. At first, I say no. My dreams from the night before are fresh, real. What if nothing is left of my town?

Lloyd doesn't understand why I would refuse to go. He'll pay for my travel. He hints at the possibility of a promotion.

Nur tells me I'm stupid if I don't go. So, I make arrangements with my mother to stay at home, and with Wardah to visit the farm. On the weekend, I drive the landlord's jalopy to my town, leaving first thing in the morning. Nur comes with me to keep me company, and because he's been dying to meet Wardah. It's a work trip, he says. No one should find fault with us traveling alone together.

He's right. No one criticizes us or looks askance—because everything is falling apart.

We drive to the farm first. Uncle and Wardah are in the farmyard, and he's yelling, his face a wall of anger. I've never seen him so red. I tell Nur to stay in the car, and as I get out, I shout a greeting, so Uncle won't be surprised.

Wardah is crying. Uncle is surprised to see me.

"We've come to give Auntie Wardah good news!" I get Nur from the car, introduce him, and rummage in my bag for the letter from Lloyd. But Uncle doesn't want to hear what I have to say.

"Go home to your mother," he tells me.

I look at Wardah. She nods. I tell her I'll be back tomorrow.

"Something's very wrong," says Nur when we're back in the car. A rooster is crowing. Auntie Wardah and Uncle have disappeared from the yard.

There's a lull in the strangeness that evening. We spend the night at my mother's, my sisters and brothers come over for dinner, and they tease Nur as though he is one of us. Everything's perfect.

The next morning, before we head to the farm, Auntie Wardah texts me.

"Safe travels home," the message says.

"The meeting is off," I tell Nur. We drive home. We don't talk about what happened at the farm. It's the height of winter, and the lavender fields are well past their bloom.

Just as I drop off Nur at his apartment, my phone buzzes against my butt in my back pocket.

I look, and then can't look away. My sister has texted that the farmer is dead—most likely a victim of the Night Killer.

How is that possible?

He was visiting his grandson at the hospital

Murdered at the hospital?

No—in the parking lot

The only one killed?

Yes

I just saw him yesterday afternoon.

. . .

Why him?

They say . . . you're going to be upset

Tell me

He beat his wife

No

That's what they say

Auntie Wardah? How could I not have known?

Maybe it's not true

Has anyone spoken to her?

You're the best one to do it. You should call her

I should have known. I should have known. He was yelling at her. Of course he beat her.

At the store that day, I can't bring myself to sell Wardah's perfumes to customers. Telling her story helps me sell her perfumes, but I can't tell the whole story now. Mentioning her husband's murder seems obscene; I'm reeling from the news. Thank God it's Nur's day off, and I don't have to tell him what happened. At lunchtime, my mother and Lajwa call me. They tell me to come home to visit Wardah during the mourning period.

"I was just there. I can't skip work. Has she asked for me?"

"No, but Layla, she's got so much grief, so many things to take care of."

"I'll think about it."

I ask Nabatean Goddess for a day off. I tell her Wardah's husband has been murdered.

"Oh," she says. "Oh. Poor woman."

I see a glimmer of humanity in Nabatean Goddess that I haven't seen before.

"She might be relieved," I say. "Relieved that he's dead."

"I'm sure she's devastated," says Nabatean Goddess.

"I hear he beat her."

Nabatean Goddess adjusts her scarf and touches my shoulder. "Are you OK? You knew him. It sounds like you trusted him."

I pick up a sample bottle and spray its fragrance into the air. The scent soothes me. The Nabatean Goddess breathes in too, and then her lips turn down and her brows squinch. Something has occurred to her. She's thinking. We are in a dark well of scent and silence, and Nabatean Goddess decides she must pull us out of it. When you come out of a hole, it's never graceful. You tumble, you scramble, you trip. We do that together now, her voice the rope that pulls me up, her hand holding mine.

"Do you think she...wanted him dead?" Nabatean Goddess says. "Do you think she's glad he's gone?"

She's whispering. A loved one's death being the only way for their victim to be free and happy is not something we should speak of.

I dust myself off, metaphorically. I'm standing tall.

"I wish I'd killed him," I say. "I wish I'd been the one to save her."

I expect Nabatean Goddess to be shocked and tell me I shouldn't say such things.

She puts her arms around me. "The bad ones deserve whatever they get," she says. "Whatever the case, your friend needs your comfort. Of course, you can take the time to go home this weekend."

When my shift ends, I walk to a park nearby, where there's a bench across from a fountain, a place I can think. The phone in my hand buzzes. There's a text from Susu, whom I haven't heard from in ages. She's just had a baby. The naming ceremony will be this weekend.

She never told me she was pregnant.

I think Susu, by inviting me, wants to make a gesture of reconciliation. Of grown-up friendship.

Be there for sure! I write.

My life is here, not back home. I owe Wardah a lot, but for flowers to keep growing, you have to deadhead the wilted ones.

Children play in the fountain, running around in their

underwear with dripping hair and goofy smiles and silly wobbles and foot splashing.

Auntie Wardah answers on the first ring.

"So sorry for your loss," I say. "So sorry I can't make it
home."

CHAPTER 17

Road Rage

Death of a hitchhiker.

If only the young man had listened to his grandmother, who'd read in his coffee grounds years ago that he would die enflamed. He would perish from his own folly.

"Both?" he'd asked. "Are you saying I immolate myself?"

"I'm telling you, 'Steer clear of strange women.'"

Everyone agreed her fortunes never made sense, but still her family, friends, and neighbors let her tell her tales and fill them with dread. Her grandson tucked her premonition in the breast pocket of his mind, like a pen or a note on a slip of paper, but never let it keep him away from cigarettes, joints, bonfires, hot women, sweaty nights.

He was on his way from town to the city, to spend a weekend with friends and see his darling, Muna, a girl he'd met visiting the city a few months ago. He'd had a car, and last week it had broken down, and all the friends with cars had driven away for good now, moved to the city forever. No one was left to give him a ride.

He'd never hitchhiked before, but he wasn't afraid of strangers and he had no other option, so he decided to do it. When the electric blue roadster pulled up, he almost thought the driver was her—his girl from the city. The long black hair, the black dress. Unlike the girls he knew in town, who wore bright colors—lipstick red, tangerine, mulberry, deepest pink—Muna only wore black. But especially, when he got inside the purring car, the smell reminded him of her. A rose perfume just like the one that clung to her pulse.

He got in, slid his arm over the driver's shoulder like he knew her, like she *was* his girl. Her neck was warm, and she flinched and giggled. She was ticklish, just like Muna, whose name stayed on the tip of his tongue the whole ride. He would not say her name out loud while he rode with another woman. He was just hitching a ride, didn't mean anything by it, although he'd parked his arm on her shoulder, touched her skin, smelled her rosy scent, imagined biting her swirly shell of an ear.

The beautiful driver asked what he did for a living, and he said he shoveled muck for a farmer with a single donkey and a dozen chickens, a guy who could hardly pay for his services. The factory had shut down and there was nothing much else to do. Except move to the city.

"Why don't you?"

She braked to a stop, in the middle of the road. They were outside town, where green dotted the brown of the valley, still on the local roads, not yet on the highway to the city. She leaned over to sniff his neck.

"You smell like a girl—like you've been with a girl."

He touched her thigh then. Its wiry muscularity gave him a thrill. Now he smelled something animalic about her. A leathery, floral scent.

"I know what they say about me." She touched his head, moved her fingers into his mouth. The taste of her skin stunned him with lust. "They say I seduce men at night. With my scent, and my hair."

When she pulled her fingers out of his mouth, longing took their place. She licked his spit off her fingers and shook her hair over her shoulders, like a model. He caught a jasmine whiff, a hint of cinnamon and vanilla, and something more ominous. Soot, blood?

She clutched his face with two wet hands and squeezed. He didn't know why he couldn't move.

"They say I'm not all human. Knives for hands, donkey legs." She let go of his jawline, wiggled in her seat. "A tail, even. I'm hiding it from you, right?"

He nodded. He felt a bit bold, disgusted and turned on at the same time by the vision of an ass's bottom on this beautiful woman. He'd never considered such a fantasy before: a truly animal woman. Her lashes were thick as a camel's lashes, her hair coarse and thick like fur. Her teeth were squared off and equine.

It wasn't true that she had donkeys' legs, he could see that.

He played along. "Show me," he said. His hand slid back to her thigh, as close to her rump as he could get while she was seated behind the wheel. She playfully slapped it away.

"They don't even believe the stories they tell. They tell them to scare children. Teenagers. Young men and women. The scare tactics don't work. You go out at night. Meet girls in the dark. Your girl puts on make-up, perfume, parades herself in front of other men. Children will be children, right?"

What was she talking about? He couldn't move.

247

She put the car into gear, pressed the gas, and they shot forward.

"What's happening?" He laughed. It seemed like a joke, this woman driving him to see his girl. He should have taken the bus.

The woman flashed two obscene fingers at him. "You know I'm going to kill you, right? And you got in the car anyway."

He didn't know, though. He'd never suspected a woman could overpower him, could inflict violence on him. It was his job to hurt *her*, wasn't it?

"First I f____ you, then I kill you." She swallowed all but the first consonant of the vulgar word. "Like all the others who've been with me."

With great effort, he reached into his pocket for his phone.

"Call for help. It'll never come. Try to videotape me, and I'll vanish from the recording before anyone sees it."

Were there drugs in her perfume? His head reeled, his stomach roiled, and an invisible fog enveloped him. Moisture beaded on his skin. The car sped faster and faster. To the right, the road dropped off into a copse of evergreens. He lunged for the steering wheel. Her hands raised, glinting. They were blades now, fingerless, threatening, the most frightening thing he'd ever seen. They hurtled toward his face, his chest, his groin. The pain galloped over him like a herd of donkeys. Is that what you called them? A herd? Where had the blades come from? How had she stabbed him while driving? How had she kept the car from swerving off the road?

She was so beautiful. Her scent had perverted his mind.

She was not driving anymore. The car lifted itself off the road and into the valley—or maybe, an army of wadi jinn lifted

it—and twisted them into burning metal, into fire. As he was
dying, burning to death, screaming in the worst pain of his life,
he knew she would walk away, leaving hoofprints and a sickly
floral scent that made you horny even in the face of death.

The stories were true.

CHAPTER 18

Heart Notes

Layla goes to a party, falls in love.

When I get to this part of my story, I spiral. I'm flung around and around a tornado's eye, an absence of *something*. Too afraid to pinpoint what that something is. I can't think chronologically, logically. Then, I stop, listening to an uncanny silence, a pressure in my ears. I'm trying to forgive myself. So, bear with me as I return to the beginning.

In my first memory of Susu, we're hanging upside down from the monkey bars on the playground, skirts held between our knees, our ponytails brushing each other's faces. Our hearts are innocent, our minds and spirits free. One of us falls and scrapes her palms and knees. Am I the one who falls, or is it Susu? The memory goes one way or the other. Other, earlier moments we shared hide in nooks and corners of my mind, under mounds of thoughts like piles of dirty clothes, stacks of unwashed dishes. My thoughts, like my flat, have become a mess the longer I'm away from my mother and sisters, with their meticulous tidiness and their refusal to wallow. My hidden memories might emerge if I talked to my mother about Susu.

Memories of a time before the murders, before Susu's father died, before our town's grief and horror sunk our childhoods into the ground and buried us alive. I call my mother most nights, but we never discuss the past, as though mentioning it would allow it to haunt us. We talk about what's happening now and what might happen in the future. We speak in questions.

My mother: How is work? When are you coming home?

Me: How is home? When are you coming to visit me in the city?

My mother: When will you get married?

Me: When will you teach me the recipes I love?

After I tell Susu I'll come to her daughter's party, I waffle, as is my habit where social events are concerned. Susu and I are not really friends, have seen each other only a few times since I moved, at parties and gatherings and group movie outings. I suspect she has not forgiven me for skipping her engagement party. I still feel guilty, even four years later, and I'm a bit surprised to have been invited to her daughter's mawlid. I guess she's forgiven me enough to want me at her daughter's special event. We're both twenty-five—and in completely different moments in our lives. I'm floating, alone, still trying to find my bearings after several years in the city, living in the same small apartment, working at the same job. She's established as a wife, and now a new mom, settled in a small villa with a walled garden in a row of small villas behind walls. White marble, a bit modern, on a street lined with bushy jacaranda and almond trees. Her husband, Arham, is a civil engineer who smells like pistachios and organizes card nights once a month. I want to be friends with Susu the way we used to be, but I don't think I deserve Susu's friendship. And I've lost the ability to ask for the things I want, the way I did when I was seven and I wanted a donkey.

I ask Umaymah what to do. She says, "You don't have to ask for Susu's friendship. She's offering it to you. Go to the party. Stop overthinking and being such a shut-in."

"I'm not a shut-in," I say. "I just don't like people very much after I've spent all day here, catering to rich people."

I've worn a bob for years, but now I have this flash of myself with long hair, showing up at a party like Mayyadah in costume, dressed to kill. This version of me spends time alone not because she distrusts people, but because they fear me. They warn their children about me. They say I lurk in the dark, when really, I'm at home watching YouTube and mixing fragrances.

"Stop being a misanthrope, then, and go to the party," Umaymah says. "Maybe you'll meet the love of your life."

Some people have the gift of foresight. I've never been able to see the future.

OK, I tell Umaymah. I'll ignore my shame, be a big girl, and go to the party.

The day of the party, I wear a long, traditional-style dress with a transparent overlay. It makes me feel elegant and stylishly old-fashioned. On my skin, rose perfume, not from Wardah, but my own concoction using her essences. I spritz a little more on my pulse points after getting out of the rideshare, as I stand on the sidewalk checking the address one more time. It's mid-afternoon, a hot day. I immediately want to get back in the air-conditioned car—to escape the heat and the party. No chance, though; the driver has sped off to his next job. I steel myself for the party by smelling my own scent. It's satisfying. The top notes will linger long enough for the people I meet here to catch them. They'll think I'm seductive. As the afternoon goes on, my scent will mature. They won't be able to figure me out.

When I walk into the flat, the chatter of children and parents signals I've entered an unfamiliar country. Susu's mother greets me at the door, takes my handbag and sets it on a bench, and steers me around the room, introducing me to people. She pats my cheek and calls me "Susu's oldest friend."

Susu, her mother, and her sisters are the only people I know at the party. They're the only people here who've been to our town, who know the violence we've experienced there. In that way, they're like me. But they left after the second murder. Which means: They don't know how ingrained the fear is. Should I take into account the fact that their husband and father was murdered, that they live with that every day? Because I avoid talking to them about our town or the murders, my view of them has calcified. I won't try to change it.

Susu's mother runs off to see if Susu and the baby are ready, and I stand alone, not driven to talk to any of the people I just met. A streaming music channel plays pop versions of traditional children's songs. The baby sleeps in another room. Soon, she'll be paraded out to the sound of drumming and children singing out of tune.

A young man my age with a round face hovers at the food table, scooping hummus onto a paper plate. He looks up and smiles like the moon.

My heart tells me he's the reason I'm here.

Susu appears and kisses me on both cheeks. "I didn't think you'd come," she says.

"Of course I came."

She sees Hani standing patiently to the side, not eating his hummus.

"You haven't met before, have you?" she says.

"No." His eyes on me. I examine the olive oil rivulets on his hummus.

Susu introduces us, winks, and excuses herself.

We chit-chat. He glows from within. I blink against his light, then stare straight into it. From time to time, his nostrils flare slightly. My perfume has invaded him. Standing over the food table, getting a second helping of finger foods, he takes a deep breath, as though he's never smelled anything like me before. He puts his plate down and leans in. The gesture is a little bit impolite, a little bit flattering.

"I don't usually notice perfumes—is it rude to tell a girl she smells nice? Is it creepy?"

"No. I'm a perfumer."

"You smell nice."

He's surprised when I say I designed my perfume myself. I tell him about the department store. He listens, like I'm the most normal and interesting person in the world.

Hani's carefree, smiles easily, and talks like he has nothing to hide. I used to be like that, I think. When he tells me he's never worn cologne—which makes him unusual among young men in this city, most of whom bathe themselves with chemical fragrances—his shoulders hunch a little with embarrassment, like he doesn't want to offend me. He uses the blandest soap possible, he says. And smells like nothing, or so he claims. I catch a bit of garlic and coriander wafting from his skin, mild perspiration, not funky. A hint of spearmint chewing gum. Plastic. The faded mint of toothpaste.

He's friends with Susu's husband, grew up in the city, and now he lives on a different side of town. He speaks of moving from one neighborhood to another as though he has made a migration of enormous consequence, a move halfway round the world.

"The restaurants are shinier where I live now, the food is arranged just so on the plates. The people are stodgier. They don't let children play football in the street."

I tease him. "The sun rises earlier and sets later."

He accepts the ribbing as though I've gifted him a watch or a bottle of cologne. "Exactly," he says. "And when children sing for rain, it falls immediately and tastes like lemonade."

Children are singing now. Baby tied to her body, Susu leads the parade of smoothly brushed heads and stiff party clothes around the food table and through the rooms of the house where people have gathered. Later, when her husband lullabies the baby to sleep for the night, and Susu's mother and sisters have left, and Hani has reluctantly waved one beautiful hand to me in farewell, Susu and I drink tea at the kitchen table. I scorch the top of my mouth, which reminds me to fear both new and familiar things.

"You like Hani," Susu says with an air of propriety, like she owns our friendship and can say what other people might dance around or try to ease out of me. She doesn't have to ask if I like him; she tells me I do. I feel myself falling back into place as her sidekick, the less-knowing of the two of us, even though in some ways I'm the more experienced one now. I've escaped the rut she's in: early marriage, early motherhood. I'm the pioneer.

She's right. I like Hani.

I don't want to admit it. "I'm afraid of him."

"He's harmless as a fly."

"I meant, I'm afraid of men."

"All men?"

"You don't know when you first meet someone whether you should be afraid. Some of them are mosquitoes, fleas, poisonous spiders, wasps."

"I suppose."

I don't tell her I'm not only afraid of men as a category of being. I'm afraid, also, of my anger at men. Fearful of the person I found myself becoming that long-ago day when I didn't go to her engagement party.

Susu asks about the store, my job, my family, our hometown. I'm holding back, not wanting to mention Wardah and her husband, and then, like it's a joke, Susu says, "Any more murders?"

The flippancy in her voice shakes me and hardens me into a position. "No," I say. Telling her about the farmer and Wardah would be too much, too complicated, too emotional. I used to tell her everything. But we were children then. We're adults with secrets now.

My suspicion—that the town and its murders and its ill-behaving men are in me more than they are in her, even with her family at the heart of the story—burrows deeper into my belly and leaves an ache there. My fears are cellular, and whatever the spiritual equivalent may be; they are the building blocks of my being and unbeing. What if I had been born in a different town or in the city? Or if my parents had packed us into the pickup and moved beyond our mushroom of a town? What if the first man hadn't been murdered? Or the second and third and so on? Or what if the police had solved the crimes, or the town had reacted differently? Had embraced us children instead of punishing us for the violence of adults? Would I be a different Layla? Would I still live near my mother and sisters and brothers?

What if the men of our town had been perfect and kind? What if I'd been born into freedom or had learned to savor the moments I had, instead of struggling to believe freedom is real?

Susu rinses dishes and loads the dishwasher, her back to me now. It feels rude, the way she won't look at me. Not being confronted with her deeply familiar face, her eyes that see me as others don't, I'm emboldened.

"What if your father hadn't been killed? Do you ever wonder?"

She turns around, leans against the sink, and wipes her wet hands on her skirt. "I'm glad my family got away from there. From the evil that people accept as though they have no choice."

"Evil is anywhere, everywhere."

"Sure," she says, and I want to kick her for not taking me seriously. "That's why we should run toward the good in life, toward joy. Don't you think? I'll give Hani your number. Unless you say no."

If our town had been different, the stress on my father's heart might not have been what it was, and he might have lived. I might have stayed closer to Auntie Wardah's roses. She might have married a better man. I might have fallen in love with one of the boys from school. I might never have met Bumbo, never have needed to covet a donkey. Freedom might have been a winged creature I could truly imagine.

I might not be here, now, in Susu's kitchen. Or we might be in a different Susu's kitchen, with a different friendship.

*   *   *

A week later, Hani and I meet for coffee. We talk for hours. About me and my interests: perfume; florals, citrus, spices, herbs, animalics, resins; the difference between top notes, heart notes, and base notes; my nephew; my father's death. We talk about Hani: his job at a bank; his love of the guitar and inability to play it; his love of the lute and inability to play it; his father's superior musicianship; his mother's mathematical genius; football; the meaning of life. We talk about siblings. We talk till blush tints the sky. Not like we've known each other forever, but like we want to know each other forever, must know every detail of each other's lives, thoughts, and feelings until now. There cannot be a day ten years from now when one of us says, "Why have you never told me that before?" Though of course, we can't talk about everything in one afternoon. I don't talk about the murders in my hometown. Or skeezy men who cat-call me in the city. Those aren't things he needs to know about. Yet.

Around us, other young couples converse and discreetly make eyes at each other. Maybe they're newlyweds, maybe not. Soft, young hands on their coffee cups, their forks and spoons; eyes on each other, but bashfully, not too brazenly. Couples come here because our conversations stay private amid the steamy hiss of the espresso machine, baristas calling orders, folksy pop music on the sound system, the swirling babble of small talk and deep talk. The husband-and-wife owners of this place, a little older than me and Hani, don't mind women and men mingling. They let us break the city's unspoken rules about the propriety of two people eating together. The husband has the tiniest bit of salt in his peppery hair. The wife dresses modestly but laughs heartily, loudly. She doesn't stay in the back of the shop like some wives might do.

We come back the next evening, and the next. I tell Hani more about my father: the kind of person he was, how he died, how he raised me. I talk a little about my town. There is still so much to say. I keep skirting around the word "murder."

On the third or fourth date, Hani says he scuba-dives, a pastime I don't know much about. I tell him I don't think I'd be brave enough to dive.

"I'm not brave," he says. "I'm scared every time I jump into the sea."

"Why do you do it?"

"I don't know. Maybe... It's quiet down there. And dark. A different kind of light. You could die if something goes wrong, but if everything's right, it's the calmest place on Earth."

Hani's square, strong shoulders give me joy. I want to cup my hands over them. He keeps talking. He adores the sea—that's the word he uses, "adores." He loves diving into the waves, cutting through the water. Feeling the weight of the water above him when he's submerged. Leaving footprints in the wet sand after he returns to land and watching them disappear as the waves lap. He loves lying on sand as the sea evaporates from his skin, leaving behind a residue of salt. He enjoys shaking the sand off, bringing it home on his towel, in his bag, in his shoes.

I imagine being under water and experiencing it the way Hani does: as thrilling and comforting, surprising and unchanging, scary and welcome.

When Hani pauses after a long rush of words, I mean to lie, to say, "Yes, yes, the sea is wonderful." Until today, I've lied by omission, by saying nothing, simply listening. Now, my tongue trips itself into hinting at the truth. I've known him barely a month, and I've heard him talk about the sea so much—sea, sea, sea, sea, sea. My heart and mouth respond.

"The sea must be so beautiful," I say.

It will turn out that Hani has a habit of catching my missteps, and I will find his ability to see the truth of me incredibly appealing and frightening. It will be hard to hide my inner secrets from him.

He's incredulous. How have I been in the city for as long as I have, he asks, yet never walked along the shore or even seen the sea from a distance?

I spread my hands in front of me, hoping for the answer to fall out of the sky into my lap. I don't know.

"I prefer the night to the sea," I say.

"Let's go now," he says.

"To the beach?"

We're staring at the foam in our cups, little hearts the barista made for us. Hani hasn't been drinking because he's been talking. I haven't been drinking because I've been listening. Our coffee has gone cold. We drink in silence, foam on our lips, while he waits for me to answer. I'm hesitating because this coffee shop is the only place we've met. I'm afraid of going out in "public" with him.

I say I need to go home.

He asks if he can drive me. I say I'll take the bus, as I've done every time we've met before, but he insists, and I agree to being taken close to home. As we walk to his car, he makes conversation about spices, the sea, our jobs, and I'm starting to feel comfortable. I feel as though I'm inhabiting both our bodies. I'm so close to him, we've merged.

I nearly walk into a woman. She steps back and I do, too.

She has long black hair, clunky black shoes, a clingy dress. The scarf half-covering her hair bunches at her neck, exposing her cleavage. A familiar scent knocks me back. A perfume built on the floral funk of jasmine.

She steps directly in front of Hani, winks, and licks her lips.

So clichéd. And shameless. I'm equally annoyed by and in awe of her.

"Excuse me, ma'am," Hani says, veering around her. I'm a step behind, and she's in my face now.

"Mayyadah?" I say, though the woman lacks Mayyadah's freckles, her sly eyes. This woman is earnestly lewd. She gestures rudely and pushes past me, disappearing into the coffee shop.

When I catch up to Hani, he's tying his shoe by the side of his car. We're the only two people in the parking lot.

"Did you see what she did?"

He thinks I mean how she came on to him, not what happened after. He stands up, opens the driver's side door. I don't move around to the passenger side.

"Didn't you see how old she was?" he says. "She could have been my mother."

I must look puzzled, because he touches the place where my eyebrows meet with his thumb and rubs. I flick my fingers to get him to move his hand away, as two men who'd been sitting a table over from us in the coffee shop pass by.

"You have nothing to worry about," he says.

"What do you mean?"

"I wasn't attracted to her."

"I never worried."

Our exchange is an admission: we like each other. But it's

261

inauspicious to have an almost-argument when we're still getting to know each other. I take his thumb and press it between my fingers, a small apology. I let go. The two men get into a red sportscar and drive away.

Sitting in the passenger seat of Hani's car as he's settling in to drive, I make sure no one's in the parking lot, then I remove his right hand from the steering wheel to finish what I started. I kiss his thumb. Nibble it. As though to say, "You're mine."

He takes a deep breath, then brings his thumb to his mouth and kisses it. Though he's not touching me, my mouth feels the brush of his lips. He drops me off four blocks from my flat.

All day the next day, I'm lost in thought at work, contemplating the sea and how it shapes this city and how we live in it.

I ask myself why I've never seen the sea. Why have I isolated myself from the beauty a few miles away? What's wrong with me? On my lunch break, I open a notepad and try to write myself into an answer, pages I may or may not show Hani later. Maybe, as someone who grew up landlocked, I fear the sea. Fear its expansiveness and what that wideness would suggest to me about the imprisonment of my youth.

But also, I'm not the problem. The city keeps me from the sea. It does not open itself to the sea. It distances itself from the waves and the depths.

From my flat, I would have to take three buses and travel for over an hour to arrive at the shore.

I've heard the folklore: Old folks say the people of this city by the sea are descended from mer-people, or jinn of the sea, who flopped onto the beach where the city port would one day rise up, shed their scales and tails, and became human.

I'd like to believe it's true, that some of us humans are descended from jinn, and that's why we feel an affinity for elements other people fear: the sea, the dark of night, the forest, the mountains, the desert.

But I saw a documentary once, and talking heads said the truth is more likely this: generations ago, hundreds of years ago, or thousands, a group of fisherpeople founded the city on the shore. As others migrated here, they built their houses farther and farther inland. The city developed as a patchwork of ugliness and splendor. Some neighborhoods bloomed, others festered.

I do not mean to say the city grew organically, like a weed or a thorny vine or a huddle of trees in an oasis. People built the city with purpose.

Near the sea: slums.

Overlooking the sea: mansions.

Near the center of the city: more slums.

At its true center: glittering shopping malls and high-rises.

Dotted throughout the city: working-class neighborhoods.

And ringing the city: the walled villas and compounds of people who grew up in the neighborhoods and fled the working class. The rich but not ultra-rich. The people who shop at the department store where I work.

Before I met Hani, I stayed in my proper places in the city: the neighborhood where I live and the neighborhood where I work.

Hani has been contemplating my relationship to the sea, too, and he's not giving up. In text messages, he insists he must take me to the closest urban beach. He promises pistachio or mastic ice cream, whatever I prefer, from a cart a man pushes down the promenade. He promises to teach me to fly a kite. The idea of taking me to the sea seems to embolden him to push against the social rules that bind us. He wants to pick me up in his car and bring me home after. *No,* I write. I don't want my neighbors or coworkers to know I have a friend who is a boy. He has seemed to understand. *I want to go, but you can't come here,* I write now. After an hours-long break in messages, after I've decided he'll never text me, and wondered if I should text him, but decided not to because his silence after two texts from me will cut even deeper, he writes: He will give me money for a rideshare. We'll meet on the beach.

I'm not in love with him, yet. I want to be. I type, *OK. I'll go.*

On my day off, we meet. The light sparkling on the sea surprises me with its glory. The wind is a love-spirit rubbing against our bodies. The smell of fish and tang of salt spray in my nose erase all thoughts from my mind except: *Sea, sea, sea.*

Hani and I scramble over a rock wall. We take off our shoes and dig our toes into the wet sand. I see something floating in the distance, a human head. A flash of arms. Someone swimming. The tiny figure dives into the water, and I think I see a tail.

That can't be.

I point toward the horizon and ask Hani if he saw a swimmer. Or a porpoise.

"Not so close to shore," he says.

If I say I saw a mermaid, will he think I'm crazy? Something about the way he talks about books and movies, as though he could walk into those worlds, suggests he might believe imaginary beings hatch from an egg of truth.

I ask if he believes in mermaids.

"Do you?" He laughs like the lapping of waves on the shore.

I tell him about the stories from my town, about a chimerical woman who smells like jasmine and gardenia, or oud, or musk. Who kills.

"Kills like the Greeks' sirens, and other imaginary creatures? Men in every time and place imagine women are half-animal and out for blood."

I tell him women told the stories, too, as often as men did. Mothers, grandmothers, aunts, and older sisters warned boys, my brothers included, to stay away from women with dark hair, fragrant skin, strong legs, sharp and dangerous desires.

"A woman like that sounds beautiful to me, and erotic," he says. "You're like that."

I act offended, lightly slap his cheek. "Are you calling me a monster? A seductress? A killer?"

I mean for him to laugh, to understand I'm joking.

Instead, he looks and sounds offended. He narrows his eyes and huffs. "Of course not. I'm calling you beautiful and strong."

To many men, *beautiful* and *strong* are dangerous attributes in a woman. I'm afraid if I say so out loud, he'll become more annoyed. More angry.

"Never mind," I say. "I'm sorry."

He asks if I want to sit on the beach to watch the sun set. I say OK. I smell popcorn and frying oil and street-food condiments: vinegar, mustard, ketchup. From the small amusement park up the street come the sounds of children and carnival music and screaming teenagers. Nearer by, the breeze, and the waves, and Hani's breathing. We're quiet, no need to say anything now we've patched up our small disagreement. When we catch each other's eyes, we smile. We hold hands, hidden in a little cove away from other beachgoers. Sunset sweeps across the sky in shades of cotton candy and tangerine and blood orange and deep plum. I feel as though I've fallen into the sea, and he's holding me afloat.

As dark diffuses around us like ink and streetlights flicker on, my mind goes to death in the dark. How men at home are afraid of women at night. I think back to the woman who stalked my town for years. If she's real, how old is she now? What fragrance does she wear these days?

Hani asks what I'm thinking about.

"Murder," I say.

The word's effect is immediate. I've changed the energy of the conversation from fun to frightening. Hani's surprise and shock, his grief for me when I explain how many murders my town experienced—they're unbearable.

"Unh," he says, like the wind has been knocked out of him.

He looks devastated. His bereft-ness leaves me bereft and hollow. Murder is a thing that happens in TV shows, not in real life. Now we're caught in the horror of my childhood.

It was different when I talked to Nabatean Goddess. She didn't recoil from my pain. She absorbed it.

"I'm sorry for bringing it up," I say.

"No, I'm sorry," he says. "I can't imagine."

Can't you? How does one live in the city, the full-of-people city, and never know violence? Know very little grief? This difference in our knowledge of the world's suffering lays a trench between us, a trench I see and he doesn't.

The trench between us widens. I fear it gobbling me up. He gets so close to the edge I want to push him away from it, to save him from my pain. But pushing him away means leaning over the trench myself.

I wonder if I'll ever recover from the fear ground into my bones.

"Maybe she's real, that donkey woman." Hani smirks. "Just like the mermaid."

I say, "The killings were real."

My four words are enough for him to see he's erred. He apologizes. We leave the beach and forget the mermaid or porpoise, or whatever she was. Once you step away from the sea in this city, inland neighborhoods pull you magnetically and you're trapped, unable to glimpse the sea from your window.

If you're brave enough to leave your prison, if you inch toward the coast, the sea pulls you in. The closer you get to the shore, the stronger the pull. Once the waves kiss your toes, you want to throw yourself into the aquamarine, choppy water. Not to drown, but to swim. To move forward with powerful strokes and kicks, toward everything else in the world, everything beyond the city. Toward other cities and far shores, distant lands. Whether you arrive or not is not the point.

Maybe, to people on another shore, we are the beyond. Maybe they want to journey toward us.

I don't know how to swim or sail. I don't know how to escape this place and go to the other shore.

When I moved to the city, I expected unlimited freedom. But even in this less-conservative-than-my-town place, boys and girls—young women and young men, really—are supposed to court in private. We are supposed to be introduced and chaperoned by our families. We are surveilled. Large cities and small towns are not as different as people make them out to be. Loneliness seeps into everyone's life at one point or another. Unfreedom ties us at the wrists and ankles. Some have what they need to live a good life and others do not; some take and others lose. How much sadness can moments of joy save us from?

But young people go out anyway. Who's to say they aren't married? Over the next year, not yet in love, but meandering our way toward it, Hani and I go out two or three times a week. He wants to correct all my mistakes of getting to know the city. Because he grew up here, he wants me to know it's not just department stores and fancy malls, flashy movie theaters and art galleries. He wants me to understand the heritage of this place. I occasionally feel like he's lording it over me about how wonderful the city is, compared to a small, murder-ridden town like mine. He never says that. I infer it. We go to the old city, a stone's throw from the sea, where tall, drooping buildings are built of coral and teak. Here, we can hear the sea, though we can't see it. He leads me up the winding staircase of a museum in a historic building, to the roof. The cool breeze from the shore embraces us. Here, we can see the sea and hear it. He says as a boy he imagined being able to walk on air from this rooftop to the beach. This is his family's former home, he explains, which they converted to a museum to showcase the city's history and culture. No one lives here, only memories. Dusty wooden and silk furniture, and on the third floor an artist's workshop. Inside, shuttles dart on looms, a man is making headdresses, a woman is embroidering ankle-length dresses, and fluorescent lights augment the mosaic of sunlight coming in through the wooden windows.

When I tell Hani I've never been to the spice market, he takes me there. It's back the way we came, in the old part of the city. I close my eyes, inhale the fragrance of spices in the little scooper, which he holds under my nose. He challenges me to guess the spice: paprika, pepper, cardamom, cumin, cinnamon, lichen, cloves, ginger, mastic, frankincense, myrrh. I correctly identify every scent.

On one of our walks through the old city, we discover a tiny perfumery, skinny as a bowling alley, overseen by an old man with no teeth and old-timer's clothes. The walls are lined top to bottom with shelves stacked with vials. Every fragrance you could want. Pure fragrances, unadulterated. Some vials are worth thousands.

She brushes past me, walking into the store as Hani and I leave. The Mayyadah look-alike. Hair loose almost to her waist. I stop to stare. Is she really the same woman? Hani doesn't notice that he's left me behind.

With Hani, I'm less alone, but I can't shake a feeling that I'm not who he thinks I am. And not who *I* think I am.

On the first anniversary of our meeting, Hani and I meet in a green park with flowering trees. He arrives a few minutes late, and while I wait, I drag a bough to my nose and sniff the tiny, orange-red blooms. I don't know their name. They smell chemical, like poison or cleaning fluid. I'm embarrassed because I didn't expect such an unpleasant scent from these flowers. As a perfumer, I should know: Beauty doesn't equal fragrance.

Hani enters the uncrowded park deep in thought. His face lights up when he sees me. We stroll, holding hands until we catch sight of someone older than we are, someone we view as an auntie or uncle or grandmother or grandfather. Someone we should behave respectably in front of. We disentangle our fingers, walk a bit farther apart.

On this day in the park, joy is the fact of being together. The warm sun invites us to sit on a bench. We chat, hands at our sides, flat on the wooden slats, fingertips touching but not holding. Our conversation is like water flowing through a dry valley after a downpour. When Hani turns his moon-shaped face away from me to look straight ahead, I crane my neck so I won't lose sight of his clear brown eyes, his finely drawn lips, his bumpy nose, his smooth eyebrows and long lashes.

By now, I'm in love with Hani, but I don't tell him I love him. He also holds on his tongue, like an aspirin tablet, the words that would bind us together. The next few weeks, I have dreams of falling. Dreaming about something means it will happen. I dream scents like I did when I dreamed about Habeeb. The scents are green and woodsy. Strong and pungent and sappy.

One morning a few weeks later, when I wake up, I could swear there's a pine tree growing outside my window. I throw open the curtains, yank up the window, and breathe in. The dream scent dissipates, and what I truly smell is jasmine climbing toward the sky. I look down toward voices on the sidewalk. Hani stands beneath my window. He's never come to my flat before, and I wonder if he's come to tell me something. To break up, or propose. Are there any other reasons he would break our routine and our code of secrecy? My landlord could very easily see him and demand I stop dating him or he'll evict me.

Hani's talking to someone, I can't see who, and then she steps from behind the corner of a building. Is it the woman from the coffeeshop and the perfumery, from weeks ago? Up here, I can't smell her, or see her face.

She's harassing him, saying she doesn't believe he really has a girlfriend. Her words are distinct, Hani's mumbled and unclear.

He looks up and sees me. He looks guilty. What does guilt look like? Like fear. Like a man seduced. Is there a man who will stay faithful? Who will stay true? Who will not hurt a woman, her body, her heart, or her mind?

There's a text from Hani saying he's downstairs. I send a surprised response. By the time I dress and go downstairs, she's gone.

"I love you," Hani says.

When I ask about the woman, he says, "Poverty is growing in the city, especially in your neighborhood. Beggars are everywhere."

My landlord leans off his balcony. "Take your confession elsewhere," he says. But he doesn't evict me, and from now on, Hani picks me up at the flat, brings me home. He never comes upstairs.

CHAPTER 19

Copycat

Murder in the city.

When Hani and I have been seeing each other for a little over a year, a man is found brutally murdered in an alley behind the department store, with his heart carved out. The news travels all the way to my mother, who calls me and says, "It's just like the first murder."

I don't remember, I say. "I was seven, and you and Baba never talked about the murders."

"I know in my bones who stabbed this man dead. *She* did it."

My mother doesn't realize how close the dead man lay to where I work. She tells me to lock my door at night, which of course I already do. I hear Lajwa and Rana in the background, urging me to come home.

The murder is all over the news, on our TVs and phones. The city police call it a copycat crime, "modeled on a small-town murder more than two decades ago." They don't release the name of the victim for several weeks. My friends at the store gossip about why that might be.

"He's been so defaced they can't place him," Nur says.

The murdered man turns out to be the distant cousin of the department store's owner. He gathers the staff and tells us we must carry on. We won't let this incident keep customers from coming to the store. He says nothing to us about his grief or fear.

My coworkers organize a buddy system for coming to work and going home. I tell them it's only the men who need to be careful. Nur tells me I'm cold.

"I grew up with this," I say. "You get used to the vigilance."

I wake up from nightmares in which Hani is killed. Some nights, the bloody knife that killed him is in my hand.

At coffee a few weeks after the murder, Hani tells me to stop working at the store. He says, "Marry me." The proposal doesn't surprise me; it seems inevitable. Hani says he'll help me open my own perfumery. The new manager has canceled the Wardah contract, so moving on makes sense to me. I've made my way up to perfumery manager, and there's nowhere else to go. Most of my friends have moved on. The Nabatean Goddess married and had children and opened a bridal boutique. Lloyd flew back to his home country. Only Nur is left.

People want foreign scents, the manager says when he breaks the news to me. In our increasingly artificial world, they don't lean toward the natural. He's wrong. I've done good business selling fragrances out of my flat, which some days smells like flowers and others like civet and hardly ever like food. I eat out with Hani or at his flat, sneaking in through a back staircase so his neighbors won't comment or report us to his mother. I don't want onions or garlic or acidic tomato to ruin the scent of my three rooms.

"Now's the time," Hani says as we sit at our favorite table at the coffee shop. Steam rises from the espresso machine behind him, and I think about spirits and jinn, an empty well in a neglected neighborhood in a sometimes-forgotten town, dead fathers. For a moment, I don't remember who I am. Hani's smiling; his stubble invites me to touch his face, and I do. He puts his hand on mine.

"No, I'm not ready," I say.

"For what? Your own store? Marriage? Embrace the future, Layla!"

"What do you mean?"

"You've been 'adjusting' to life in the city for years. You're an urbanite now. You belong here. Stop fighting it."

Have I been fighting belonging to the city? To Hani? Sometimes, I daydream about going home, where there's less traffic and smog. Where I used to be a person who stood up for herself. Wasn't I? Now I feel afraid all the time—I felt that way long before the murder behind the store.

Hani sees me thinking, and it seems to dawn on him that he should be offended. "Are you going to break up with me? Tell me now."

No, I love him, I don't want to leave him. I always set aside my daydreams of home as nostalgic. Unrealistic. There's so much more for me in the city—whatever that means.

"I just need a little time to decide," I say. "I don't want to feel pressured."

Hani says he understands.

A month after the murder, rumors continue to spread. My customers and coworkers tell me stories: The officers smelled not death and trash but roses and jasmine. The murderer rode—what the heck?—a donkey. Or a motorcycle. Left bloody hoofprints.

"With our own eyes, we see how quickly urban legends begin," one TV talking head quips, though similar stories have been infecting my town and spreading within it like cancer for more than twenty years.

For the next few weeks, I go down a rabbit hole, watching videos of reporters dredging up old stories from the "infamous small town" no one had heard of. My town. The reporters drive from the shore into the countryside to interview the towns-people and are "shocked" to learn the details of the string of unsolved, brutal, unimaginable murders. Hardened reporters sob at the end of interviews.

I wonder if these stories are distressing to Susu, if she's able to avoid them popping up on her phone.

The reporters all want to know this: Why were the victims all men?

"Female vengeance," Lama Murad, who was in my year at school, tells one of the camera crews.

Her statement becomes a meme people from the city share with a wink and a nod.

In some of the videos, people in town, people I know, describe their nightmares and fears in vivid detail. Reporters observe how townspeople hid their sons and secrets behind closed doors for a generation. Hundreds, maybe thousands, of people have migrated to the city over the past few decades from a town with a population of ten thousand. Not for opportunity, but to escape the horror.

"The murderer leaves a message every time, always too vague

to lead to a breakthrough in the crime investigation," a reporter says, standing in front of the old Murad store, which remains vacant to this day.

The copycat in the city left nothing but the dead man and his still-beating heart.

When reporters ask about suspects, their subjects clam up. The police have searched for an answer for more than twenty years, they say. Every lead has been followed. The perpetrator couldn't be anyone in town.

Following the story back to the city, one frustrated and intrepid reporter finds, in a working-class neighborhood, a son of the very first victim, a young man named Anwar whose family moved to the city when he was very small. He says he visited relatives in the town every summer until he was old enough to refuse. He grew up on stories about his father's death and those that followed. He looks familiar to me, like I've seen him on the street or playing on the rooftops or at an evening gathering hosted by one of my mother's friends.

"My mother thought we would be safer in the city," he says in a video millions of people have viewed. "But we're not safe anywhere. We thought the horrific crimes were a curse on the town we left. Now every man in the city should ask himself what he can do to protect himself, whether she will find a reason to stalk him."

"She?" asks the off-screen reporter. "How do you know it's a *she*? And *reason*? What do you mean? Are you talking about motive?"

Anwar asks the reporter to stop filming.

The reporter agrees. The screen goes dark. But secretly, the reporter has recorded Anwar's voice, and the audio goes on.

THE NIGHT IS NOT FOR YOU

Anwar tells the stories I've known all my life: A woman with black hair, fragrant as a garden on a warm day, misshapen legs. A creature. Men accused. Including his father—though Anwar's mother never talked ill about the man, Anwar's aunts and cousins did. Not to hurt the son of the victim, they said, but to warn him. To force him to become better than his father was.

"It can't be true," the reporter says. "Those are crazy stories. Completely made up."

"Don't call me a liar!" Anwar says. "You're questioning the stories the women of my family raised me on. You're questioning our values."

"Calm down," the reporter says—words that have never calmed anyone down. "Don't you want justice for your father? For the men mowed down. Not by a monster, but by a monstrous human?"

Anwar tells the reporter to go to hell, but he keeps talking about the horrible stories he has been told throughout his life, causing him lifelong nightmares that don't leave him even for a night. He's lived alone for years, but now he thinks he should move back in with his sister. Or he should get married, to someone who doesn't know his story.

Now, though, everyone knows his story. We listen, even though we know the reporter got his scoop unethically.

Anwar tells the reporter about finding photos online purporting to be his father's crime scene, posted by a police officer from town who lamented the injustice of the crime never being solved. Maybe someone would see the photos and identify the murderer. Anwar had barely been able to make out the hole in his father's chest. He'd clicked away before he could see more. But now, instead of having an intact picture of his father in his mind, an image he could hang his grief on, he is haunted by the thought of his father's final moments.

"We're not safe anywhere," he says to the reporter.

I think he means everyone, anyone who lives. Anyone he would ever love. His future wife, his future children, his current and future friends. On the audio, he breathes deeply several times, trying to calm himself.

"Do you smell that?" he says. The reporter says, yes, he smells incense.

Anwar says his neighbors burn oud when they have a party or deep-clean their flat.

The scent usually soothes him, disperses peace throughout his body, he says. Tonight, it does not.

Silence stretches for long seconds on the audio, and I wonder what the two men are doing. Are they staring at each other? Is the reporter comforting Anwar?

Just when I'm about to click "stop," Anwar screams, in grief and pain. "Where can I go? Where can I go?"

The audio ends.

I listen to Anwar's testimony dozens of times, after work, on nights when Hani is busy. I cannot get enough of it. I start to have false memories, flashbacks of being in the alley behind the Murad store, seeing blood splattered everywhere.

One night, after these several weeks of bingeing on all these videos about my town, and thinking about whether to marry Hani, and not being able to decide, I call Rana and confess my addiction to the videos. I tell her about Anwar. Does she remember him from school? Was he her age, or my age?

"That can't be right," she says. "I need to ask Mama."

"What about?"

"The first victim. I don't think he had children."

I step to my window and stare at the bougainvillea, breathe in the jasmine.

"You mean it's not true?"

"That reporter was duped," she says. "Or that reporter is duping you."

CHAPTER 20

Monstrous Night

Another night of violence.

Hani and I set our wedding date for the anniversary of the day
we met, a few weeks after Susu's daughter's second birthday.
Susu is giddy at the idea of us getting married. She takes credit
for introducing us, for making a beautiful match. Hani helps
me find a little shop in a corner of a high-rise mall in the old
city, and Nur has agreed to quit his job at the department
store, too, and work for me. We install shelves all the way to
the ceiling. The back room becomes my perfume lab. Hani's
brother is good with wood; he builds me a perfume organ as
a wedding gift. I'll open the store after my wedding and week-
long honeymoon. Hani and I have rented a cottage on the beach,
an hour north of the city. Hani's going to teach me to snorkle.

My last day at the department store is a week before the wedding. All day, my stomach clenches, unclenches, turns over. Too
many new things are beginning at once. I have a bet with Nur:
he will buy me coffee if I can sell the most expensive bottle of
perfume in the store, a large bottle the size of a baby's torso
from a famous French company, by a perfumer every fragrance

geek can name. It's not his best scent, but it combines all the most exotic and expensive ingredients. Gold, the essence from the glands of an endangered animal, a sap that can only be collected when the tree is infected and dying, a lichen that grows under a certain type of ledge in the Himalayas, essence of an exotic orchid that grows only in the middle of a desert. Or so Nur and I guess, because the ingredients are super-secret. The scent's beauty makes me woozy, the way the top notes swoop in, and then the heart notes rise up and swirl, and the base notes linger and linger, as though I'm lying on the floor of a forest for hours. I love this scent. We're only allowed to give customers the tiniest whiff from a sample strip that itself would be worth hundreds on the black market. The strip lives in a safe when we're not sharing it with customers.

I start the day scoping out customers, on the hunt for the richest-looking women. Jewelry and handbags are the best clues, but I have to be subtle. They expect to be upsold, and they don't always like it.

I hit them with the most sincere honesty. "It's my last day, and I need the commission because I'm saving up to open my own shop," I say, my business card cupped in my hand as I slip it to them so the store manager won't see.

I nearly make the sale to a woman with fox-red hair, dried-blood-colored fingernails, and winking platinum and diamonds on her ears, her waist, her wrists, her ankles, her fingers, and her toes. She's intrigued by the unusual scent, especially when I say she'll be the only woman she knows to wear it. In the end, she calls the bottle "too huge, too gaudy." Lately, she says, she has become enamored of a minimal look in her home.

Nur pulls me aside. "I'll be angry with you if I win too easily.

Go after the men, that guy with a Rolex, or the one who looks like his wife's about to leave him."

"How can you tell?"

"His expensive haircut has gotten shaggy and he's hungry to spend money."

"I'm afraid," I tell him.

He asks what's on my mind.

My life's about to change in every way.

"You'll still be with Hani. You'll still be a perfumer. Sure, you might have babies soon, but that's just a small thing."

He's laughing at me. Weeks ago, he told me I should take more time before the wedding, not get married a week after leaving the store, with my own store opening in less than a month.

"Go home," he says. "Start your new life."

He unlocks the cabinet where the baby's-torso perfume is kept. He's already paid for it with his life savings. I can't accept such an expensive gift, I tell him. I don't want it, actually. I want to make and collect tiny bottles of perfume made by my own hand.

"Display it in the store," he says. It will be an inside joke for the two of us.

Perfume in my arms, I say goodbye to the store and the more-and-more artificial and chemical smells of the perfumes we sell.

Since the murder behind the store, we've gone from one old security guard at the front door to a dozen young guys ringing the building. Still, I hate walking through the parking lot alone at night, even as bright as it is, even though I could call the guards and they'd scuffle to my rescue in their flak jackets and heavy boots, guns at the ready. Tonight, I'm on edge, and I jog all the way to the bus stop. I pant, clutching Nur's gift to my pounding heart.

I notice a man noticing me. Is his smile threatening or friendly? Are his eyes wolfish or witty? I wish I could stand at a bus stop unnoticed, invisible. I don't want to assume every strange man is an enemy or predator. I can't help but make the assumption, though, because men in the city cat-call women like me night and day. Women who walk or ride the bus, women who walk alone, women who go out in public at all. At home, where I knew a man's cousins and uncles and aunts and parents, I knew what family he came from, and could demand respect and threaten to call a guy out if he harassed me. No one ever did.

This man is handsome in a middle-aged way, clearly an athlete or former athlete. A man who lifts things: weights, children, his wife, heavy jugs of water at the office, bags of rice his wife requested from the store, cases of soda. Maybe he plays street football with his buddies or volleyball on the beach or racquetball in a private club. He knows he's handsome. He wants women to acknowledge his handsomeness.

He needs a haircut; he might be the man from the store, the guy with the shaggy hair. I can't say for sure.

I stand at one end of the bus stop and he's at the other. He sidles nearer to me, about an arm's length away. I smell him now, middle-of-the-road cologne. Not expensive and complex, not overzealously applied aftershave. A muddy fragrance, unpleasant to my practiced nose. I imagine his wife bought it for him. I imagine she would like to buy him nicer things, but they can't afford them.

He's sniffing me, too.

"You smell nice," he says. "Going to see your boyfriend?"

I take a seat on the bench and pointedly stare at my phone, reading, scrolling. Can I text Hani without the man seeing what I write? He sits next to me. Our thighs touch and I bounce to the side.

"Apologies," he says snidely. "What are you reading?"

I want to be left alone. Where's the damn bus? I stand up, put my phone in my pocket, and look up the street.

He won't back down.

"Where do you work?"

I have an easy lie at my fingertips. "At the department store."

"I like to shop for my wife there. I'm taking the bus because my car broke down and my brother can't pick me up."

He's lying. He stretches his arms, then his legs, like he's limbering up for a run.

It's a busy road. Cars' headlamps light up the man's eyes; shadow darkens them. I look away, at anything but him, so he'll leave me alone. A crushed soda can under a tree, a cockroach scurrying nearby, a poor mangy cat. I mew at her, rummage through my purse for a treat for her. Nothing but mints.

"You like cats?" the man says. "Me too."

The bus is late, and I don't want to ride it anymore, I don't want to be in an enclosed space with this man. I could walk, but he might follow me. The street is well lit, but shadows lurk.

I text Hani: *Can you pick me up?*

The man says, "Who are you texting? Can't we just talk?"

Hani doesn't respond immediately. I stand and order a rideshare. The man stands beside me and watches me set up the request.

"The bus is coming," he says. "I promise I'm not a bad man."

I've tried not to look at him. Yes, he's handsome, but his eyes are bloodshot and I smell something foul on him now. Where has he gotten liquor in this place where it's forbidden? His nails are clean, his speech hardly slurred enough to be noticeable. Everything about him except his eyes is respectable. He touches my arm. I step aside, because slapping him would not be seemly. But I want to slap him, right across the face. I want him to leave me alone.

I exhale. I've been holding my breath. Several men dressed for the office stand to the side. I'm the only woman here.

One man steps in. "Are you OK, Summer?" He's pretending he knows me.

"I think I've missed my bus. I think I should walk."

He offers to walk with me, but why trust him? I tell him I'll be fine.

The red-eyed man has disappeared. I start in the direction of my flat, a forty-five-minute walk I've done once or twice before on cool evenings—not a humid, warm night like tonight.

As I walk, I watch the tiny car in the rideshare app go up and down a street two blocks away. I cancel it, and then wish I hadn't. I could have caught up to the car, sent the driver a message.

Before I can request another ride, I get to the corner, and the man from the bus stop is there.

"Hello, beautiful," he says.

He walks very close to me, and if I move, he moves too.

He's stuck to me like a shadow. I cannot get away.

"Leave me alone," I hiss. I want to transform myself into a serpent queen, fearsome, monstrous, able to devour this man in one swallow and slither away.

But I'm a woman, and I have a heavy, expensive bottle in my arms.

The man puts his hand on my shoulder and starts to rub. "Doesn't this feel nice?" he says.

I pry myself away. There's no one around to help me, no one around to witness what is happening between us. For a moment, I think I might keep walking. But I remember the night of Susu's engagement party. The guy I shoved.

"Want to see what's in the box?" I say.

"Not really."

I open the box and take out the exquisitely crafted bottle. It's tall, twisted and spiraled, with a round top. The liquid a bright rose-gold. I raise the bottle up high.

The man watches me smash the glass against the sidewalk. He doesn't know what's happening.

I stab the jagged glass into his belly. Surprise grips his face. My powerful arm keeps jabbing; I'm full of adrenaline. Five, six, seven. Eleven, twelve.

Blood gurgles from his throat, spills from his veins. Is he dead yet?

I lean in, examine what I've done. He's twitching, but he's dead.

The fragrance Nur bought me envelops me. It smells like funk, like Bumbo, like jasmine and coriander and roses and the sea and Hani and my family and my flat and my city and my broken heart and my sweat-slicked skin.

On the wings of this exotic fragrance, I imagine, I shall rise up above the earth, fly far away.

No, I'm merely human. I can't fly.

I can kill, though. And I can write.

I coat my hands with his blood, rub them together, rub the blood on my face like rouge.

She's always left a message. *I've* always left a message. I use the blood on my hands, drag my fingers and palm against the rough sidewalk:

> "THE NIGHT IS NOT FOR YOU.
> THE NIGHT IS MINE."

Life will continue as it is, was, and has been. No fragrance or violence will save me or free me.

I will wipe my hands on the lifeless man's pantlegs. I will undo my ponytail. I will shake my hair till it shrouds my face, and walk away from my victim and predator.

Walk away from everything that used to be, into the monstrous night.

ACKNOWLEDGMENTS

In the United Arab Emirates and other parts of the Arabian Peninsula, Umm Ad-Duwais is a terrifying figure. Typically, she's a jinn with a human head and torso, long, beautiful hair, sickles for hands, and a donkey's legs and tail. In the shadows of night, she seduces men with her mysterious scent and beauty—and murders them when they give in to temptation.

She's been a cautionary tale told by mothers to their young children: "Come back before it gets dark."

She's been a warning to young men: "Don't wander the streets late at night."

She's been an epithet lobbed at young women who are deemed too alluring: "Don't wear perfume in mixed company."

But who is she really?

This novel would not be possible without the centuries-old folk traditions of the Arabian Peninsula and the many storytellers who gave birth to Umm Ad-Duwais and other scary jinn that go bump in the night. Thank you also to the Maldivians, who began and continue the annual tradition of Maali Hingun, which inspired me to give Layla's town a Monster Parade.

Two books helped me better understand scents now and

throughout history, as well as the lives, senses, and practice of perfumers: Tanaïs's *In Sensorium: Notes for My People* and Mandy Aftel's *Fragrant: The Secret Life of Scent*. The "Odours" issue (#135) of *Espace* magazine was also helpful.

Thank you to Necessary Fiction for publishing "The Well" in slightly different form.

The book you hold in your hands would not exist without the hard work of publishing teams on both sides of the Atlantic. In the U.K., Areen Ali, my editor, has my undying gratitude for her invaluable partnership on the writing of this folklore-inspired, coming-of-age horror tale. Thank you also to the rest of the Wildfire team: Hannah Whittaker in marketing, Federica Trogu in publicity, Alice Clark on cover design and art direction, and Vicky Lord on typesetting and production.

In the U.S., my editor Alyea Canada has my eternal thanks for her incredible passion and excitement and her spot-on reading recommendations. Thank you also to the rest of the Orbit U.S. and Run for It team: Tim Holman at the helm; Alex Lencicki, Kayleigh Webb, Natassja Haught, and Ellen Wright in marketing and publicity; and Lauren Panepinto and Alexia Mazis in the art department.

Thank you to Steven Chudney for always having my back.

Thank you to my family for their unconditional love and undying support.

MEET THE AUTHOR

Hillary Deane

EMAN QUOTAH's debut novel, *Bride of the Sea*, won the Arab American Book Award for fiction. Her writing has appeared in the *Washington Post, USA Today,* and many other publications. She lives outside Washington, DC, with her family.

if you enjoyed
THE NIGHT IS NOT FOR YOU

look out for

RED RABBIT GHOST

by

Jen Julian

Eighteen years ago, an infant Jesse Calloway was found wailing on the bank of a river, his mother dead beside him. The mystery of her death has haunted him all his life, and despite every effort, he has never been able to uncover the truth.

Now someone is promising him answers. An anonymous source claims that they'll tell him everything. But only if he returns to the hometown he swore he'd left in the rearview.

But in Blacknot, North Carolina, nothing is as it seems. It's a town that buries its secrets deep. Jesse's relentless investigation garners attention from intimidating locals, including his dangerous ex-boyfriend. And he'll soon discover that this backwater town hides a volatile and haunting place on its desolate edge.

*The Night House is calling. Some secrets are better
left buried....*

1

Jesse keeps his dead mother's things in an old Tarbarrel tin. Pork jerky smell, black pepper and molasses, contained alongside photographs. His mother's senior yearbook picture—her sharp, toothy grin. A Polaroid of her and Aunt Nancy toilet-papering the Confederate Memorial in downtown Blacknot. Nancy was seventeen then, his mother nine, both dressed in bell sleeves and fringe like it was still the 60s, though the Polaroid was taken by Jesse's grandmother in 1982. On the back, an inscription: *Nancy Jane & Constance Louise, getting in trouble.*

Also inside the tin: twelve postcards addressed to Nancy while she was in graduate school, messages in his mother's affected teenage voice—*If you find a man in the Queen City, bring him home so that we might sacrifice him to the swamp gods and ensure the harvest.*

Also: one bracelet of black wooden beads, which he guesses his mother must have worn.

Also: a series of articles from the paper about how they found her, dead, on the banks of the Miskwa River eighteen summers ago, and a small notebook of inscrutable thoughts, facts, and fantasies (Jesse couldn't remember his mother, so he resorted to inventing details), which he wrote when he was a kid. *River highest since 1980—average water temp 71°—she had* black hair, pretty face, archy eyebrows—5 foot 1—shoe size 6 1/2, bad at singing—loved Wizard of Oz, X-Files, will-o'-the-wisp, animals—spoke French <u>and</u> Spanish—laughed at weird stuff like ghosts—smelled like cinnamon, fixed eggs better than Nancy, came home from work wearing costumes, played chess—

And so on.

There are many things the tin does not include. According to Nancy, Connie burned a lot of keepsakes and photos in the years leading up to the final breakdown that killed her, including pictures of her and Jesse together. That is his least favorite detail about her, aside from being dead.

Remarkably, he didn't take the tin with him to college. When he packed last August, he decided to leave it right there on the upper shelf of his closet, its time-honored home. Now, after driving back the four hours from Greensboro, he finds that Nancy has used his monthslong absence as an excuse to pack up his bedroom to turn it into an office/meditation studio. All his posters and books and old school projects are stuffed away in boxes, the walls now hung with calming beach photographs, the closet clean of his baggy high school clothes and red Miskwa High sweatshirts.

And the tin, which is not where he left it.

"Where'd you put it?" he asks Nancy, trying not to panic.

His aunt stands in the doorway, looking sheepish. "I mean." She gestures to the boxes. "I put away a lot of shit, hon. It's probably here."

"Probably?"

"I did throw some things out. Your old running shoes were biohazards. What did the tin look like?"

"Like a *tin*," he says. "It looked like a tin. Red. A red tin. It had the Tarbarrel logo on it. It had—all her stuff was in there."

"Her stuff?" Nancy says.

Jesse dives into the boxes. Some are open, some already taped shut. His aunt knows what he's talking about, of course, but in the face of his alarm, she stands calm. Or at least pretends to.

"I'm sure it's here somewhere."

On principle alone, he doesn't like that she's done this, just crunched down and packed away his entire childhood like a whole lot of junk. Trophies for cross-country crammed in with mix CDs, the complete films of Bogart and Bacall. In one box, he finds the many amusing pulp fiction book covers he hunted down in flea markets all over the county, then, digging deeper, a glass hand pipe containing the charred residue of some backwater ditch weed. He bristles at the thought of Nancy finding it. Sure, they used to sing along to Peter Tosh's *Legalize It* on car trips, but that doesn't mean he wants her to have a firsthand view of his indiscretions.

But then, maybe the invasiveness was the point. Maybe her whole meditation studio plan was just an excuse to go through his stuff, to try to understand him one last time, unravel his secrets, account for his high school misery.

"Oh, stop being so *frantic*," she says. "I'll help you."

"Don't!" he says. "Please, don't touch anything else. I'll find it myself."

"But you *know* I wouldn't have thrown that out."

"You just said maybe you did."

She laughs. Her expression is becoming strained.

"But I didn't trash anything *important*, sweetheart. Do you really think I'd just throw out—*that*?"

"Connie's things," he says. "My mother's things."

There's no official moratorium on mentioning his mother's

name, though he realizes it's been a long time since it was uttered aloud in this house. Nancy steps back, no longer smiling. Her face flushes with indignation.

After a minute, she says, "You know, you've caught me off guard, Jesse, just being here. You insisted you were staying out in Greensboro for the summer. Since November, that's been your plan, right? Get a job, get an apartment. What happened?"

He can't even tell if she's happy to see him. Sure, when he first got in, she rushed out to the driveway to meet him, and when Dick, his red 1998 hatchback, let out its usual tricky sputter, she laughed and said, "Now, *there's* a sweet sound." All the neighbors must've heard it, too. Must've thought, *Oh, that's Jesse Calloway. Antsy Nancy's boy. He's back from college, finally.* Because he didn't come back for Thanksgiving, Christmas, or Easter. Nancy, who taught film and public speaking at the community college in Kneesville, had all the same breaks he did, so each time she'd drive out to see him, and they'd stay with Minerva, her old roommate from grad school, a silver-haired lesbian. And during every visit, Nancy praised the "culture" of the city (i.e., Greensboro) in comparison to the hick trashfire of Miskwa County, and then she drank too much wine and said she would be happy enough to see Jesse survive his freshman year without alcohol poisoning or gonorrhea, which he guessed was meant to take the pressure off or something. But in all that, there was never any talk of Jesse returning home. Nancy took him at his word.

"The plan," he says to her, "changed."

"It changed," she says. "What changed? You were *adamant* about not coming back here."

He rips up packing tape in snaky strips, one box after another.

"What *changed*?" she asks again.

He finds a plastic bin of photos: Jesse and Nancy at the carnivorous plant garden in Wilmington, another one of him and his grandfather at the Fort Fisher Aquarium, then a few with his former high school friends in their ninth-grade Halloween costumes, grins with retainer wires.

"I wanted to see friends," he says.

"Which friends?" asks Nancy.

" 'Which friends?' Why does that matter?"

"Because. Some of your friends have a history of getting you in trouble."

He laughs. "Well, there you go. You got me. I drove four hours to get lit at some redneck barn party. Nothing like the *scene* in metropolitan Blacknot. Endless ragers. Orgies day and night."

Nancy's flush deepens.

"You had a plan," she says firmly. "You changed your mind so fast, that's all I'm saying."

"For all you know, I've been thinking about it for weeks. And anyway, that's got nothing to do with you culling out my shit without asking."

"Oh, Jesse, stop it. Just stop. I didn't—do you seriously think I'd do that on purpose, throw out those things, my *sister's* things…?"

She trails off, her voice breaking. Tears fog up her glasses.

Little fucker, says a voice in Jesse's head. First night home, and you have lied to Nancy and made her cry. Fine work.

"I didn't say you'd do it on purpose," he says, trying to be nicer. "It's fine. It's got to be here somewhere."

"I mean," she says tearfully, "you didn't even take it *with* you. How was I supposed to know?"

In hindsight, yes, maybe the tin would've been safer if he'd brought it with him to college. But he never missed it there. Until a month ago, he was hardly thinking about Connie Calloway at all. Back at school, he was an actual adult, savvy and queer and experienced. He got props for liking David Lynch and owning a discontinued car. It's 2015 and the 90s are cool again. Everything comes back around. Everything reincarnates.

That's what changing your life is like, he assumes: a reincarnation.

Nancy lifts her glasses, squeezes her fingers against her eyes. "I didn't throw it out, I didn't," she keeps saying. "At least, I don't think I did."

And he keeps saying, "It's okay, it's okay, I'm sure you didn't," though really, he just wants to find the damn thing so they can stop talking about it and she can stop crying.

Then, finally, hiding under a pile of Dashiell Hammett novels, there it is. The Tarbarrel mascot—a rosy-cheeked cartoon pig—beams goofily at him from the tin's candy-red lid. He takes a breath.

"It's there?" Nancy asks.

"It's here."

"Good." She leaves the room, swiping at her tears and muttering, "Came all the way back here to fucking worry me."

Sometimes, Nancy takes Jesse's bad decision-making personally, and that is not his fault.

What did she say back in August when she took his shoulders in the campus courtyard? She was crying then, too, their clothes damp with sweat from carrying his stuff upstairs in an elevator-less dorm. She hugged him like he belonged to her, a compact little yin-yang, light and dark. Nancy is honey haired and pink faced, and Jesse inherited his mother's wiry dark curls and brown eyes and sandy-brown skin. But they shared a cringey optimism there, in that courtyard.

"I knew you'd get out of there," she said. "You are going to kick the shit out of this place. You're smart. You bounce back. You always have." Something like that. He remembers looking around at everyone else squirming in the face of similar talks from parents, grandparents, siblings. Everyone is tough. Everyone is the most genius genius.

"I'm just lucky," he told Nancy.

"You're *not* just lucky," she said. "You'll show them. You're *resilient.*"

Then the fearsome Minerva swung back around in her SUV, driving without patience (she and her ex-wife had already seen their two children off to college), and she loaded up Nancy and the empty dolly and the bungee cords, and then, with a kiss and a blink, his aunt disappeared into the shaky summer heat.

Jesse was relieved to see her go. He carried his last box up to his room, a care package Nancy assembled: rolls of quarters, double-ply toilet paper, condoms (*I know you can get these at the health center,* she wrote in a mortifying note, *but still*). He met his roommate, a kid from Cary who introduced himself with a strong handshake, as if they were making a business deal: "Alex Khan. Poli-sci."

"Jesse Calloway," Jesse said. "Undeclared."

"You on Wipixx?"

Wipixx was a social media app Jesse had never heard of, so he didn't understand the question. At the time, he assumed Alex could discern immediately that he was a backwoods clown from a trashfire county.

"I'm sorry, man," he said. "Did you just ask me if I'm *on whippets?*"

Reincarnation indeed.

Jesse reclaims his room. He takes down Nancy's tranquil photos. Goodbye, sand dunes and softly waving seagrass. He tapes up all his pulp book covers in their place. There are at least forty of them, an impressive collection. However, when he steps back to admire them, he's disheartened to see that they don't look as cool or eclectic as he remembers. They look like a mess.

As he rearranges them, trying in vain to make them more aesthetically pleasing, Nancy sticks her head in the doorway.

"Did you even eat dinner?" she asks sharply. "You're like a rail."

He looks at her, startled. "I had something on the road."

"Well, if you get hungry, you know, there's a chess pie in the fridge. That's still your favorite, right?"

Jesse feels suddenly ashamed of himself.

Later, when he goes to the kitchen, he finds the pie in the fridge: a pristine golden disc of butter and sugar. He's not hungry, but he takes the pie out and stands in the kitchen doorway with it, fork in hand.

Nancy is grading finals in the den. The local news plays on mute. The windows are open to the night air of late spring, filling the room with an eggy smell. Nancy notices him standing there, sets aside her papers, and holds out an arm. He comes to sit by her.

"Sorry," he says.

"Same," she says. "I shouldn't have gone through your stuff without asking."

On the news, a young teacher leads a camera crew around his old elementary school. The hallway is lined with scribbly drawings of animals. Jesse experiences a wave of nostalgia. He pokes the chess pie with his fork.

"I know you can't help it," he says, "but you don't need to worry. I won't go anywhere near Pinewood. I promise."

"Hmm," Nancy says. "Thing is, sweetheart, it's Blacknot." She pronounces it the way the old locals do, like Black-*nut*. "If you're here, you're near everything."

Jesse shrugs and looks down at the pie in his lap. He begins to eat it, so sweet it feels like it's burning his tongue.

"You're not going to cut a piece?" says Nancy. "You're just going to eat it like that, like a monster?"

He licks the fork. "Uh-huh."

She digs in herself, and they sit like that for a while, trading the fork back and forth until there's a huge hole in the pie, as if an alien burst out of it. Jesse stares at the hole. Already, his stomach is telling him this was a mistake.

"Of course," Nancy says, "I'm happy you're here. Stay as long as you need."

"Thank you. I know."

"But you should know you won't find a job. Merle hired out your spot at the diner."

"I won't be here long enough to get a job. A couple days, tops."

She reaches out and brushes the hair off his forehead. "This new haircut... I don't know about this haircut. It's a little hipster-y."

He bats her hand away. "No, it isn't."

"What do you think they'll say about you when you're waltzing around downtown Blacknot looking like this?"

"They'll say, 'That kid has his shit together.' I mean, come on, I cleaned off the nail polish. What's the issue?"

She squeezes his cheek. "I just want you to be careful."

"I will, I will. Don't fuss."

He can see in her face that she doubts him; not that he's lying, but that he's making a promise he can't keep. This is often the soul of her doubt, and the soul of his deceit. He believes wholeheartedly any promise he makes to anyone, every time.

He goes to bed early that night. The drive wore him out, he says. By three AM, he's wide awake, listening to Nancy's snores on the other side of the house and staring once again at the collage of book covers on his wall. They're almost disturbing to him now; why is that? He lights a candle. His room is dark and hot. Most of these he didn't even find himself, actually. The best ones—*Alligator-Women from the Swamp Planet*, which features the tagline "They're here... and they're *horny!*" and *Attack of the Mutant Mushrooms*, in which the monsters resemble dildos—those were gifts from Harlan. Thrifting is one of few gay activities a closeted man can enjoy in this county.

If Jesse wanted to, he could find other pieces of Harlan all around the room. A pair of jeans, pierced in the crotch by a spring in Harlan's couch. A Union army coat button, which Harlan's uncle found at the battlefield over in Kinston. But only Jesse would know the significance of these things; Nancy wouldn't be able to pick them out.

God help him if she could.

But he's not here for this. He doesn't need this collection. He's not a fucking kid anymore. His aunt's impulse to cull, he feels it, too—though in a different, more volatile way. One by one, he tears the book covers away and takes them down the hall to the bathroom. There, he begins to burn them in the sink. The Alligator-Women curl up and turn black; the Mutant Mushrooms shrivel. The fire flares up unexpectedly and nearly catches the hand towel, and he is forced to open the bathroom window and let the smoke out into the night—

Whoosh. A flood of swamp stench hits him hard in the face. Low tide and hog farm. Confederate jasmine. Stale hot air. The assault seems personal, like this place has been waiting for him. Like it *sees* him. He never wanted to come back here. This stinking, suffocating place.

A rising wave of sugar burns the back of his throat. He leans over the toilet, and it comes up fast. A full-body retching. An exorcism.

That's a bad sign. A terrible idea all around, this trip. But then he returns to his room, drained and shaky, and he sees his phone lit up on the bedside table.

A Wipixx message from Cat:

> *Welcome home*
> *You want still pictures of your mother?*

His heart hammers. This. This is what he's here for.

Yes

Please

Tomorrow come town to bridge 9am

Tell no one

RAISING READERS
Books Build Bright Futures

Thank you for reading this book and for being a reader of books in general. As an author, I am so grateful to share being part of a community of readers with you, and I hope you will join me in passing our love of books on to the next generation of readers.

Did you know that reading for enjoyment is the single biggest predictor of a child's future happiness and success?

More than family circumstances, parents' educational background, or income reading impacts a child's future academic performance, emotional well-being communication skills, economic security, ambition, and happiness.

Studies show that kids reading for enjoyment in the US is in rapid decline:

- In 2012, 53% of 9-year-olds read almost every day. Just 10 years later, in 2022, the number had fallen to 39%.
- In 2012, 27% of 13-year-olds read for fun daily. By 2023, that number was just 14%.

Together, we can commit to **Raising Readers** and change this trend. How?

- Read to children in your life daily.
- Model reading as a fun activity.
- Reduce screen time.
- Start a family, school, or community book club.
- Visit bookstores and libraries regularly.
- Listen to audiobooks.
- Read the book before you see the movie.
- Encourage your child to read aloud to a pet or stuffed animal.
- Give books as gifts.
- Donate books to families and communities in need.

Books build bright futures, and **Raising Readers** is our shared responsibility.

For more information, visit **JoinRaisingReaders.com**

Sources: National Endowment for the Arts, National Assessment of Educational Progress, WorldBookDay.org, Nielsen BookData's 2023 "Understanding the Children's Book Consumer"